SHE DIDN'T SO MUCH WALK AS GLIDE ON THOSE LONG ELEGANT LEGS, BLAINE THOUGHT.

Mallory moved like a dancer, vist and turn, every smooth pivot. I dropped the bombshell the fallout. He knew mply wasn't up to it.

"Someth He hoped if she was g messenger, she aimed high.

"I *knew* there was something." Mallory came to an abrupt halt. "I've been picking up vibes something wasn't right. I can see by your face you'd prefer not to be having the upcoming conversation." Normally she spoke quietly. She never sought to draw attention to herself, but with Blaine, her usually controlled manner became by comparison nearly theatrical.

"How right you are. I don't think you could guess, so I'll get right to it. Jason Cartwright has a job at Moonglade. On the farm."

The shock was so great she felt like ducking for cover.

"Hey, are you okay?" Blaine showed his concern.

For a moment she was too dumbfounded to reply. "Okay? I'm actually delirious with joy. My ex-fiancé, who got another woman pregnant before our wedding, is working at my home! What luck!"

Also by Margaret Way

Her Australian Hero

His Australian Heiress

Published by Kensington Publishing Corporation

POINCIANA ROAD

MARGARET WAY

ZEBRA BOOKS
KENSINGTON PUBLISHING CORP.
http://www.kensingtonbooks.com

ZEBRA BOOKS are published by

Kensington Publishing Corp.
119 West 40th Street
New York, NY 10018

All Kensington titles, imprints, and distributed lines are available at special quantity discounts for bulk purchases for sales promotion, premiums, fund-raising, educational, or institutional use.

Special book excerpts or customized printings can also be created to fit specific needs. For details, write or phone the office of the Kensington Sales Manager: Attn.: Sales Department. Kensington Publishing Corp., 119 West 40th Street, New York, NY 10018. Phone: 1-800-221-2647.

Zebra and the Z logo Reg. U.S. Pat. & TM Off.

First Printing: November 2016
ISBN-13: 978-1-4201-4170-2
ISBN-10: 1-4201-4170-8

eISBN-13: 978-1-4201-4171-9
eISBN-10: 1-4201-4171-6

10 9 8 7 6 5 4 3 2 1

Printed in the United States of America

For Diana Palmer: guardian angel

Chapter One

Mallory knew the route to Forrester Base Hospital as well as she knew the lines on the palms of her hands. She had never had the dubious pleasure of having her palm read, but she had often wondered, was palmistry no more than superstition or was there something to it? Her life line showed a catastrophic break when one had actually occurred. If she read beyond the break, she was set to receive a card from the queen when she turned one hundred. As it was, she was twenty-eight. There was plenty of time to get her life in order and find some happiness. Currently her life was largely devoted to work. She allowed herself precious little free time. It was a deliberate strategy. Keep on the move. Don't sit pondering over what was lodged in the soul.

The driver of the little Mazda ahead was starting to annoy her. He was showing excessive respect for the speed limit, flashing his red lights at every bend in the road. She figured it was time to pass, and was surprised when the driver gave her a loud honk for no discernible reason. She held up her hand, waved. A nice little gesture of camaraderie and goodwill.

She was almost there, thank the Lord. The farther she had travelled from the state capital, Brisbane, the more drag on her emotions. That pesky old drag would never go away. It was a side effect of the baggage she carted around and couldn't unload. It wasn't that she didn't visualize a brave new world. It was just that so far it hadn't happened. Life was neither kind nor reasonable. She knew that better than most. She also knew one had to fight the good fight even when the chances of getting knocked down on a regular basis were high.

It had been six years and more since she had been back to her hometown. She wouldn't be returning now, she acknowledged with a stab of guilt, but for the unexpected heart attack of her uncle Robert. Her uncle, a cultured courtly man, had reared her from age seven. No one else had been offering. Certainly not her absentee father, or her maternal grand-parents, who spent their days cruising the world on the *Queen Mary 2.* True, they did call in to see her whenever they set foot on dry land, bearing loads of expensive gifts. But sadly they were unable to introduce a child into their busy lives. She was the main beneficiary of their will. They had assured her of that; a little something by way of compensation. She was, after all, their only grandchild. It was just at seven, she didn't fit into their lifestyle. Decades later, she still didn't.

Was it any wonder she loved her uncle Robert? He was her superhero. Handsome, charming, well off. A bachelor by choice. Her dead mother, Claudia, had captured his heart long ago when they were young and deeply in love. Her mother had gone to her grave with her uncle's heart still pocketed away. It was an extraordinary thing and in many ways a calamity, because Uncle Robert had never considered snatching his life back. He was a lost cause in the marriage stakes. As was she, for that matter.

To fund what appeared on the surface to be a glamorous lifestyle, Robert James had quit law to become a very popular author of novels of crime and intrigue. The draw card for his legions of fans was his comedic detective, Peter Zero, never as famous as the legendary Hercule Poirot, but much loved by the readership.

Pulp fiction, her father, Nigel James, Professor of English and Cultural Studies at Melbourne University, called it. Her father had always stomped on his older brother's talent. "Fodder for the ignorant masses to be read on the train." Her father never minced words, the crueller the better. To put a name to it, her father was an all-out bastard.

It was Uncle Robert who had spelled love and a safe haven to her. He had taken her to live with him at Moonglade, his tropical hideaway in far North Queensland. In the infamous "black birding" days, when South Sea Islanders had been kidnapped to work the Queensland cane fields, Moonglade had been a thriving sugar plantation. The house had been built by one Captain George Rankin, who had at least fed his workers bananas, mangoes, and the like and paid them a token sum to work like the slaves they were in a sizzling hot sun.

Uncle Robert had not bought the property as a working plantation. Moonglade was his secure retreat from the world. He could not have chosen a more idyllic spot, with two listed World Heritage areas on his doorstep, the magnificent Daintree Rainforest, the oldest living rainforest on the planet, and the glorious Great Barrier Reef, the world's largest reef system.

His heart attack had come right out of the blue. Her uncle had always kept himself fit. He went for long walks along the white sandy beach, the sound of seagulls in his ears. He swam daily in a brilliantly blue sea, smooth as glass. To no avail. The truth was no one knew what might happen next. The only certainty in life was death. Life was a circus; fate the ringmaster. Her uncle's illness demanded her presence. It was her turn to demonstrate her love.

Up ahead was another challenge. A procession of undertakers? A line of vehicles was crawling along as though they had all day to get to their destination. Where the heck *was* that? There were no shops or supermarkets nearby, only the unending rich red ochre fields lying fallow in vivid contrast with the striking green of the eternal cane. The North was sugar, an area of vibrant colour and great natural beauty. It occurred to her the procession might be heading to the cemetery via the South Pole.

Some five minutes later she arrived at the entrance to the hospital grounds. There was nothing to worry about, she kept telling herself. She had been assured of that by none other than Blaine Forrester, who had rung her with the news. She had known Blaine since her childhood. Her uncle thought the world of him. Fair to say Blaine was the son he never had. She *knew* she came first with her uncle, but his affection for Blaine, five years her senior, had always ruffled her feathers. She was *more* than Blaine, she had frequently reminded herself, the only son of good friends and neighbours. She was *blood*.

Blaine's assurances, his review of the whole situation, hadn't prevented her from feeling anxious. In the end Uncle Robert was all the family she had. Without him she would be alone.

Entirely alone.

The main gates were open, the entry made splendid by a pair of poincianas in sumptuous scarlet bloom. The branches of the great shade trees had been dragged down into their perfect umbrella shape by the sheer weight of the annual blossoming. For as far back as she could remember, the whole town of Forrester had waited for the summer flowering, as another town might wait for an annual folk festival. The Royal Poinciana, a native of Madagascar, had to be the most glorious ornamental tree grown in all sub-tropical and tropical parts of the world.

"Pure magic!" she said, aloud.

It was her spontaneous response to the breathtaking display. Nothing could beat Nature for visual therapy. As she watched, the breeze gusted clouds of spent blossom to the ground, forming a deep crimson carpet.

She parked, as waves of uncomplicated delight rolled over her. She loved this place. North of Capricorn was another world, an artist's dream. There had always been an artist's colony. Some of the country's finest artists had lived and painted here, turning out their glorious land- and seascapes, scenes of island life. Uncle Robert had a fine body of their work at the house, including a beautiful painting of the district's famous Poinciana Road that led directly to Moonglade Estate. From childhood, poincianas had great significance for her. Psychic balm to a child's wounded heart and spirit, she supposed.

Vivid memories clung to this part of the world. The Good. The Bad. The Ugly. Memories were like ghosts that appeared in the night and didn't disappear at sunrise as they should. She knew the distance between memory and what really happened could be vast. Lesser memories were susceptible to reconstruction over the years. It was the *worst* memories one remembered best. The worst became deeply embedded.

Her memories were perfectly clear. They set her on edge the rare times she allowed them to flare up. Over the years she had developed many strategies to maintain her equilibrium. Self-control was her striking success. It was a marvellous disguise. One she wore well.

A light, inoffensive beep of a car horn this time brought her out of her reverie. She glanced in the rear vision mirror, lifting an apologetic hand to the woman driver in the car behind her. She moved off to the parking bays on either side of the main entrance. Her eyes as a matter of course took in the variety of tropical shrubs, frangipani, spectacular Hawaiian hibiscus, and the heavenly perfumed oleanders that had been planted the entire length of the perimeter and in front of the bays. Like the poincianas, their hectic blooming was unaffected by the powerful heat. Indeed the heat only served to produce more ravishing displays. The mingled scents permeated the heated air like incense, catching at the nose and throat.

Tropical blooming had hung over her childhood; hung over her heart. High summer: hibiscus, heartbreak. She kept all that buried. A glance at the dash told her it was two o'clock. She had made good time. Her choice of clothing, her usual classic gear, would have been just right in the city. Not here. For the tropics she should have been wearing simple clothes, loose, light cotton. She was plainly overdressed. No matter. Her dress sense, her acknowledged stylishness, was a form of protection. To her mind it was like drawing a velvet glove over shattered glass.

Auxiliary buildings lay to either side of the main structure. There was a large designated area for ambulances only. She pulled into the doctors' parking lot. She shouldn't have parked there, but she excused herself on the grounds there were several other vacant spots. The car that had been behind her had parked in the visitors' zone. The occupant was already out of her vehicle, heading towards the front doors at a run.

"Better get my skates on," she called with a friendly wave to Mallory as she passed. Obviously she was late and by the look of it expecting to be hauled over the coals.

There were good patients. And terrible patients. Mallory had seen demonstrations of both. Swiftly she checked her face in the rear-view mirror. Gold filigrees of hair were stuck to her cheeks. Deftly she brushed them back. She had good thick hair that was carefully controlled. No casual ponytail but an updated knot as primly elegant as an

Edwardian chignon. She didn't bother to lock the
doors, but made her way directly into the modern
two-storied building.

The interior was brightly lit, with a smell like fresh
laundry and none of the depressing clinical smells
and the long, echoing hallways of the vast impersonal
city hospitals. The walls of the long corridor were off-
white and hung with paintings she guessed were by
local artists. A couple of patients in dressing gowns
were wandering down the corridor to her left, chat-
ting away brightly as if they were off to attend an in-
hospital concert. To her right a young male doctor,
white coat flying, clipboard in hand zipped into a
room as though he didn't have a second to lose.

There was a pretty, part aboriginal young nurse
stationed at Reception. At one end of the counter was
a large oriental vase filled with beautiful white, pink-
speckled Asian lilies. Mallory dipped her head to
catch their sweet spicy scent.

"I'm here to see a patient, Robert James," she said
smiling, as she looked up.

"Certainly, Dr. James." Bright, cheerful, accommodating.

She was known. How?

An older woman with a brisk no-nonsense air of
authority hurried towards Reception. She too appeared pleased to see Mallory. Palm extended, she
pointed off along the corridor. "Dr. Moorehouse is
with Mr. James. You should be able to see him shortly,
Dr. James. Would you like a cup of tea?"

Swiftly Mallory took note of the name tag. "A cup
of tea would go down very nicely, Sister Arnold."

"I'll arrange it," said Sister. Their patient had a

photograph of this young woman beside his bed. He invited everyone to take a look. "My beautiful niece, Mallory. *Dr.* Mallory James!"

Several minutes later when she hadn't even sat down, Mallory saw one splendid looking man stride up to Reception. Six feet and over. Thoroughbred build. Early thirties. Thick head of crow black hair. Clearly not one of the bit players in life.

Blaine!

The mere sight of him put her on high alert. Though it made perfect sense for him to be there, she felt her emotions start to bob up and down like a cork in a water barrel. For all her strategies, she had never mastered the knack of keeping focused with Blaine around. He knew her too well. That was the problem. He knew the number of times she had made a complete fool of herself. He knew all about her disastrous engagement. Her abysmal choice of a life partner. He had always judged her and found her wanting. Okay, they were friends, having known one another forever, but there were many downsides to their crotchety, often stormy relationship. She might as well admit it. It was mostly her fault. So many times over the years she had been as difficult as she could be. It was a form of retaliation and a deep-seated grudge.

Blaine knew all about the years she had been under the care of Dr. Sarah Matthews, child psychologist and a leader in her field. The highly emotional unstable years. He knew all about her dangerous habit of sleepwalking. Blaine knew far too much.

Anyone would resent it. He wasn't a doctor yet he
knew her entire case history. For all that, Blaine was
a man of considerable charisma. What was charisma
anyway, she had often asked herself. Was one born
with it or was it acquired over time? Did charismatic
people provoke a sensual experience in everyone
they met? She thought if they were like Blaine, the
answer had to be yes. One of Blaine's most attractive qualities was his blazing energy. It inspired
confidence. Here was a man who could and did get
things done.

Blaine was a big supporter of the hospital. He had
property in all the key places. The Forrester family
had made a fortune over the generations. They were
descendants of George Herbert Forrester, an English-
man, already on his way to being rich before he left
the colony of New South Wales to venture into the
vast unknown territory which was to become the
State of Queensland in 1859. For decades on end,
the Forresters pretty well owned and ran the town.
Their saving grace was as employers they were very
good to their workers to the extent everyone, right
up to the present day, considered themselves part of
one big happy family and responded accordingly.

She heard him speak to the nurse at Reception. He
had a compelling voice. It had a special quality to it.
It exactly matched the man. She saw his aura. Her
secret: She was able to see auras. Not of everyone.
That would have been beyond anyone's ability to
cope with. But *certain* people. Good and bad. She saw
Blaine's now. The energy field that surrounded him
was the familiar cobalt blue. She knew these auras
were invisible to most people. She had no idea why
she should see them, *feel* them, as *heat* waves. The gift,

if it was one, hadn't been developed over the years. It had just always been there.

Once, to her everlasting inner cringe, she had confided her secret to Blaine. She was around fourteen at the time. There he was, so handsome, already making his mark, home from university. She remembered exactly where they were, lazing in the sun, down by Moonglade's lake. The moment she had stopped talking, he had propped himself up on his elbow, looking down at her with his extraordinary silver eyes.

"You're having me on!"

"No, I swear."

He had burst out laughing. *"Listen, kid. I'm cool with all your tall tales and celestial travels, but we both know auras don't exist."*

"They do. They do exist."

Her rage and disappointment in him had known no bounds. She had entrusted him with her precious secret and he, her childhood idol, had laughed her to scorn. No wonder she had gone off like a firecracker.

"Don't you dare call me a liar, Blaine Forrester. I see auras. I've seen your aura lots of times. Just because you can't see them doesn't mean they're not there. You're nothing but an insensitive, arrogant pig!"

He had made her *so* angry that even years later she still felt residual heat. She had wanted him to listen to her, to share. Instead he had ridiculed her. It might have been that very moment their easy, affectionate relationship underwent a dramatic sea change. Blaine, the friend she had so looked up to and trusted, had laughed at her. Called her a kid. She *did* see auras, some strong, some dim. It had something to do with her particular brain. One day science would prove the phenomenon. In the meantime she continued to see auras that lasted maybe half a minute before they faded. Blaine's, the unbeliever's aura was as she had told him all those years ago, a cobalt blue. Uncle Robert's was a pale green with a pinkish area over his heart. She couldn't see her own aura. She had seen her dying mother's black aura. Recognised what it meant. She had seen that black aura a number of times since.

A moment more and Blaine was making his way to the waiting room. Mercifully this one was empty, although Mallory could hear farther along the corridor, a woman's voice reading a familiar children's story accompanied by children's sweet laughter. How beautiful was the laughter of children, as musical as wind chimes.

As Blaine reached the doorway she found herself standing up. Why she did was beyond her. The pity of it was she felt the familiar involuntary flair of *excitement.* She was stuck with that, sadly. It would never go away. She extended her hand, hoping her face wasn't flushed. Hugs and air-kisses were long since out of the question between them. Yet, as usual, all her senses were on point. "Blaine."

"Mallory." He gave her a measured look, his fingers curling around hers. With a flush on her beautiful skin she looked radiant. Not that he was about to tell her. Mallory had no use whatsoever for compliments.

The mocking note in his voice wasn't lost on Mallory. She chose to ignore it. From long experience she was prepared for physical contact, yet as always she marvelled at the *charge.* It was pretty much like a mild electric shock. She had written it off as a case of static electricity. Physics. With his height, he made her willowy five feet eight seem petite. That gave him an extra advantage. His light grey eyes were in startling contrast to his hair and darkly tanned skin. Sculpted features, an air of sharp intelligence, and natural authority made for an indelible impression. From long experience she knew Blaine sent women into orbit. It made her almost wish she was one of them. She believed the intensity of his gaze owed much to the luminosity of his eyes. Eyes like that would give anyone a jolt.

He gestured towards one of the long upholstered benches as though telling her what to do. She *hated* that as well. It was like he always knew the best course of action. She realized her reactions were childish, bred from long years of resenting him and his high-handed, taken for granted, male superiority, but childish nevertheless. No one was perfect. He should have been kinder.

Blaine was fully aware of the war going on inside Mallory. He knew all about her anxieties, her complexities. He had first met her when she was seven, a pretty little girl with lovely manners. Mallory, the adult, was a woman to be reckoned with. Probably she would be formidable in old age. Right now, she was that odd combination of incredibly sexy and incredibly aloof. There was nothing even mildly flirtatious about her. Yet she possessed powers that he didn't understand. He wondered what would happen if she ever let those powers fly.

She was wearing a very stylish yellow jacket and skirt. City gear. Not a lot of women could get away with the colour. Her luxuriant dark gold hair was pulled back into some sort of knot. Her olive skin was flawless, her velvet-brown eyes set at a faint tilt. Mallory James was a beautiful woman like her tragic mother before her. Brains and beauty had been bred into Mallory. Her academic brilliance had allowed her to take charge of her life. She had a PhD in child psychology. Close containment had become Mallory's way of avoiding transient sexual relationships and deep emotional involvement. Mallory made it very plain she was captain of her own ship.

The aftershock of their handshake was still running up Mallory's arm to her shoulder. She seized back control. She had spent years perfecting a cool façade. By now it was second nature. Only Blaine, to her disgust, had the power to disrupt her habitual poise. Yet there was something *real* between them; some deep empathy that inextricably tied them together. He to her, she to him. She was aware of the strange disconnect between their invariably charged conversations and a *different* communication she refused to investigate.

"I'm worried about Uncle Robert," she said briskly. She supposed he could have interpreted it as accusatory. "You told me it was a *mild* heart attack, Blaine. I thought he would be home by now. Yet he's still in hospital?"

"He's in for observation, Mallory. No hurry." *Here we go again,* he thought.

"Anything else I should know?" She studied him coolly. The handsomeness, the glowing energy, the splendid physique.

"Ted will fill you in."

"So there's nothing you can tell me?" Her highly

sensitive antenna was signalling there was more to come.

"Not really." His light eyes sparkled in the rays of sunlight that fell through the high windows.

"So why do I have this feeling you're keeping something from me?"

Blaine nearly groaned aloud. As usual she was spot on, only he knew he had to work his way up to full disclosure. "Mallory, it's essential to Robb's recovery for you to be *here*, not in Brisbane. He's slowed down of recent times, but he never said there was anything to worry about. It now appears he has a heart condition. Angina."

"But he never told me." She showed her shock and dismay.

"Nor me. Obviously he didn't want it to be known."

Without thinking, she clutched his arm as if he might have some idea of walking away from her. He was wearing a short-sleeved cotton shirt, a blue and white check with his jeans, so she met with suntanned warm skin and hard muscle. She should have thought of that. Blaine had such *physicality* it made her stomach contract. He further rattled her by putting his hand on top of hers.

"You believe I have a moral obligation to look out for my uncle as he looked after me?"

"I'm not here to judge you, Mallory," he said smoothly.

"Never mind about that. I'm always under surveillance." Blaine had established the habit of meeting up with her whenever he was in Brisbane on business, which was often. His lawyers, accountants, stock brokers among others were all stationed in the state capital. He made sure she was always contactable.

As a man he was even more highly esteemed by her uncle, for whom he clearly stood in.

His hand dropped away first. He had only just beaten her to it with his swifter reflexes. It had made her uncomfortable feeling the strength of his arm and the warmth of his skin, but she wasn't about to waste time fretting about it.

"That's in *your* head, Mallory. It's not true. More like I've tried my hardest to be a good friend to you." *You difficult woman, you.* He didn't need to say it, Mallory heard it loud and clear.

"Anyway, you're here now. You can give Robb your undivided attention for a few days."

"Whatever you say, Blaine. You're the boss." Heat was spreading through her. In the old days she had let it control her. Not now. As Dr. Mallory James, she was used to being treated with respect. "Uncle Robert and I are in constant touch, as you well know. Anyway, he has *you*," she tacked on sweetly. "Always ready to help. The figure of authority in the town."

"Do I detect a lick of jealousy?"

"Jealousy!" She gasped in air. "That's a charge and a half."

"Okay, make it sibling rivalry, even if we aren't siblings. You can't rule it out. I've known Robb all my life. My parents loved him. He was always welcome at our home. I remember the first time you turned up. A perfectly sweet little girl *in those days* with long blonde hair tied back with a wide blue ribbon. My father said later, 'Those two should be painted, Claudia and her beautiful little daughter.'"

"That never happened." A flush had warmed Mallory's skin. She wished she could dash it away.

"I noticed like everyone else how closely you resembled your mother," Blaine said more gently.

"Ah, the fatal resemblance! It was extraordinary and it impacted on too many lives." She broke off at the sound of approaching footsteps. Sister Arnold was returning with tea.

Blaine moved to take the tray from her. "Thank you, Sister."

"Would you like a cup yourself, Mr. Forrester?"

How many times had Mallory heard just that worshipful tone? Nothing would ever be too much trouble for Blaine Forrester; tea, coffee, scones, maybe a freshly baked muffin?

"I'm fine, thank you, Sister." He gave her a smile so attractive it could sell a woman into slavery.

"You could bring another cup, Sister, if you don't mind," said Mallory. There was really something about Blaine that was very dangerous to women.

"No trouble at all." Sister Arnold gave Blaine a look that even a blind woman would interpret as non-professional.

"I don't drink tea," Blaine mentioned as she bustled away.

"At this point who cares? Sister likes bringing it. Makes her day."

He ignored the jibe as too trivial to warrant comment. "You drove all this way?"

She nodded. "One stop. It would have been a whole lot quicker to fly but I don't enjoy air travel, as you know." She was borderline claustrophobic but halfway to conquering it.

"That's your Mercedes out front?"

"It is." She had worked long and hard to pay it off.

"I love my car. Just like you men. You did *assure* me Uncle Robert was in no danger."

"With care and the right medication Robb has many good years left in him."

"I hope so." Mallory released a fervent breath.

"Ah, here's Sister back with my tea."

"Don't forget to give her your dazzling smile."

"How odd you've noticed," he said, his sparkling eyes full on hers.

An interlude followed filled with the usual ping-pong of chat, largely saturated with sarcasm, most of it, hers. Dr. Edward Moorehouse, looking like an Einstein incarnation with his white bush of hair and a walrus moustache, hurried into the waiting room. A highly regarded cardiac specialist, he possessed a sweetness of heart and an avuncular charm.

"Ah, Mallory, Blaine!" He saluted them, looking from one to the other with evident pleasure. His head was tilted to one side, much like a bird's, his dark eyes bright with more than a hint of mischief. "How lovely to see you together. I hear such good things about you, Mallory."

Mallory kissed him gently on both cheeks, feeling a sense of warmth and homecoming. "Dr. Sarah set my feet on my chosen path."

"Bless her."

Dr. Sarah Matthews had guided Mallory through her severe childhood traumas; her terrible grief over the violent, sudden death of her adored mother which she had witnessed, the later abandonment of her by her father, compounded by irrational feelings of guilt that she had lived when her beautiful mother had died.

"Wonderful woman, Sarah!" Moorehouse's voice

was tinged with sadness. Sarah Matthews had died of lung cancer a couple of years previously when she had never smoked a cigarette in her life. "We would always have a job for you if you ever come back to us, Mallory. No one has taken Sarah's place with the same degree of success. There are always cases needing attention, even here in this paradise."

She was aware of that. "Blaine tells me Uncle Robert has had a heart condition for some time. I didn't know that."

"Robb wouldn't have wanted to worry you." Moorehouse darted a glance at Blaine, then back to Mallory. "He has his medication. Robb is the most considerate man I know," he said, in his soothing manner.

Mallory wasn't sidetracked. "He *should* have told me. I needed to know."

"Don't agitate yourself, Mallory. With care and keeping on his meds, Robb has some good years left to him."

"Some?" She had to weigh that answer very carefully.

"All being well." Ted Moorehouse spoke with a doctor's inbuilt caution. "You must be longing to see him. I'll take you to his room."

"I'll stay here." Blaine glanced at Mallory. "You'll want to see Robert on your own."

"I appreciate that, Blaine," she said, gracefully. "Give us ten minutes and then come through."

They found Robert James sitting up in bed, propped up by pillows. An ecstatic smile lit his still-handsome face the moment Mallory walked in the door. As a consequence, Mallory's vision started to cloud. Outside his room she had steeled herself, concerned at how he might look after his heart attack.

Now his appearance reassured her. She felt like a little girl again, a bereaved child. Uncle Robert was the one who had been there for her, taking her in. She couldn't bear the thought of his leaving her.

The ones you love best, die.

She knew that better than anyone.

Robert James, gazing at the figure of his adored niece, felt wave after wave of joy bubbling up like a fountain inside his chest. She had come back to him. Claudia's daughter. His niece. His brother's child. His family. He was deeply conscious of how much he had missed Mallory these past years, although they kept in close touch. He had accepted her decision to flee the town where he had raised her. She had strong reasons, and he accepted them. Besides, clever young woman that she was, she had to find her place in the larger world. He was so proud of Mallory and her accomplishments. Proud he had been her mentor. His whole being, hitherto on a downward spiral, sparked up miraculously.

"Mallory, darling girl!" He held out his arms to gather her in. What he really felt like doing was getting out of bed and doing a little dance.

"Uncle Robert." Mallory swallowed hard on the lump in her throat. She wasn't about to cry in front of him, though she felt alarm at the lack of colour in his aura. Love for him consumed her. He looked on the gaunt side, but resplendent in stylish silk pyjamas. Robert James was elegant wherever he was, in hospital, in private. Like her father, he was a bit of a dandy. There were violet shadows under his eyes, hollows beneath his high cheekbones and at the base of his throat. But there was colour in his cheeks, even if it was most probably from excitement. He had lost much needed weight, along with strength and vitality, hence his diminished aura.

"It's so wonderful to see you, sweetheart, but you didn't have to come all this way. Ted says I'm fine."

"You *are* fine, Robb." Ted Moorehouse quietly intervened. He knew how much his friend loved his niece. Her presence would do him a power of good. "I'll leave you two together. You can take Robb home around this time tomorrow, Mallory." He half turned at the door. "I expect you're staying for a day or two?"

Mallory tightened her hold on her uncle's thin hand, meeting his eyes. "Actually I've taken extended leave."

"Why that's wonderful, Mallory." Moorehouse beamed his approval. "Just what the doctor ordered." He lifted a benedictory hand as he headed out the door.

"Extended leave! I feel on top of the world already." Robert's fine dark eyes were brimming with an invalid's tears.

Mallory bowed her head humbly at her uncle's intense look of *gratitude*. It was *she* who had every reason to be grateful. She pulled up a chair and sat down at the bedside. Her touch feather light, she smoothed his forehead with gentle fingertips, let them slide down over his thin cheek. "I'm so sorry if I've hurt you with my long absence, Uncle Robert. I know Blaine finds it so. He's outside, by the way."

"He's always there when you need him." Robert's voice was full of the usual pride and affection. "To be honest, I don't know what I would have done without him. He's been splendid, a real chip off the old block. Not that D'Arcy ever got to grow old."

Mallory bowed her head. She wasn't the only one who had lost a beloved parent. Blaine too had suffered. D'Arcy Forrester had been killed leading a clean-up party after a severe cyclone. Too late to be spotted, he had trodden on fallen power lines that had been camouflaged by a pile of palm fronds. His passing had been greatly mourned in the town. The reins had been passed into Blaine's capable hands.

Robert James's hollowed-out gaze rested on his niece. "Does Nigel know about me?"

Mallory's smile barely wavered. "I've left messages. I'm sure he'll respond."

"I won't count on it." Robert spoke wryly. "Stripped of the mask of learnedness, my brother is not a caring man. What heart he had went with your mother. I would have liked to see him, all that same. We *are* blood."

Unease etched itself on Mallory's face. "Goodness, Uncle Robert, you're not dying." She tightened her grip as if to hold him forever. "You've got plenty more good years left to you. I'm here now. Father will be in contact, I'm sure." She was certain her father would have received her messages. But her father hated confronting issues like illness and death.

Some minutes later Blaine walked through the door, his eyes taking in the heart-warming sight of uncle and niece lovingly holding hands. "How goes it?" An answering affection for the older man was apparent.

"Wonderful, thank you, Blaine," Robert responded, eyes bright. "Ted says I can come home tomorrow."

"That's great news. I can pick you up in the Range

Rover. To make it easy for Mallory, I can pick her up on the way."

So it was arranged and they left the room.

She didn't so much walk as glide on those long elegant legs, Blaine thought. Mallory moved like a dancer; every twist and turn, every smooth pivot. It was high time he dropped the bombshell and then stood well back for the fallout. He knew Robb hadn't told her. Robb simply wasn't up to it. It was part of Robb's Avoidance Program.

"Something I should tell you, Mallory." He hoped if she was going to shoot the messenger, she aimed high.

"I *knew* there was something." Mallory came to an abrupt halt.

"Your psychic powers?" he suggested, that irritating quirk to his handsome mouth.

"Why don't you double up with laughter? What powers I have—which you *don't believe* is true—do work. I've been picking up vibes something wasn't right. I can see by your face you'd prefer not to be having the upcoming conversation." Normally she spoke quietly. She was quiet with her movements as well. She never sought to draw attention to herself, but with Blaine her usually controlled manner became by comparison nearly theatrical.

"How right you are. I don't think you could guess, so I'll get right to it. Jason Cartwright has a job at Moonglade. On the farm."

The shock was so great she felt like ducking for cover.

"Hey, are you okay?" Blaine showed his concern.

For a moment she was too dumbfounded to reply. "Okay? I'm the expert on okay. I'm actually delirious with joy. Jason at the farm! What luck!" Her blood pressure was definitely soaring well above her usual spot-on 119/76.

He didn't relish this job, but he had promised Robb he would bring Mallory up-to-date. Robb tended to pull in the favours. "I'm sorry to spring it on you. Robb has never told you for his own reasons, but it's something you obviously need to know now that you're here."

Take your time.

Stare into space for a minute.

She felt more like shouting, only that would be so utterly, utterly unlike Dr. Mallory James. "I love Uncle Robert dearly, but we both know he evades difficult issues like the plague. I *knew* he was keeping something from me."

"Your psychic powers didn't fill you in?"

"Oh, bugger off, Blaine." Abruptly she stalked off to her car, unlocking the doors with a press on the remote. She felt like driving back the way she came.

Blaine caught her up with ease. "We can handle this, Mallory."

"*We?*" she huffed, rounding on him. "*We* will, will we? I love that. Your offer of support only grates."

"It's well meant. I've another surprise for you."

Her dark eyes flashed. "Don't hang about. Get it out. It's a bigger surprise than Jason working at the farm?"

For a woman who hated to lose her cool, Mallory's dark eyes gave her, the enigma, away. They were *passionate* eyes. "He *runs* it," Blaine bit off. "No point in stretching things out."

She tried to find words. None came. "Well, he's had such a rotten time, he deserves a break," she said, finally.

"I share your dismay."

"Then why didn't you stop it?" She was trying without success to dampen the burn inside her. "You can do *anything* when you want to. I've seen plenty of evidence of that over the years. You're the Fixer. You run the town."

"I've never said that."

"You don't have to. Does Queen Elizabeth tell everyone she's the queen? She doesn't have to."

"Are you hearing yourself?" He too was firing up. "Be fair. It was Robb's decision, Mallory. It was never going to be mine. I couldn't take matters out of his hands. Robb owns Moonglade and the business. I've never been a fan of Jason's but he's not a criminal."

"He *is* a criminal!" Mallory declared, fiercely. "He betrayed me. He betrayed his family, Uncle Robert, even the town. That's criminal in my book. Honestly Blaine, this is too much."

He agreed, but he wasn't about to stoke the flames. "I can't expect you to be happy about it. He's good at the job. He works hard."

Mallory shook her head. "The golden boy! That makes it okay for my married ex-fiancé to live and work on the doorstep? I suppose I can be grateful he wasn't invited to live in the house. Why couldn't Uncle Robert tell me himself? I don't give a damn how efficient Jason is. Uncle Robert—oh, don't bother." She broke off, in disgust. "It's the Avoidance

Syndrome. It's rife among men." She propped herself against her car, in case she slid ignominiously to the ground. "Why does chaos follow me?"

"You're doing okay," he said briskly.

She waved his comment off. "What is *wrong* with Uncle Robb's thinking?"

"Obviously, it's different from yours."

"Ss-o?" She rushed so fast into words she almost stuttered.

"If someone's decisions are different from our own, then we tend to assume it doesn't make a lot of sense."

"There's nothing wrong with my thinking, thank you." She became aware she was beating an angry tattoo on the concrete with the toe of her shoe. This wasn't like her. Not like her at all. Blaine found the terrible weak spot in her defences. "You didn't understand Uncle Robert's decision, did you?"

"The milk of human kindness? Blessed are the merciful and all that?"

"I love the way you guys stick together."

"Oh, come off it, Mallory," he said, exasperated.

"We never know people, do we? Even the people closest to us. We always miss something. Uncle Robert needed to tell me. *You* of all people should know that. Damn it, Blaine, Jason's working at Moonglade is an outrage. It chills my heart. So don't stand there looking like business as usual."

He rubbed the back of his tanned neck. "It won't help to see it like that, Mallory. It's a done deal. You'd moved on. You didn't come back. It was well over six years ago."

"An astonishing amount of time. So you're saying

I'm the one who is acting badly? Or am I an idiot for asking?"

"I don't think you're likely to hear the word 'idiot' in connection with you in a lifetime. Robb has a notoriously kind heart. He gave your ex-fiancé a job after it became apparent Harry Cartwright had disowned his only son. Robb is a very compassionate man."

"A sucker for a sob story, you mean. Okay, okay, *I* was a sob story. A seven-year-old kid who had lost her mother. A kid who was abandoned by her greatly admired gutless father because I'm the spitting image of my mother. He couldn't look at me. I might have had two heads. I was his little daughter so much in need of a father's comfort, but my appearance totally alienated him. It was like I should have had plastic surgery, changed the colour of my hair, popped in baby blue contact lenses. Ah, what the hell!" She broke off, ashamed of her rant.

"Mallory, I can't think of a single soul who didn't find your father's behaviour deplorable. You had a tough time but you've come through with flying colours."

"An illusion I've managed to create."

"We all create illusions. I do get how you feel."

She raised her face to his, not bothering to hide her agitation. "How do you get it? Selma didn't run off from your wedding, so be grateful for that. Jason was an assassin. He stabbed me in the back, right on the eve of our wedding, remember? You should, you were there. You're *always* there, letting me know what a fool I am. Will you ever forget how the news of Kathy Burch's pregnancy spread like wildfire around the town? The disgrace. The humiliation. The shame.

To make it worse, Uncle Robert had spent a fortune ensuring a fairy-tale wedding for me."

"I did warn you."

She felt the screws tighten. "Yeah, prescient old you! You must get great satisfaction out of knowing everything you said about Jason came true."

"He wasn't the most desirable candidate for your hand. Certainly not the husband of choice."

"Not your choice for me."

"Not Robb's choice either, even if he avoided saying so, which is a great pity, but seriously not worth getting into now. It didn't make me *happy* to say what I said then."

"I don't believe that for one moment. You relished the breakup. I was under so much stress, but you, superior old you, had to punch my stupidity home."

An answering heat of anger was rising in him. A certain amount of conflict with Mallory was par for the course. "How unfair can you get? If I'd told you I thought Jason Cartwright was absolutely *perfect*, you might have broken off the engagement."

She stared at him, wondering in consternation if he had spoken a truth. "There's always friction between us, isn't there?" she said, angrily puffing at a stray lock of her hair. "Bottled-up forces."

"That's what *you* want, Mallory. Not me." Blaine stared down at her. Radiance had a way of playing around Mallory. The hot sun was picking out the gold strands in her hair and at her temples. The delicate bones of her face he found not only endearing, but intensely erotic.

"Jason was kicked out of his home and the thriving family real estate business for reasons unknown. Was it money?" Mallory pondered. "Money causes big problems. Were the twins robbing their father on the side? Surely Uncle Robert pressed Jason for some explanation?"

"None forthcoming to this day." Blaine fixed a glance on her narrow, tapping foot.

She stopped the tapping. "You've always been able to get to the bottom of things."

"Wasn't my place, Mallory, as I said."

"Well, I can't accept you don't have *some* idea as to what the breakup was all about. You have your little network. All the businessmen in town want to hook up with you. They all know Harry. What about the grapevine?"

"Oddly the breakup hasn't become the talk of the town. It's a mystery, destined to remain so."

She gave another dismissive wave of her hand. "I don't like mysteries, especially when they impact on my life. His parents doted on Jason. Could the fallout have been because of *me*? That would make me very uncomfortable indeed."

"I think not."

"How can you be so sure?"

"I know that much, Mallory."

She felt another quick surge of anger. "Of course you do, and a whole lot more you're not telling. Jason married Kathy Burch. They have a little girl."

"Her name is Ivy, a cute little kid. Kathy, however, is a very subdued young woman these days. Marriage and motherhood have—"

"Taken their toll?"

"The short answer is yes. Kathy is very much under Jessica's thumb."

She took a deep breath. Counted to ten. "A bigger bombshell is coming? Jessica is still on the scene?"

"Try to pry her away from her brother," Blaine said, his tone bone-dry.

"Can no one kill her off? Or at least start looking into it?"

"No way of doing it without landing in jail," Blaine said, laconically. "Those two were always joined at the hip. Jason and Kathy live in the old manager's bungalow, by the way. Robert remodelled it up for them."

Mallory put her fingertips to her aching temples. "I didn't come prepared for these disclosures, Blaine. To think of all the phone calls, the emails, the visits and never a word."

"Not so surprising, is it?"

She shook her head. "Not really. We both know Uncle Robert avoids unpleasantness. It's his problem area. As for *you*! You too left me completely in the dark."

"Mallory, I couldn't go over Robb's head."

"I had rights, didn't I?"

"You left, Mallory, telling us you were never coming back."

"Who would blame me? You're not the most compassionate man in the world, are you?"

"Compassion wasn't, still isn't, what you wanted," he said, testily.

Mallory gave up. She would never win with Blaine. "I can't believe the Cartwrights would turn their backs on their only grandchild. Kathy might remain the outsider, but cutting off the little girl, the innocent victim, their own flesh and blood? The Marge Cartwright I remember was a nurturing woman."

"Maybe Jason is hitting back at his parents by not allowing them to see the child. She has a few problems apparently."

"Problems? What sort of problems?" Immediately

Mallory started ticking off childhood disorders in her head.

"Health problems, and I believe she's a little wild. The whole town knows. Kathy is always at the hospital with her."

"How very worrying." Mallory's stance had softened considerably. "Is the child on medication? There are so many underlying reasons for behavioural problems. Sometimes it can be hard for a GP to differentiate. Kids are hyper for a wide range of reasons."

"I'm sure you're right, Dr. James."

Ah, the suavity of his tone! "Helping problematic children is my area, Blaine," she reminded him sharply. "I'd like to point out, while we're on the subject, I didn't allow bitterness over what happened to me and Jason to eat me away. What's past is past."

"Faulkner didn't see it that way."

"Okay, the past is never past. That way of yours of constantly having the last word drives me crazy."

"As I've suggested, it could be your bad case of 'sibling' rivalry. You were lucky you didn't marry Jason. He didn't break your heart."

"Did Selma break yours?"

He only shrugged. "Forget Selma. Look, I'm not in the mood for this, Mallory."

"Then you're welcome to go on your way. I'm not stopping you." She tilted her chin.

"Take a chill pill, why don't you."

She flared up. "Chill pill? I don't pop pills." She had been on antidepressants for some years. Occasionally she had panic attacks, but she worked to contain them without medication.

"Oh, for God's sake, Mallory! Why do you work so

hard to misunderstand me? You're a psychologist. You know all about chill pills to control moods. I know this is difficult. If it helps, Cartwright is working hard. *Jessica* too."

For a split second she allowed her shoulders to droop. Then she straightened. No way was Blaine going to see her crumple. She'd do that when she was alone.

"Jessica Cartwright mightn't be a bucket of fun, but she's extremely competent," he went on. "She's far better than Jason at getting the best out of the staff."

"That's her big rap, is it? Jessica Cartwright gets the best out of the staff. Does she do it with a whip? Jessica was the nastiest kid in the school. She tormented the life out of Kathy Burch when Kathy suffered enough with that appalling father. Dare I ask how she wrangled the job?"

"Good question."

"With no good answer. Uncle Robert never liked her. He once called her a little monster."

"Tell me who did like her? Being pleasant never caught up with Jessica. She needed a job. The prospect of her finding work in town was uncertain at best."

"Most people had had kids in school with Jessica," Mallory said, tartly.

"She mightn't have a winning personality, but Jason's life doesn't seem to be complete without her."

"Repressed development. Jessica is the alpha twin. She's always been in charge. But Jason is a married man now. If Jessica is around, she probably spends her time ensuring every day is a real *bad* day for her sister-in-law. It's cruel for Jason to subject his wife to Jessica's TLC. God forbid he did it on purpose." Mallory felt up to her neck in unwelcome disclosures. "She's not his identical twin. They don't share identical genetic material. They express their DNA differently. Jason was as pleasant as Jessica was downright nasty. Having said that, twin-ship is a deeply symbiotic relationship. I hope it's not too rude to ask, what now? Is there a way out?"

"Not at the moment. Jessica lives in an apartment in town."

"I expect you own the complex?"

"I expect I do," he said.

"Modesty doesn't come in your size, does it?"

"If you say so, *dear* Mallory," he drawled. "To try to balance the good with the bad. Jessica has stuck by her brother."

"She'd stick with him if he were a total nutter. I really liked the Cartwrights."

"And they *loved* you." He went heavy on the *loved*.

"It was what it was," she said soberly. "So you got me here knowing all this?"

"I got you here for *Robert*. You owe him."

Memory after memory was sidling up. All of them full of angst. "I do so love you when you're righteous!"

"Me, righteous?" He spread his shapely hands.

"That's one of your big problems, Blaine. You're most righteous when you're in the wrong. And this is wrong."

"Would you have come back had you known?" He pinned her with his luminous eyes.

"So you deliberately kept me in the dark?"

"What would you have done had I told you the truth?"

She averted her gaze. "You don't know the workings of my mind, Blaine."

"You don't know mine, either."

"What's that supposed to mean?"

"You're smart. You'll figure it out. One piece of advice. Take it slowly."

She searched his face. Blaine was a central part of her life, but hunkering down inside her bolt hole had become a habit. "You make that sound like I could be steering into dangerous waters."

"And so you could be." He made the sombre observation.

"They know I'm coming?"

Blaine nodded. "I expect they're feeling their own brand of trepidation. But life has moved on. *You* have moved on, Mallory. You're Dr. James now, a highly regarded professional in your field. You could even be of help to the child."

The thought took the edge off her upset. "Only I'm certain Jason and his wife wouldn't want any help from me. Jessica was *never* my friend."

"I did tell you that as well."

"You did indeed." Between the heat and her sizzling emotions, she felt compelled to get away from him. "You know I've always thought you a complete—"

He cut her off, opening her car door. "No need to say it, Mallory. I can fill in the dots. And it wasn't *always*. Once we were good pals until puberty got in the way."

"Puberty? Whose puberty?" she demanded, incensed.

"Why yours, of course. I'm not a fool, Mallory. I know you hate it, but I know you too well."

"You'll need to do a lot of catch-up." With practised grace, she swivelled her long elegant legs as she settled into the driver's seat. "You find this funny?" She caught the glint in his eyes.

"Not at all. I just hope you're relatively okay with it."

"Like I'm relatively okay with a Force 5 cyclone. What time tomorrow?"

"Say eleven o'clock. Robert has a new house-keeper. Mrs. Rawlings. She lost her husband, Jeff, to cancer."

She nodded. "Uncle Robert did manage to tell me. I'm sorry. He told me plenty about your goings-on as well. We do so know he thinks of you as the son he never had. What did go wrong between you and Selma anyway?" Her voice was edged with malice, when malice didn't come naturally to her. "I would have thought she was madly in love with you?"

"You've managed to make that sound like one would have to wonder why."

"Just trying to spin your wheels. Besides, I didn't think you cared all that much what I thought."

"I'll let that one go as well. It was Selma who de-cided against an engagement," he offered with no loss of his ironclad composure.

"It was the other way around, I fancy. She loved you, but you found you didn't love her, or not enough to get married. Had you a new conquest in mind?"

He made to close her door. "Let's swap stories at another time, shall we, Mallory?"

"Nothing for you in it, Blaine. I'm a closed book."

"Unknowable to everyone but *me*."

She could have cheerfully slapped him. Instead she found herself tightening her body against the odd tumbling inside her. "I assume that's your arro-gance talking?"

"Not entirely. See you tomorrow."

He shut her door.

He walked away.

He didn't look back.

It wasn't the way it was supposed to be. But it was the way it was. She started the engine. She and Blaine were like a couple of tectonic plates doomed to scrape away at one another.

Twenty minutes later she arrived at the estate by way of Poinciana Road, one of the most beautiful country roads anyone could travel anywhere in the world. Thanks to the foresight of the town's founding fathers, the Forresters, of course, the magnificent shade trees had been planted in great numbers all over the district as well as being chosen to line the scenic drive just north of the town. It was the poinciana that gave Forrester its special character.

For Mallory on that hot afternoon, it was like driving through a dreamscape. The trees were a flamboyant scarlet against the burning blue sky. The lush emerald green of the open fields were sprigged with lovely little lavender wildflowers that visited periodically.

The avenue came to an end a hundred yards from the entrance to the estate. The high wrought iron gates were open in preparation for her visit. The name of the plantation house, *Moonglade,* was inscribed on a shiny brass plaque set into one of the stone pillars. Her heart swelled as she drove straight through, looking up at the towering Cuban Royals that lined the broad driveway up to the house. She had already pushed the button to wind her window down so she could hear their great fronds clattering in the breeze. She liked to think they were applauding her arrival.

Gorgeous tropical parrots and little lorikeets soared and darted between the trees, their exquisite multicoloured plumage gleaming like jewelled silks. She remembered, as a little girl, the wild symphony of birdsong waking her up to a new day. Moonglade had entered her imagination early. She had always loved everything about it. Moonglade was a magical place.

At the end of the gravelled drive sat the house in all its golden tranquillity. The site was marvellous. It had been built on a headland that jutted into the Coral Sea with a secluded crescent bay at the foot of the cliffs. Access to the beach was by way of a steep series of steps, with an iron railing to hold on to. As a child she had always chosen to skip down those steps as sure footed as a mountain goat. She had expected the sight of the house to somehow sadden her; all she felt was a profound sense of homecoming.

Doesn't everyone long to go back home at some point?

Slowly she turned the car into the circular driveway. She needed a period of solitude, a quiet space in her head to get a clear overview of the situation. Jason, his wife, and their little girl on the very doorstep? Worse, Jessica was still around to make trouble. And her uncle had kept it a secret! She was aware of the build-up of emotions inside her, but they were pale shadows of what once they had been.

The Cartwrights had doted on the twins, even though Jason had been the clear favourite. The good-looking Jason had been a popular figure in the town, a very pleasant and courteous young man. The same couldn't be said of his twin. Jessica had never come across as a poppet. The truly bizarre thing was, Kathy Burch had always been Jessica's main target for humiliation. Kathy, the town's little temptress, but as far as anyone knew at the time of her brother's engagement, Jessica had never had a boyfriend. She appeared to live in an emotional vacuum, or maybe she had a secret relationship no one was supposed to know about. It could have been an older, married man in the town. Loving her brother the way she did, it wasn't difficult to explain Jessica's resentment of his fiancée. Jealousy was a terrible force. It could do a power of harm.

In the blazing sunshine, the big white house shimmered like a mirage. The two-story building, colonial in style, was supported by series of pillars, six in all, wreathed in jasmine. The huge corrugated iron roof was painted dark green. The drumming of rain on that roof was locked into her memory, the smell of ozone. The rooms on the upper floor opened out onto a broad wrap-around veranda, the railings embellished with ornate white cast iron. French doors hung with tall shutters were painted a matching green to the roof. The spacious porch on the ground floor was similarly decorated with white cast iron.

Afterwards, she was grateful she had been travelling at a crawl. Her eyes had shifted from the house to the three-tier baroque-style fountain. The fountain had always been there. Its playing filled the hot summer air with delightfully cool, babbling sounds. She wondered if it was playing especially for her arrival. In the next instant a small child—it could have been either a boy or a girl from the unisex clothing—came running full tilt around a corner of the house and straight onto the drive.

Bloody hell!

Mallory felt her heart quake as all her old fears surged. The child wasn't at all close to being hit, but her reaction was a result of her own childhood trauma. Besides, children were just so unpredictable. She slammed on the brakes, mastering the panic that jumped into her throat. Engine off, she threw open the door and got out. She thought the child was a girl. There was something about the little knock-kneed run.

"Hello, little girl! Hello!"

Could this be Ivy?

The child skidded to a halt at the sound of Mallory's voice, almost losing her balance. She regained it by putting one hand down on the gravel.

Ouch, that must have hurt.

At the same time, a lean fair-haired woman rounded the corner of the house as if a gale force wind was behind her. She had a bundle of what looked like dried flowers in her hand. Clearly she was in furious pursuit of the child. Or had she panicked the child might run into the car? Mallory didn't have to wait long for an answer.

"Wait up, Ivy, you little brat," the woman yelled, swishing the bundle of flowers hard against her side like a jockey on the home run.

So this was Ivy, the problematic child. How could anyone so small evoke adult *fury*?

The child, a scrap of a thing in the land of plenty, ran directly at Mallory, hurling herself at Mallory's legs and wrapping her puny arms around them. Mallory found herself hugging the small curly blonde head to her waist. It was an extraordinary moment. No doubting who the father was.

"Well, well, well," the woman called, still flapping her bundle in manic fashion. "Our princess returning. *Quelle* surprise!"

The bright, jokey tone contrasted sharply with the taut piano-string body language. No difficulty seeing Jessica's aura. It was a blinding orange. She recalled Van Gogh had once said orange was the colour of insanity.

"You knew I was coming, Jessica?" Mallory asked pleasantly, with no intention of spending a lot of time with Jessica, who had always hated her.

"Of course. Of course. The beautiful and brilliant Dr. Mallory James, alive and well!" A smile was plastered on Jessica's face.

"Alive at any rate." Mallory thought the smile wouldn't fool anyone. She bent to check on the little girl. "Let me have a look at your hand." Her voice was full of tenderness and concern. Instantly the little girl put her hand up for Mallory's inspection, watching as Mallory brushed specks of gravel away from her palm.

"Thank you," the little girl said sweetly, staring up into Mallory's face with a kind of wonderment.

"You're welcome." Mallory returned the endearing smile. She had a great liking and a strong protective feeling towards children. No aura to this child. Not as yet.

"Long time no see, Mallory." Jessica's lips now formed a thin line.

"It *has* been a long time, Jessica." There had always been volcanic activity about Jessica. From her years of study, Mallory now began to consider Jessica with her history of highs and lows might well be undiagnosed bipolar. "How is life treating you?" she queried. Good manners made the world go round.

"I've known better times." Jessica looked like she wanted to wallop someone.

"I'm sorry to hear that." Jessica had always had a grievance. "What has this little person been up to, to make you so angry?" she asked, keeping a reassuring hold on a small sticky hand.

Jessica feigned shock. "*Moi*, angry? Who said anything about angry?"

"Cross certainly." Mallory took a good look at Jessica. She looked washed out, posture rigid as though she didn't have a clue how to relax. Not yet thirty, Jessica could have been mistaken for several years older. The absence of any effort to look good didn't help. Jessica had gone to no pains. Her thick blonde hair, a real asset, had darkened. It was scraped back. She wore no make-up, not even a skerrick of lipstick which would have protected the sensitive skin of her mouth. She was dressed in a dark red T-shirt that had a clinically depressed blue dolphin on it leaping half-heartedly through a hoop. The shirt hung so loosely on Jessica's thin, yet athletic body, it had to belong to her brother, and her wrinkled khaki rollup cargo pants looked like they needed a good wash. Jessica wasn't looking good. She had to wonder if Jason was faring any better.

"You *are* angry. You are angry, you, you, you!" The little girl broke in with a show of spirit. For good measure she kicked up a spray of white gravel, aiming deliberately at her aunt's thin brown legs. "That's why I ran away." She raised a mucky little face to Mallory. She was all Jason. Bright blue eyes and a bubble of white-blonde hair curling around her head in the manner of Renaissance *putti*. There was no trace of her mother, the extremely pretty, sable-haired, hazel-eyed Kathy, Mallory remembered.

"Don't take any notice of her," Jessica warned, not about to be short listed as Aunty of the Year. "She's always trouble."

Ivy's bottom lip started to tremble, so Mallory increased the gentle pressure on the child's hand. "She couldn't be that, Jessica. Why isn't she at school?"

Ivy twisted her curly head to look up at Mallory. "What day is t'day?" she asked.

"It's Wednesday, Ivy."

"Then I been home three days," Ivy said. "I been sick. I'm always home sick," she confided as though Mallory had come with the right medicine to cure all her ailments. "I vomit a lot." She clutched her little stomach.

"You're not sick now?" Instantly Mallory bent over the child, concerned.

"Nuthin' left to come up." The child gave her a perky grin.

"She's one sickly kid!" Jessica said in disgust. "Kathy is always at the hospital with her."

"That's no good." Mallory frowned. "It needs looking into, Jessica."

Jessica bridled ferociously. "It *has* been looked into." The look blared, *don't interfere.* "As far as I'm concerned, Kathy is responsible."

"Kathy?" Mallory was taken aback. "In what way?"

"The kid looks anaemic."

Ivy's skin was indeed pallid and paper thin. She was definitely underweight.

"If there's a problem, it needs to be sorted out." That was her job, sorting out children's problems. She was dedicated to it. "There's no shortage of good nourishing food around here. Has any medication been prescribed for Ivy?"

"Mede-kay-shun. Mede-kay-shun." Ivy was trying the new word out on her tongue.

"How should I know?" Jessica responded tartly. "I'm the aunt, not the mother. It's Kathy's job to feed her."

"But you take a keen interest?"

"I have work to do," Jessica bit off. "Looking after Ivy isn't high on my list of priorities. She has her mother, only Kathy spends her life nursing her headaches."

"Migraines?" Migraines could be hell.

"Who cares!" Jessica was in a flurry of impatience.

Ivy butted in. "You give me juice. I don't like it. It's yucky."

"Vitamin C," Jessica pronounced, still banging away with the bundle of dead flowers. *Swish, swish, swish.* Their decapitated heads flew about like confetti, blanketing the gravel.

"She shouldn't be short on vitamin C. Plenty of fruit to eat and enjoy."

"Ivy doesn't like fruit." Jessica spoke as if she were being tested beyond endurance.

"I do too!" Indifferent to her own safety, feisty little Ivy spoke up again, thrusting out her bottom lip. Mallory found her show of spirit cheering.

That did it for Jessica. "Come here to me, Ivy," she cracked out.

But Ivy wasn't about to obey. She shut her eyes tight like she was wishing her aunt would go up in a puff of smoke. When she opened them she looked up at Mallory, her new best friend. "Aunty Jessy is a cranky old thing. Are *you* a princess? You look like the princess in my picture book. You have the loveliest hair. It has sparkly gold through it."

"Thank you, Ivy." Mallory smiled. "When I was your age I was nearly as blonde as you. My hair has darkened over the years."

Jessica kept her eyes trained on the child, her expression sending out the message: *This is no joke.* Jessica was not well pleased by the turn of events. She was seething to haul the child away, especially as Ivy was now busy doing a good job of mimicking her aunt's swishing actions with her hand.

"Kathy needs day in, day out support," Jessica said, her tone showing contempt for her sister-in-law. "She's no woman of substance, I can tell you that. You might remember the Burches came up real short on brain cells. Kathy lets Ivy run wild."

"*I* ran wild around here," Mallory said, gazing about the splendid grounds any child would adore. There was a man-made lake with its flotilla of waterlilies, its borders deep in thick stands of iris and arum lilies. A swimming pool was at the rear of the house. The lake would be off limits, but surely not the swimming pool with an adult present? "Can you swim yet, Ivy?" Mallory knew all Queensland schools had a swimming program.

Jessica snorted, but Ivy said proudly, "Daddy taught me. I'm never allowed to go near the lake. It has mucky things in it. Besides, I can't get past all them lilies. I'm not afraid of water. We have lessons at school."

"That's good. Do you like school?"

"It's okay." Ivy nodded. "I'm in grade two. Some of the kids aren't very nice to me."

"Their loss, Ivy. I'd like to see you swim one day. Perhaps in the swimming pool?"

"She's not allowed into the swimming pool." Jessica was busy tugging at her T-shirt like she wanted to pull it down over her knees.

"Certainly not on her own, but with an adult present?"

"As though any of us have the time!" Jessica scoffed, a woman kept so busy she had no chance to lounge about.

"Where *is* Kathy?" Mallory asked. Meeting up with Kathy again couldn't be as bad as this reunion with Jessica.

Ivy gave a little nervous giggle, while Jessica shot a glance at the child, blue eyes glaring. "She's around. We've got the farm running well. Not that you would be interested in that, I reckon. Jason took a long time to recover after you ran off."

"Ran off?" The injustice of that grabbed Mallory's attention.

"Oh, yeah, the princess!" Jessica's resentment blew wide open.

"I *know'd* you was a princess!" Delightedly Ivy intervened, clapping her hands.

"No, Ivy." Mallory gave the child's shoulder an extra pat. "I'm an ordinary person."

Jessica gave a final swish to the decapitated bunch of dried flowers. "Nothing ordinary about you. My brother worshipped you. Only Kathy tricked him into marrying her, the cunning little—"

Mallory glanced meaningfully at the child. "Please don't pursue this, Jessica," she warned.

Jessica made some effort to compose herself. "Blaine Forrester used his influence to get the business under way. He's the Big Man. He's got connections all over the state." She broke off abruptly, as though she had said more than enough. "Come here to me, Ivy." She thrust out her rigid free arm, preparing to frog march the child off. "The lady has things to do."

"I'm Mallory, Ivy." Mallory introduced herself, putting out her hand. "I'm Mr. Robert's niece, like you are Aunt Jessica's niece."

"The doctor?" Ivy took hold of Mallory's extended hand, looking up at her in awe. They exchanged a grown-up handshake that made the little girl giggle.

"Not a medical doctor, Ivy. I'm what's called a psychologist, a big word for a little girl. My patients are children."

"Can I be one of your payshens?" Ivy asked hopefully. It was obvious she was regarding Mallory as her new friend and protector.

"Ivy, come here to me." Jessica's tolerance level had hit zero.

Ivy raised her thin little arms like someone anticipating attack.

Bruises.

Not good.

Not good at all.

"You don't want me to tell your father you've been a naughty girl?"

It was a threat that made the child shrink. She cringed against Mallory, who put a protective arm around her. A woman of Jessica's temperament had to be the worst possible caregiver for the child. "You seem stressed, Jessica. Why don't you let me look after Ivy for a while? She can come into the house with me."

"I'm not allowed in the house, Mal-Mal—"

"Mally will do," Mallory said.

"I'm only allowed into the kitchen, Mally," Ivy said, looking like she was about to cry. "I'm not allowed in the front door, but I've run in plenty of times. It's a *bewdiful* house."

"Filled with *valuable* things a little girl could break," Jessica said.

"*I* never broke anything," Mallory said. "I'm sure Ivy won't break anything."

"I'll be very, very careful," said Ivy, bright blue eyes solemn.

"You could do something for me if you would, Jessica," Mallory said. "Have someone bring my luggage into the house." There had always been a full-time gardener with at least one off-sider.

"Can't carry it yourself?" Jessica asked.

"Jessica, I don't *need* to," Mallory stated, mildly. "If you've something else to do, I'll ask the housekeeper to attend to it."

"Don't bother, Your Highness. I am, as always, your humble servant." Jessica executed a mocking bow.

"Aunty Jessy don't like *you* neither," Ivy observed shrewdly. At six years of age, she was already on top of the situation.

"Who asked you?" Jessica rounded on the child as if she were a woman.

"Jessica, I'm here for my uncle," Mallory intervened. "I'll be here for some weeks."

"*Weeks?*" Jessica gave such a shriek it caused panic among a dozen or so rainbow lorikeets feeding on some bottlebrushes nearby. They took off with a battery of emerald, cobalt, ruby, and golden wings.

"Something worrying about that?" Jessica's over-the-top reaction hadn't been lost on her.

"That's one big fuckin' *yes*."

Shocked for a second, Mallory didn't show it. Was there any word in the English language that *hadn't* lost its shock value, she wondered. But never in front of a child. Probably a few other groups. "Jessica, please don't use that word in front of Ivy," she said, pressing the child's head against her just in case Jessica started up with the F-word again.

Only Ivy had heard. "Ooh, Aunty Jessy *swore*," Ivy crowed, clearly delighted at catching her aunt out. "Daddy was real mad at her when she called me a fuckin' dumbo kid." Ivy, a natural mimic, got her aunt's voice off pat.

"I think it's time you shut your mouth, young lady," Jessica warned.

Mallory ramped up her disapproval. "You can't be forgetting Ivy is only six."

"Six going on sixty," Jessica snorted.

Jessica hadn't much love for her niece, and that wasn't going to change any time soon. Mallory had to wonder how the two women, Jessica and Kathy, had related to each other over the past few years. It couldn't have been easy. The bully and the victim.

"You're a lovely lady, Mally," Ivy was whispering, having swiftly identified Mallory as an ally.

"Come along now, Ivy," she said with gentle but firm persuasion. "Everything's fine." She spoke over the child's head to Jessica. "It's okay, Jessica, Ivy can come with me."

"I'll get someone to bring in your luggage." Jessica spoke so tartly, it was like having a door slammed in one's face.

Chapter Two

It had to be Mrs. Rawlings who was hurrying down the short flight of stone steps and onto the drive. Ivy must have felt comfortable with the approaching woman because her little face lit up. "Mrs. R. makes me fairy cakes," she told Mallory with a big grin about due to become gap-toothed.

"How kind of her. She might make some for me."

"Oh, she will. She's real nice. Mummy likes her too."

"Dr. James." Dorothy Rawlings was a five-foot-nothing, kindly looking woman, early sixties, blue eyes, a cloudburst of soft grey curls, and a fairly serious weight management problem. She wore comfortable lace-up shoes and a blue button-down dress with a white collar, much like a uniform. She was panting and red faced by the time she arrived. "I was in the kitchen. I didn't realize you were here," she gasped out.

Mallory smiled, wanting to put her uncle's housekeeper at ease. Her aura was a delightful blue. "No problem, Mrs. Rawlings. I was sorry to hear Mr. Rawlings passed away. My sincere condolences."

"Thank you."

"What's passed away?" Ivy turned her eyes on Mallory with interest.

"Gone to heaven, love," said Mrs. Rawlings, a bit distractedly as though she had other things on her mind.

"I don't go to church," Ivy confided. "Grandma Burch says, 'That kid of yours, Kathy, will never get through the pearly gates.' I don't do nothing wrong either." Ivy showed anger at her grandmother on her face. "Well, not always."

"One doesn't have to go to church to go to heaven, Ivy."

"That's what Mummy says." Ivy was pleased with the backup. "She says Grandma is always pushin' her buttons."

Mrs. Rawlings held up a hand as Ivy, childlike, got set to launch into more family revelations. "That will do, Ivy, lovey. How is Mr. Robert?" She addressed Mallory. "I rang early."

"We'll be bringing him home tomorrow."

"Oh, that's great news." The housekeeper bestowed on the child a worried glance. "What are you doing here, Ivy?"

The gentle tone couldn't have been more different to Jessica's hectoring.

Ivy was bursting to tell. "I was running away from Aunty Jessy." She gave them a big grin of triumph. "She don't love. I haven't had a bath for two days."

Mallory started to get glimmers of the big picture. "Aunt Jessica bathes you?"

Ivy giggled. "Mummy doesn't let her in case she drowns me. Mummy is going to give me a bath tonight.

She's had a really bad headache. That's why Jessy was running after me. She likes to give me a wallop. She don't love me."

"That can't be so, Ivy!"

Mallory well knew pretence didn't work with kids.

Mrs. Rawlings flashed Mallory an embarrassed glance. "Of course she does, lovey. It's just she's so busy all the time."

"You know she don't, Mrs. R.," Ivy said, wedging herself up against Mallory's legs. "I can tell the way she looks at me. She never kisses me and I'm glad. She don't like Mummy either. She says Mummy's trash. No kiddin', I heard her say it. She's always telling Mummy she's a stupid cow. Mummy isn't a *cow*, she's a *lady*. Aunty Jessy is the stupid one."

With prior knowledge of Jessica Cartwright's less-than-sunny nature, none of this came as any great surprise to Mallory. "Well, we won't talk about that now, Ivy." Mallory thought it best to leave things there for the time being. "I'll be minding Ivy for a while, Mrs. Rawlings. If you take Ivy into the house, I'll shift the car." The Mercedes was still standing in the drive with the driver's door open. "Ivy startled me running around the side of the house."

"Gettin' away from Aunty Jessy." For a moment Ivy looked as though she was about to cry. "Mally saved me."

Mallory patted the child's shoulder. "Go with Mrs. Rawlings now, Ivy."

"Got some cake for me, Mrs. R?" Ivy tilted her curly blonde head.

"Never mind that now, little lady. We'll get you cleaned up first."

As they walked away Mallory exhaled a breath of

relief. Mercifully Mrs. Rawlings was on Ivy's side. She was beginning to feel considerable sympathy for Kathy, the young woman she had once thought of as a traitor.

It was an hour or so later. Ivy was in her element chattering away, telling Mallory all sorts of things—some of which made Mallory glance up sharply—when they heard heavy footsteps coming down the hallway.

Clearly a man's footsteps. The reunion. Mallory felt her throat tighten. The tightening continued down her body. She experienced for a moment the old roaring river of rage, the way her blood had pumped wildly in her veins, the hazy red mist in front of her eyes.

"I don't know how to tell you, Mal. It's like a bad dream. You know I love you. I worship you. It kills me to dump it on you, but Kathy Burch is pregnant. By me. Can you believe it? I've never looked twice at her. God knows what happened. I can't remember much about it. I was drunk. Off my head."

The really odd thing was, the Jason she had known back then was no heavy drinker. The whole town would have known. At the time, in the red rawness of her frenzy, she had never followed up his remark. Jason drunk? She had never stopped to consider. Now she thrust those humiliating images from her mind. Jason had made Kathy Burch pregnant, yet he had spoken as if a stroke of colossal bad luck had engulfed him. His self-pity had been so nauseating she had answered with a burst of unprecedented fury. What bond they'd had totally disintegrated on the spot. All trust was gone.

It was Blaine, needless to say, who had broken things up, racing down from the house and getting a good hold on her while her uncle stood transfixed by the sight of sunny-natured Mallory shouting so alarmingly and struggling in Blaine's strong arms. Afterwards shouting at Blaine to let her down, Mallory had cried out to her distressed uncle, "I can't live here anymore!"

Jason's behaviour had turned life squalid.

Jason hadn't broken her heart, but he had abandoned her. Abandonment was a crime in her book. She had to wonder if she could handle this encounter with equanimity. Her hands were trembling. She knew the signs. She had seen Jason's abandonment as a continuing pattern in her life. Her father had abandoned her when she had been desperate for a father's loving comfort. Her grandparents had abandoned her. Not a backbone between the lot of them. She had spent years before she had arrived at a stage where she felt in control. In the eyes of the world, she was a high achiever. On the outside. She kept the inside out of sight.

Behind her, Ivy had flopped down onto the day bed, hiding her curly head half under a pillow. "That will be Daddy," she said, her piping voice muffled and low in her narrow chest.

The child's reaction surprised and dismayed Mallory. Surely Jason hadn't turned into a strict disciplinarian? In the old days he'd had such an easy-going temperament. It was Jason's *mildness* that had drawn her to him in the first place. Marriage might stand a chance of lasting a lifetime with an easy-going, tolerant person. At least that was what she had convinced herself of back then. A fraught moment more and Jason loomed in the doorway.

An instant dark yellow aura that nearly made her whole body sag engulfed him. Like his twin, Jason's appearance had undergone serious change. From handsome, comfortable in his skin, he appeared enraged, grief stricken, both? Was there even something *hunted* in his attitude? He was lean to the point of thinness, his clothing flecked with dust and fruit stains. His electric blue eyes were fixed on *her* with an intensity she didn't welcome. The truth was she had never wanted to see Jason again. One powerful reason why she had kept away. The sense of utter failure was still present.

Instead of searching out his little runaway daughter, Jason's sole focus was on *her*. A red flush was moving from his tanned throat to his forehead.

She had to wait until his aura faded. She had to break up the dramatics. If Jason still thought he was in love with her, the issue had to be dealt with.

Jason stood motionless. "All these years later, and you've finally come home."

"You're not going to leave it at that surely?" she said. "How are you, Jason?"

"What do *you* think? Look at me, Mallory."

She wasn't about to be caught up in any drama. "What are you hoping I'll see? I *was* hoping you're getting on with life, Jason. As I am." She wanted to hurdle these moments. Get them out of the way. Clear the decks. All the scenarios, the rehearsed confrontations, nothing approaching any of them happened. There was no sick racing heart. No upsurge of remembered emotion. No feeling of regret for the what-might-have-beens. Only clear confirmation she, at least, had moved on. "Before today, I had no idea you and Kathy were living on Moonglade," she said, moving back so as to reveal more of Ivy. "As you can see, Ivy and I are getting acquainted."

"Come here to me, Ivy." It was an order.

Mallory looked back at Jason with dismay. The harshness with his child, a little girl moreover, was unexpected. It might have been Jessica who had barked the order.

"I'm sorry if she's bothering you," he said, his tone short, unapologetic. "She got away from Jess. She does it all the time."

"Ever wonder why?" Her words shot out like a thrown plate. Clearly Jason was not the man she had known. Where was all the old gentleness? Today he was a man under a lot of stress, perhaps even mentally exhausted by it.

"I've no idea what you mean." He held out his hand to Ivy, who was noticeably reluctant to get up. In fact she dug further in.

"I want to stay with Mally." Ivy shook her head. It was obvious she was readying herself for a burst of histrionics. Mallory knew she would make a good, loud job of it.

"She's quite all right with me, Jason." She quickly intervened. "You or Kathy can pick her up late afternoon." She was happy to give the Jolly Psycho Aunt Jessica a miss.

"She can come now." There was a smouldering anger in his blue eyes. "It would make things very difficult for us, Mallory, if you undermined my sister."

Ah, the unbreakable bonds of twin-ship! Mallory had perfected calm with just about everyone outside Blaine. "You're talking nonsense, Jason. I feel nothing but a desire to help out and get to know your little daughter. Has Jessica suggested otherwise?" She left that one up in the air. Mallory turned towards the child with a gentle smile. "Daddy wants you to go with him now, Ivy. I promise you we'll spend more time together."

Ivy unwound herself, standing on her feet, but the look of mutiny was still on her small face. "I want to stay here with Mally." She was exhibiting a stubbornness that Mallory thought could be a developing part of her nature. Time would tell.

"God give me patience!" Jason looked at the end of his tether.

Everything in his life appeared to be just awful. Mallory found herself taking pity on him. "I told you, Jason. It's fine with me for Ivy to stay here."

"You're the expert on children, aren't you?" he said with startling bitterness.

Mallory swallowed a curt rejoinder. If Jason was hoping for emotion from her, he would hope in vain. "Working with children is my vocation, Jason. Ivy has been helping me put my things away."

"Jess tells me you're staying for *weeks*?" He speared a hand through his hair. He'd been doing that at regular intervals since he arrived.

"Is that a problem?"

"You can't see it?" His blue eyes were devouring her.

No similar response could ever have been foreseen. She refused to be dragged back into the unhappy past. "If there's a problem, tell me what it is." She already knew the answer. He still fancied himself in love with her. Men always did want what they couldn't get.

"You're the problem, Mallory."

It sounded like a mantra he said every morning.

"I'll take Ivy now. Her mother can look after her. Come here to me, sweetheart. Daddy isn't cross with you. I was worried, that's all."

Mallory nodded reassuringly to the child. "Go with Daddy."

"I can come back again, Mally?"

"Of course you can." Mallory glanced across at Jason. His fevered blue eyes were still fastened on her, an agony of regret in their depths. She may have escaped Jason for a new life, but she had left unfinished business behind her. "Surely Uncle Robert allows Ivy into the house? He loves children. I can't accept he would bar Ivy from visiting."

"Robert has been more than kind to all of us," Jason responded. The statement held a jarring note, as though deep down Jason resented Robert James's many kindnesses. "Jess's concern is Ivy will break something. She *does* knock into things."

"Do *not*!" Ivy whipped out. Not so much a protest, as a heroic defence. "Aunty Jessy is the clumsy one." Ivy turned to Mallory, her new-found friend and confidante. "See that bruise on my arm? She done that." Ivy rolled up her short sleeve, turning her arm so Mallory could examine a large multicoloured bruise. "I dint break the pottery elephant neither. *She* done that as well." An expression of real anger flitted across her face.

"Ivy!" She was instantly reprimanded by her father, who had sucked in his lean cheeks, resembling the painter Munch's *Scream*. "That's not true. And it's *did*, not done."

"*Did* too!" To Mallory's trained ears, that came

close to adult despair. "I'm tellin' the truth. Swear. Swear. Swear. Cross me heart."

Mallory felt a wave of compassion. "Why would you say that, Ivy?" She had treated many children who spun elaborate tales, so she had learned to rely heavily on intuition. She believed Ivy.

Emboldened, Ivy was only too eager to oblige. "'Cause she said, 'Just look what you done, you clumsy little bitch!' I dint do nuthin'," Ivy fretted. "*She* must have rocked it over to get me into trouble."

Jason's expression showed outright rejection of Ivy's story. "Ivy," he said testily, "I've told you a hundred times not to tell fibs."

Ivy buried her blonde head against Mallory. "*You* tell Aunty Jess," she piped up bravely, hands bunching Mallory's skirt. "She's the big fat liar. Not me. She tells lotsa lies to make bad things happen. Mummy knows I told the truth about the elephant. I loved that elephant. It had its trunk up. That means it's happy. Mummy loved the elephant too. Mummy says Aunty Jess is a horrible person. She's got a wicked tongue. That means—"

"We know what it means, thank you, Ivy," Jason thundered. "You're being silly now. And you're giving Mallory the wrong idea. Come here to me."

"Go along now, Ivy," Mallory said, gentle but firm, steering the little girl towards her father. She could not interfere.

To Mallory's huge relief, Jason bent and swept his little daughter into his arms. Ivy put her arms around his neck. He kissed her on the forehead. "Mummy will play with you, okay?"

"Doesn't she have a headache anymore?" Ivy asked, tenderly stroking her father's tanned cheek.

"It's gone, sweetheart. But you must behave for her."

Ivy's blue eyes opened wide. "I'm always a good girl for Mummy. It's only Aunty Jess I hide from. I know lotsa places Aunty Jessy don't know," she crowed.

Jason's strain was apparent. "Say thank you to Mallory."

"Thank you, Mally," Ivy said very sweetly, reaching out a hand.

Mallory took it. "You're always welcome here, Ivy," Mallory assured her. "I'll make some arrangements with your mother."

"Better if you *don't*," Jason told her brusquely. "I can see Ivy will get fond of you, then you'll go away. You're good at that."

Mallory might have retaliated only it would be futile. She had seldom seen a man look so *alone*. Again her heart stirred with pity. Was she supposed to have stuck around to offer support to the man who had betrayed her? Blaine had told her she'd had a lucky escape. She was able to see with great clarity she could now offload that unhappy part of her life. Jason had chosen his path. She had embarked on another.

And never the twain shall meet.

It took all of ten minutes after they had gone before she could go on with her unpacking. Jason's harsh tones still rang in her ears, yet she was aware of a sudden *quietude* within herself. Her meeting with Jason had been easier than she had anticipated.

Since she had lost her mother at so young an age, and in such a sudden, violent way, she had lived with her fears. The fear of *loss* was uppermost in her mind.

Loving meant *loss*. Her mindset, she knew, had been strongly influenced as well, by her fear of passionate relationships such as the obsessive love her father and uncle had borne for her mother. It explained a great deal about the relationships she'd had, starting with Jason. Her choice of a certain type of man was her way of protecting herself. She aspired to being a woman who took pride in charting her own course.

She never wanted to be at the mercy of any man.

She didn't trust them. Neither could she forget the results of a respected survey that asked both men and women what they feared most about the opposite sex. The men: They laugh at us. The women: They kill us.

Dot Rawlings, one hand stuffed into her pink and white checked apron pocket, stood at the top of the steps, the other waving a white napkin à la Pavarotti. Mallory's mouth curved in wry amusement. Dot had to be a romantic at heart. She clearly saw Mallory's return to Moonglade as heralding something *new* and interesting. Like a romance. One couldn't condemn her for it. Romance as a cure-all was a widespread illusion.

"Dot likes you." Blaine held the door as she slipped into the passenger seat.

"What's not to like?" she challenged.

"More than my life's worth to do that."

On such a blazing hot day Mallory looked as cool as a lily. That ethereal quality she possessed probably had something to do with the brightness of her psyche. "You're not one to reach out."

"Too precarious."

He shot her a sideways glance. "How hard is this for you, Mallory?"

There was nothing between them but the charged air. It vibrated with sensual energy. His, not hers. He had it in abundance. "Since when did you become my honorary confessor?"

"Way back."

"I thought you'd resigned."

"More like sacked."

"I admit you've been loyal, Blaine." She allowed her eyes to rest momentarily on his striking profile. Blaine had one of those faces that was hard to forget.

"I've met Ivy and Jessica," she said, waiting for the question she knew was coming.

"Not Jason?" He shot her another laser look. "Are you going to tell me or do I have to pry it out of you?"

"Ah, yes, Jason."

"Well?" he prompted.

"Well *what*, Blaine?" She felt one of the flares of temper that only Blaine could set alight. "Why do you do this to me? Are you expecting me to say I went to pieces?"

"Not these days, *Doctor* James," he returned suavely. "So how did it go?"

She dropped all pretence. "Not that well. Jason is still struggling with old issues. Ivy is the image of him. I couldn't see anything of Kathy at this stage. Of course children change. She's a smart little kid. She has spirit, but she's woefully underweight. It needs to be checked out."

"I'm sure it has been, Mallory."

"Still, I think I'll find out for myself."

"If there's something wrong, wouldn't it show up in blood tests?" he argued.

"That can be checked out. I'm not prepared to let go. There should be answers to the child's vomiting, for a start. I'm a person who has to *know*."

"I would never, *ever* have guessed!"

She ignored the sarcasm. Both of them were veterans. "There appears to be quite a bit of trauma going on in her young life. She doesn't get on with Aunty Jessy. Jessica really should have been christened Krakatoa."

"She could do with a course on anger management. I guess not all women are good with kids."

Mallory was well aware of that. "Sad for Ivy, don't you think? Jason is stern with her as well."

"You'll find out soon enough, the marriage isn't going well."

"Then I'm sorry to hear that." Mallory's response was genuine. "Not easy to hurdle a bad start. It might go better if Jessica butted out. Ivy divulged among other things, Jessica had called her an effing dumbo kid and her mother a stupid cow. Ivy took that insult literally. Jessica was the stupid one since her mother was a *lady*."

"Careful where you go with this, Mallory," Blaine warned. "Your interest could be seen as unwelcome interference."

"You're saying don't get involved? I *am* involved. If Ivy has behavioural problems then there's a root cause. If she vomits frequently, that needs to be more thoroughly checked out. I should have asked what time of the day she vomits, that's important, and whether she suffers from childhood migraines. Kathy apparently has migraines. I'll speak to Ted."

"Whoa! Back up a step. How did Jason react when he first saw you?"

Her response was brisk. "What are you asking precisely? Is he still in love with me? Or fancies he is?"

"He *is* still in love with you," Blaine told her with his usual bluntness. "It's a literal fact."

"Or a self-indulgent fantasy."

"I'm glad to hear you say that. Jason certainly didn't love poor little Kathy, but he did what he thought was the honourable thing. He married her. But it hasn't worked out. No big surprise there. Marriage is difficult enough, but without love! Then again, Kathy could never have managed on her own. Her mother has been a battered woman for all her married life, and her father is a hopeless alcoholic. No support system within that family."

"It would have been very hard for her. All the more despicable then is Jessica's bullying. The Jessica I remember would *hate* anyone who married her brother. I believe she hated *me*. Probably still does. Jessica wants sole sway over her twin. Kathy doesn't stand a chance with Jessica ruling the roost. What's wrong with Jason he can't tell his sister to stay out of his marriage? It might give it a chance."

"When did he ever lock out his sister?" It was a statement, not a question.

"Maybe it saved a lot of wear and tear. Jason has always allowed Jessica to dominate him. I believe Jessica goes into crisis mode when her relationship with her twin appears threatened. It's not all that unusual, human nature being what it is. Jason can never hope to become an individual with Jessica forever on the scene."

"Would you say they're an extreme case?" Blaine shot her a keen glance.

"Not really." Mallory gave vent to a sigh. "I treated twelve-year-old identical twins, girls, who are genuinely hostile towards one another. Each is pathologically jealous of the other. Sadly I would say the hostility will grow stronger as they move further into adolescence. The signs are not hopeful, even with treatment. As for me, it's a huge relief to realize I never *loved* Jason."

"I know that," he said with terrific emphasis.

"That's it! Go for broke. There are no lingering feelings whatever."

"Good."

"Proof I didn't—and still don't—truly know myself, but I'm getting there. What about you and Selma? I mean you two were the town's big item. You didn't love her?"

"Maybe *you and I* should have married," he suggested, looking straight ahead at the mirage-hazed road.

"There's a comic suggestion! We're incompatible. Chalk and cheese."

"Are we?" He shot her a glinting glance. "Are we really?"

"At least I acknowledge it. Besides, I would never give you power over me." As soon as she said it, she knew it was a big mistake.

Blaine reacted angrily. "What the devil are you talking about, Mallory? *Power over you?* Get real."

She was immediately on the defensive. "I don't want to carry on this conversation."

"Of course you don't. You might have to confront a few hard facts about yourself."

"I know a woman's vulnerability gives a man power."

"And women don't use their power?" he countered. "Women can get men to do just about anything. You're highly intelligent. A trained psychologist. Why don't you turn your analytical eye on yourself? You keep to yourself far more than any woman I've ever known."

"And you've known a few," she said, tartly.

He ignored her comment as having no worth. "The only reason you got involved with Cartwright is because, given your history, you didn't want to expose yourself to *real* emotion. Falling passionately in love was out of the question."

She made a shushing sound. "Might I remind you who's the psychologist here? What about you? Who are you to analyse me? Why do *you* continue to vacillate between women friends? Don't you want children?"

"I certainly do." His retort was immediate. "Your biological clock can't be ticking too merrily away?"

Emotions were stirring. She did long for a child. "What if it is? The difficulty, however, is finding the right man. If indeed such a man exists," she added waspishly.

He gave a taut laugh. "To your own exacting standards. You won't find the right man until you bulldoze down the barriers, Mallory."

"Thank you, Dr. Forrester. Who says I need a man at all? Relationships can be brutal. I think our time's up."

Despite the air-conditioned interior, the atmosphere

inside the Range Rover was heating up. "We're always arguing when we meet," she added. "Doesn't that prove we're incompatible? The irony is, I want you in my life. Only contact brings conflict. Everything gets too heated."

"Well, I'm pretty sure I know why if you don't," he said crisply, then fell silent.

That suited her just fine. Trying to find the answer would be like opening up a whole slice of her psyche.

Robert James was dressed and waiting for them by the time they arrived. This morning he looked a shade hyper, his prominent cheekbones flushed. He was going home. His Mallory would be staying with him, at least for a time. The joy of it was there for all to see.

Ted Moorehouse was on hand to see them off, which was fortunate, because Mallory wanted a private word with him, and not only about the care that should be given to her uncle. She wanted to speak to him about Ivy Cartwright.

Aren't you butting in here?

Blaine's searing gaze was boring a hole in her. He was reading her mind again, digging deep for the morning's agenda. She touched her uncle gently on the shoulder. "You go on to the car with Blaine, Uncle Robert. I just want a few words with Dr. Ted. Won't be long."

Blaine continued to stare at her as if he wanted to ask a lot of questions. Nevertheless he proceeded to push Robert, who was making use of a hospital wheelchair, out into the corridor.

Ted Moorehouse gave Mallory a comforting smile.

"Robb knows exactly what he has to do, Mallory," he said, thinking that was her concern. "If you have any worries, you can ring me at any given moment. I'll call out to the house from time to time. Robb is a good friend as well as my patient."

"I know that, Ted," Mallory said gratefully. "I really wanted to have a word with you about Ivy Cartwright."

"Ivy Cartwright?" Ted's bushy eyebrows shot up in surprise. "Not *my* patient, my dear. I'm a cardiologist, as you know. You should be speaking to Dr. Marisa Farnsworth. She's in the building. Do you want me to put out a call?"

Mallory shook her head. "Not for the moment, Doctor Ted. I met Ivy yesterday. She's an intelligent, perceptive child. She told me she's sick a lot."

Ted Moorehouse tugged a drooping corner of his luxuriant moustache. "Her mother does bring her too often, I have to say. Overanxious, overprotective. Kathy is a young woman with self-esteem problems. It all lies within her extremely unhappy upbringing. Poor girl is in need of some warmth and attention."

Mallory could only agree. "I remember Kathy as a very pretty girl."

"Yes, indeed, but sadly, the bloom has gone. Nothing would be left to chance, Mallory, regarding Ivy. Marisa would have checked the child out thoroughly. Marisa is a bit on the brisk side"—he could have used the word "abrasive" but glossed it over—"but she's a very good paediatrician."

"I'm sure she is. I have no problem with that, Ted. I just wanted to have a private word."

"Something specific disturbing you?" Moorehouse's expression had turned keenly professional.

"Ivy is a troubled little girl, a problematic child so

I've been told, though I can't say I've seen much sign of it. But I've only been here a short time. She's a quirky little kid, on the mischievous side. I don't hold that against her. Rather, it's a plus. I've been told Ivy is left often in the care of her aunt Jessica. Jessica—let's face it, Ted, we know from her past history Jessica is not good with children."

"So where is this heading?" Ted asked with a frown. "You want to know what the home situation is?"

"In the land of plenty she's underweight and her skin tone is not good."

Ted patted her on the shoulder. "After you left, no one in the town would speak to Kathy. She was a virtual pariah for a time. Everyone's sympathy was with *you* and Robert, who is so supportive of the town. Even Jason and Jessica have long been estranged from their parents. They didn't even attend the wedding."

Shock mounted on shock. The Cartwrights hadn't attended the wedding? She was getting the story in drips and drabs. "Uncle Robert didn't mention that astounding piece of information. Neither did Blaine."

Why would they bring up such a painful subject?

"It's at odds with what I know of the Cartwrights," Mallory continued. "Ivy is their only grandchild. You can turn your back on the daughter-in-law you didn't want, but how can you possibly turn your back on your grandchild?"

Ted's brilliant, all-seeing gaze fell.

Mallory flushed. "Okay then, my father turned his back on me. His problem was psychological. I was the one who should have died. That doesn't explain the Cartwrights' reaction. Ivy is a little girl who needs all the support she can get. She could spend quality time with her grandparents when she isn't at school."

"So what are you going on, Mallory, intuition?" he asked gently.

"I *am* speculating," Mallory confessed. "We both know intuition is *not* science, but my intuitions regarding the children I've treated have never let me down. I could tell you some very sad cases I've intuited."

"Don't have to!" Ted grimaced. "I saw your strengths even as a child. Maybe you should talk to Marisa. You're not a family member, that's the thing."

"I'm a professional who has concerns. I fully understand doctor-patient confidentiality. I just want to touch base with Dr. Farnsworth."

"You could get the permission of her parents to treat the child," Ted suggested, sounding none too hopeful.

"I'm sure that would be difficult indeed to get. I'll make an appointment to see Dr. Farnsworth. I won't keep you now, Ted. I know you're busy. Thank you so much for looking after Uncle Robert."

It was lunchtime when they arrived back at Moonglade. "You're staying for lunch, aren't you, Blaine?" Robert asked as Blaine was helping him from the Range Rover. He looked at Mallory while he was speaking, obviously expecting her to second the invitation, which of course she did. Blaine hesitated, then when Mallory thought he would decline, he said, "Love to."

So that was that.

Mrs. Rawlings was on hand to greet them. It was

obvious to Mallory she had a real affection for her employer. Robert James was equally comfortable with her. It was a heart-warming state of affairs. Not that her uncle wasn't a lovable man. Mallory had never known a single soul who didn't like her uncle. Except her father, his own brother.

Blaine accompanied Robert to his room while Mallory followed the housekeeper into the kitchen. It had been redesigned for a serious cook. Mallory wasn't. The cabinetry had been replaced. There was an impressive new fridge. Attractive pendant lighting hung from the high ceiling. A tall open dresser held a collection of Worcester dessert services Mallory remembered. It was part of a beautiful nineteenth-century dinner service, green and cream ground with painted flowers. Moonglade had had a long country tradition of hospitality. Uncle Robert had always enjoyed entertaining friends. Like her father, he was a fussy eater. She supposed she was herself, for that matter.

"So what's on the menu?" She watched the housekeeper bustling about, a woman in her element.

"It was going to be roast chicken, but fresh barramundi was delivered this morning."

"Sounds great!" Mallory sat down on a kitchen chair. "Do you know there are more chickens on the planet than there are people, so you'll never run out."

"You're joking!"

"Indeed I'm not. I'm a mine of trivia. Classical, biblical quotations, chunks of Shakespeare, my favourite poets, Shelley and Keats. All of it learned at my uncle's knee."

A clever middle-aged bookish man tutoring a

clever child. Dot Rawlings got the mental picture. "You love your uncle very much."

"He's the perfect uncle."

"Mr. Robert told me your sad story. My heart aches for you."

"Losing one's mother is the worst kind of pain," Mallory said. "Only losing one's child would topple that. You'll know my mother and I were out on a shopping trip. It was a sunny Saturday morning. I was wearing a new dress. I thought I looked just beautiful, like my mother. We were so happy. An elderly man lost control of his car and mounted the pavement, ploughing into the shoppers. A man was killed instantly. My mother, acting for all mothers, threw me to safety. I will never forget it. Never in a hundred lifetimes. My father and my uncle were devastated by my mother's death. Both of them loved her. Uncle Robert took me under his loving protection. My father . . . well, my father had great difficulty looking at me. I'm very like my mother in appearance."

Dot was well aware of that. She had seen photographs of the very beautiful Claudia James around the house. "You were a brave child and a brave woman."

"And a lucky one to have Uncle Robert." Mallory sat a moment more and then stood up as if she had lots to do. She could only take so much sympathizing, however kindly.

After lunch Robert retired to his room for "a recharge." He tired quickly, a man on a physical and emotional seesaw. His heart attack had clearly taken a great deal out of him.

Mallory had decided she wouldn't broach the

subject of Jason and his family and Jason's role of
running the tropical fruit farm. She guessed Blaine
had managed to convey to his friend all was under-
stood and accepted.

Nevertheless Robert flustered an apology. "I'm so
sorry, Mallory, that I didn't tell you about Jason and
his sister."

Mallory stopped him from going further. She
grasped his hand. "Think no more about it. All that is
important is that you get well."

"How could I not when you'll be here with me?
You're the image of Claudia." His face softened into
a dream-like smile. "There hasn't been a single day in
all these years I haven't thought of her."

"I know, Uncle Robert," Mallory said, her voice
sightly strained. Obsession wasn't good. It was pro-
longed torture. It prevented one from forging ahead.
Her mother's premature death had brought terrible
grief to both brothers in different ways. She knew her
father had had women over the years. He was extremely attractive. A lot of dangerous men were.

When she went back downstairs, she found Blaine
waiting for her in the entrance hall. "I've got time.
What about a tour of the farm?" He was all business
and blazing vitality.

"Sounds like a plan. I'll let you do all the talking if
we run into the twins. They're definitely not happy
about my staying on."

"What's it got to do with them? The twins have *no*
say." Blaine's lucid gaze flicked over her. "I hope
you've got a wide-brimmed hat with you."

She made a tut-tutting sound. "Don't play big
brother. Give me a minute."

"You might change your shoes as well."

"You can't contain yourself, can you?" She turned and hurried up the stairs so as not to keep him waiting.

Mallory couldn't believe how much change had occurred over the years. The estate had always grown avocados, lemons, limes, lychees, passionfruit, paw-paws, pineapples, and bananas. The *earth* was every-thing. Growing things. It was wonderful to eat the plantation produce, freshly picked. No shop-bought produce could hope to compare. In the old days a great abundance of fruit had been left to fall to the ground. These days, Moonglade was a thriving busi-ness. Moonglade Plantation House now produced a wide range of tropical and ultra-tropical fruits that went by unfamiliar names like keledang, starapple, rambutan, mangosteen, rollinia, abiu, durian, malay apple, sapodilla, carambola, and many more. A lot weren't at all pretty in appearance like the everyday oranges and lemons. The delicious tasting new vari-eties had spikes, bumps, and even hair-like strings, off-putting until one actually tasted the fruit and got hooked on the flavour.

"You won't see a lot of these in the cities." Blaine lifted a hand to acknowledge a small group of itiner-ant workers busy packing exotic fruit into cardboard boxes bearing the logo *Moonglade Plantation House.*

Mallory followed suit. She accepted a piece of golden-fleshed fruit from Blaine. He had cut it with the Swiss pocket knife he had in his pocket. It was tart-sweet, the taste somewhere between a mango and a pineapple. She could see it accompanying savoury food or added to a salad for a bit of zing. It was juicy too. A trickle was making its way from her mouth to her chin.

Blaine put a forefinger to her chin, catching the juice before sliding it into his mouth.

A blast of excitement shot through her. It was a reaction way too extreme for his casual action. Only it had seemed to her incredibly *voluptuous*. It wasn't as if his hand had touched her breast. She would have freaked out. It had to be a side effect of the humid heat. Heat ignited arousal. It spiralled up and up. She knew she was going to have to live with her over-the-top reaction. Possibly for *hours*.

God, she thought. *This is ridiculous. Utterly ridiculous.* Psychological claustrophobia.

Mercifully Blaine had moved on, allowing her time to pull a tissue out of the pocket of her linen pants to dab her pulsing mouth.

They were emerging from the large shed, coming back into the blaze of sunlight. "Where does all the produce go?" she asked, surprised her voice hadn't squeaked.

Blaine's downward gaze was both cool and turbulent. "The bulk goes to the major supermarkets and restaurants here in the North, but supplies are sent regularly south. The estate is managed as an organic permaculture. You've seen the sheds. What about a walk through the orchards? Not too hot for you, is it?"

He had noticed the flush in her cheeks. He would. He always had his reasons. "I'm fine," she said tartly. He was wearing a dashing wide-brimmed straw hat, compelling her gaze to move back and forth over him. She didn't ask herself why. Better to shove it in a back compartment along with everything else.

They walked down corridor after corridor of nutty

grass with exotic fruit-bearing trees to either side. The bright colour of the fruit contrasted beautifully with the dark green of the leaves. The wonderfully fertile earth had been turned into a marvellous tropical fruit farm where everything grew. In the wild labyrinth of her childhood, this part of Moonglade had been almost a forest choked with vines, brilliantly coloured butterflies flitting everywhere, a cacophony of bird calls. Always a long muscled snake to watch out for.

"The Garden of Eden." Mallory felt in awe of the sheer bounty.

"It is indeed."

Golden shards of sunlight cut through the dense greenery. The strong scent of fruit saturated the air, making it thickly overpowering. The abundant produce was being handpicked by workers, male and female, poised high on ladders. They worked quickly and efficiently, placing the produce into Hessian slings hung around their necks. There was much waving and smiling. One of the men was whistling an Italian folk song she knew. The sound had the purity of a solo flute.

They were turning into an aisle of heavily bearing passion fruit vines when they caught sight of Jason and Jessica at the far end. Their fair heads were bent so close their foreheads might have been glued together. Each appeared to be drawing on the other's breath.

"Let's turn back." She had already started to do so. She realized with a start she didn't want to speak to them. Seeing the two of them together *unnerved* her.

"Too late." Blaine took her arm, compelling her

along. "Hansel and Gretel have seen us. Better to get this over, Mallory. You'll be here for some time. Robert owns Moonglade Plantation House. The twins work for him."

"They look like they're planning on murdering him this very afternoon."

"I grant you they're an odd pair, but I don't think murder is on their mind. Let's walk on. You're never in any peril while I'm around."

"Peril? That's a bit melodramatic!"

"There was a viper in the Garden of Eden, remember? There are nests of vipers everywhere."

They were drawing close to where the twins were standing, lean bodies facing one another. The two had always been excessively needy of one another. "To think all this has happened and I didn't know a thing about it." Mallory raised both arms above her head in a graceful arabesque.

"Well, it wasn't as though you were a frequent visitor." Blaine's attention was claimed by the grace of her willowy body. Mallory had beautiful limbs. Her white camisole was drawn taut against her small, perfectly shaped breasts. For an instant he gave himself up to just staring at her, admiring her loveliness. "Robert owned all this land, as you know, but it was lying unproductive. It made sense to start a business. Tropical fruit gardens are springing up everywhere in the North. We've always had our mangoes, pawpaws, coconuts, pineapples, bananas—you name any of the old varieties—but the public and the chefs love new tastes, new flavours. Chefs enjoy mixing the sweet with the sour. The tropical North is just right for the cultivation of most exotic fruits. As I said, I could easily have found a manager for Robert, but clearly

Jason Cartwright needed a job with a wife and child to support."

"It can't have been easy for Kathy, flung at break-neck speed into a marriage with Jessica along."

Blaine ducked the question. That riled her. She tugged on his arm, slowing his progress. "What I *really* want to know is why Jessica was given the opportunity to muscle in on her brother's marriage."

He gazed down at her hand. Her beautiful skin glowed against his dark tan.

Mallory too stared down rather helplessly at their fused hands. She had a powerful urge to entwine her fingers with his. Imagine! She removed her hand quickly, as if skin on skin caused a sizzle.

"Jason apparently needed her." Blaine carried on walking. "I can't think of many businesses in the town falling over themselves to hire her."

"She's her own worst enemy."

They reached the twins. The Cartwrights stood facing them. "How's it going?" Blaine asked, his tone casual.

They answered as one. "Fine. Fine. Fine."

Like spitting out bullets.

"We're just deciding when to transplant the young mangosteens." Jason plucked a reply out of the humid air. "They've been in the ground almost four years. They can take a more open position. We're ready to clear more of the old established areas."

"We're getting busier all the time," Jessica broke in, as always with aggression. Mallory wasn't sure if she was even aware of it. "We need more land. The more we grow, the more we'll be able to supply."

Blaine thrust a hand into the pocket of his jeans.

"Self-evident, Jessica." Coolly he turned his head to address Jason. "Where exactly were you thinking?"

"The old mandarin orchard." Jason's eyes had strayed to Mallory and never moved away.

Many a time they had strolled hand in hand through the old orchard, pausing to pick a succulent piece of fruit. Mallory had no difficulty tuning into Jason's brain waves. But there was a difference between past and present. Jason was now a married man and the father of a small child.

She spoke for the first time. "I'm amazed at the transformation. You both must have worked very hard."

"You can say that again!" Again the combative tone from Jessica. Mallory watched her place a proprietary hand on her brother's tanned arm. She radiated a totally inappropriate level of hostility, apparently unconcerned or unaware of it.

"What exactly does Kathy do?" Mallory asked.

Jessica gave a hard click of her fingers. "Fuck it!" she exclaimed crudely. "She gets these headaches constantly."

Blaine cast a cool silver gaze over her. "I'm not surprised if you use obscenities around her all the time."

Jessica's face reddened unattractively, as did Jason's at the reprimand. "Sorry, sorry, sorry," Jessica said, hammering the word hard.

"She and Ivy might benefit from a good check-up," Mallory said. She was beginning to feel very sorry for Kathy.

"As I've told you before—" Jessica began hotly, but Jason gave her a quick warning glance. Mallory was their employer's niece. Blaine was Blaine Forrester. That said it all.

"We'll let you get on with the job." Blaine's tone had turned frosty. He did frosty well. "This is Robert's first day home from hospital so I wouldn't bother him for a while. Maybe Mallory can pave the way?"

That suggestion rendered the couple of labourers in the field speechless.

They walked on in silence, their thoughts in tune. "Now wasn't that interesting?" said Blaine. "I have the feeling Jessica will say 'fuck it' on her death bed."

Mallory was barely listening. "A lot of people, even people one doesn't expect it of, use four-letter words. They get into the habit. Jessica hates me."

"And here I was thinking her capacity for friendliness has no equal."

"Her hostility is way beyond normal."

"You'll get no argument from me. It's understandable in a weird kind of way. Her brother loves you. It could even be a kind of balancing act for him."

"What on earth do you mean?" Mallory rocked to a standstill.

"Jason is an unhappy man. His marriage hasn't worked out."

"How could it with Jessica around? He's stuck in a time warp. There can be no place for me in his life. The dirty linen has been washed, dried, folded, and put back in the cupboard. We can't even resume a friendship. Why all this intensity of feeling? What's fanning it? I've been gone for years."

"You more than most people would know a few years can mean nothing. You *were* going to be married, remember?"

She laughed. Not a happy sound. "How *can* I properly understand when I didn't love *him*? He loved *me*. He was the one who suffered. It was my pride that took a king hit. Not my heart. In retrospect, I would have to plead guilty to a kind of dishonesty. I'm just so thankful we didn't have sex."

Blaine gave her a long look. "With anyone else I'd say you were having me on. But you always were paranoid about keeping your space."

"Maybe I'm suffering from some as yet unnamed syndrome," she suggested, looking him right in the eye.

So many lush scents were suspended in the humid heat they were tickling the membranes of her nose. She was even feeling a little woozy, drunk on sensations.

"Let's walk back to the house, shall we?" Blaine said. "It's very hot in the aisles."

"I could do with some of Dot's icy cold lemonade."

"You and Dot get on well?"

"We've had some very harmonious and some very funny conversations covering a range of subjects. The only person we disagree on is *you*."

"I'm sure you said that just to goad me." He could see the disturbance in her eyes.

Mallory abandoned herself to the truth. "I have to confess. I *did*. It's childish, I know, but I get a lot of satisfaction out of goading you."

"Is there any way you can wrap it up?"

Mallory got herself together. She twisted her mouth down at the corners. "I honestly don't know, Blaine. The urge goes deep."

Chapter Three

It was almost a week before Mallory was to lay eyes on the young woman who had been instrumental in changing her life. She hadn't sighted the twins. They must have wanted to steer clear of her. She hadn't caught sight of Ivy, either, which was a disappointment because she had taken a liking to the little girl. Also she wanted to get to the bottom of Ivy's recurring poor health. That seemed to her of the utmost importance. She had to *know*. She had to find solutions. It was bred in the bone.

It might have taken much longer to come face-to-face with Ivy's reclusive young mother, only Mallory walked into the kitchen earlier than usual one morning to confront Kathy Cartwright, fragrant basket of herbs in hand, moving quickly to the back door that opened onto Dot's splendid kitchen garden.

Dot looked up in surprise, flustered by Mallory's early entry, while Kathy stood rooted to the spot like a wallaby caught in a Land Rover's headlights.

No aura. Or a barely perceptible one, like a gauze. *She's more shocked than you are*, Mallory thought.

To Mallory's surprised dismay, Kathy had lost almost all her former prettiness. The look of sensuality that had once defined her was gone. Kathy was much too young to undergo such a radical physical transformation. Skin and hair lacked lustre. Her thick dark hair badly needed cutting. She was so painfully thin she could have hidden behind a cricket bat.

It had to be anorexia. Mallory felt a strong need to put Kathy at ease. "Hello there, Kathy. It's good to see you." It wasn't a lie. "I've already met Ivy. She's a bright little girl. I've seen Jason and Jessica, as I expect you know."

Huge sad eyes. A pixie. Kathy didn't look like anyone's mother, dressed in a pair of shorter than short denim shorts and a T-shirt that had started life as white but was now grungy grey. Her scant clothing only served to showcase the thinness of her limbs and her near nonexistent bust.

"Mallory, how beautiful you look!" Kathy Cartwright summoned up her voice. "You were always beautiful."

Mallory smiled, wanting to avoid a trite response.

Dot, motherly woman that she was, was making wordless noises, signifying encouragement to both parties.

"I apologize for coming into the house, but Mrs. R."—Kathy whipped her dark head around, seeking support—"always has some of her lovely herbs for me to put in the salads. Jessy grows a lot of things, but they don't taste good. Most of them are really bitter."

"Well, those won't be," Mallory said, looking down at the contents of Kathy's basket: mint, the strongly fragrant basil, dill, parsley, thyme, rosemary, sage, a bunch of spring onions, and some coriander. "By the way, Kathy, no apology is needed. You're quite welcome to come in and say hello at any time. I'm glad I caught you because I wanted you to know Ivy too is welcome."

Kathy gave a ragged little laugh. "Jessica told me the opposite."

"I assure you Jessica got that wrong. If you don't have to hurry off, why don't you stay and have a cup of tea with us?"

Kathy coloured up with a mix of pleasure and embarrassment, responding to the atmosphere of simple kindness. She hesitated, clearly tempted, then muttered, "Maybe another time if that's all right?"

"Certainly," said Mallory.

Yet Kathy continued to stand there, as though she wanted to get something off her chest. "I don't know what to say to you, Mallory," she finally burst out in distress. "I did a terrible thing way back then. It's no excuse but I was drunk."

Mallory held up a staying hand, but Kathy was on a roll. "So was Jason. You know he *never* gets drunk, not Jason."

That contentious question rose again. Jason in those days had not been a drinking man. A beer or two at the outside. He didn't drink wine.

"Jessica was with us, but she never has much to drink either."

Jessica was *with* them! Mallory was forced to let that murderous piece of information lie. Kathy had called up a demon. "It's all in the past, Kathy. You can't keep carrying this heavy burden."

"I think I'm doomed to carry it forever." Kathy's expression was full not of self-pity but of acceptance of the fact she had done something she still considered utterly unforgivable.

Dot made another one of the encouraging noises that came easily to her, while Mallory made physical contact with a hand on Kathy's arm. It seemed to calm her. "You're being very hard on yourself, Kathy. You've let negative feelings engulf you."

"People hate me." Kathy bowed her head, exposing her thin neck. She had lost all her youthful glow. Mallory wanted to bring back that glow.

"Maybe people were shocked initially, but shock wears off."

"They *still* hate me. Jessy said so."

Mallory was angered, but kept it well under control. "So if Jessica says so it must be *true*?"

Kathy's huge hazel eyes were pumping tears. "I think she likes to make me feel bad just like the old days, remember?"

"Well, *I* don't hate you, Kathy. Both of us have started new lives. We're reborn if you like. I want you to look on me as a friend."

"But you'll leave." Kathy, who had seemed genuinely comforted, pulled away.

"Kathy, I'm here for some time." Mallory spoke in her calm professional voice. "Uncle Robert needs me. If you have a problem you think I may be able to help you with, you have only to pop over and tell me."

Kathy's expressions ranged from sheer disbelief to the slow realization Mallory was *serious*. "A lot of people don't like Jessica," she said as if to balance the ledger. "But she's Jason's sister. Jason always listens to his sister before he would ever listen to me. Jess holds the reins."

"Then you'd better make a start on turning that around, Kathy."

Kathy stared towards the back door as though she fully expected to see her sister-in-law come charging in like a stampeding rhino. Even Mallory thought it a strong possibility.

"Not easy." She grimaced. "No one pays attention to me. Never did. I'm Kathy Burch, before I'm ever Kathy Cartwright. I'm the daughter of the town drunk."

Mallory winced, seeing life through Kathy's eyes. "Kathy, no child could cope with that, but you're a woman now, independent of your father. You have to let go of your old way of seeing yourself. The ridicule you were subjected to was truly cruel."

"There was no one worse than Jessica!" Kathy exclaimed, dashing her tears away with her hand while Dot grabbed a box of tissues, thrusting them towards her. "She was the big culprit. She's such a bully! Why is she such a bully?" Kathy blew her small nose like a cornet.

"Bullies are always cowards, Kathy. Remember that. You have a better understanding of life now. No child can be held responsible for the actions of a parent. As a child you couldn't control the situation, but you can now."

Kathy was visibly trembling. "I'm no match for Jessy."

"You're a woman now, Kathy. You're the mother of Jason's child. That should put you in a strong position. I understand Ivy's health isn't all that good. She told me she's sick a lot."

Kathy put the basket down. Mallory noticed Kathy's nails had been bitten back to the quick.

Mallory took advantage of the moment. She pulled out a kitchen chair, signalling to Dot, who needed no signalling, to make a cup of tea. Kathy perched apologetically on the edge of her chair, one leg balanced on a rung, the other jiggling up and down. She was silent for only a few moments, then she began to talk . . . and talk . . . and talk . . .

Open sesame.

After Kathy left, they sat at the kitchen table, heads bowed, occasionally looking up to trade exhausted glances. "Struth, I thought I was going to fall into a coma," said Dot. "Talk about a dam bursting! I don't like to make judgements, but poor little Kathy could be a wee bit weak in the crumpet."

Mallory too had her concerns. There were degrees of revelation in her experience, but what they had just witnessed was a massive tsunami. At one point Kathy had spilt some of her tea on the tablecloth. She reared back in her chair like she had engineered a flood. "I don't know what the answer is. Kathy's relationship with Jessica, ironically now her sister-in-law, has always been bad. Lucky is not Kathy's middle name."

Dot clicked her tongue. "Life can be like that for some. Never getting a break from birth to death. Born under the wrong stars, I expect. Jessica is such a bully, I can't quite grasp it."

"She's certainly a big part of the problem." Mallory didn't want to take it further. There was major pathology at work.

She stood up, making the snap decision to take a

run into town. "I'm going into town. Anything you need?"

Dot too pushed up, with a series of soft grunts. "I need a prescription filled, but I don't like to bother you."

"No bother at all. Where is it?"

"Colin Watson at the pharmacy keeps it. My blood pressure is a bit on the high side. Medication keeps it under control."

"So, ring Colin Watson and tell him to make up the prescription," Mallory urged. "Tell him Mallory James will be picking it up for you."

Dot smirked. "Colin will be thrilled about that. He has a thingy about you."

"A thingy?" Mallory was taken aback. She had never met Colin Watson in her life.

Dot was chortling to herself. "Let's say he's a big fan. Men are always interested in a beautiful woman."

It was another scorching day under a sky baked the colour of bright blue enamel. The scarlet of the poincianas was a wonderful foil for the bluer-than-blue sky. The great trees continued to cling to their glory, hazing the air with rose-pink. Squadrons of birds were on the wing, sunlight glancing off their gaudy plumage. The beautiful colourful bird life of the tropics was extraordinary.

Her journey, as ever, delighted her naturally artistic eye, but her mind wasn't at ease. Theories on an unprecedented level were taking seed. All the time Kathy had been pouring out her soul accompanied by a lot of fast gulping and fidgeting on her chair, Mallory was seriously considering if all the trips to hospital with Ivy had anything to do with Kathy's desperate need for sympathy and attention. Everything about Kathy's behaviour suggested it. Kathy appeared starved of love, even basic consideration. Ivy had been presented at hospital many times. Kathy over their cup of tea had exhibited the great concern one would expect of a loving mother. Yet it couldn't have been more obvious to her and to Dot that Kathy craved attention.

Worst-case scenario, Munchausen syndrome by proxy.
It had to be considered.

She had experience of the syndrome. She had dealt with such a case. A young patient's mother, over a period of fourteen months before she had been referred to Mallory, had been making her child ill with nothing more than kitchen salt. The mother, separated from her husband, had craved attention. As did Kathy who wasn't getting much attention. The sooner she spoke to Marisa Farnsworth, the better. There couldn't be a question of doctor shopping as had happened with her former patient's mother. As far as anyone knew, Kathy had brought Ivy to Base Hospital on all occasions. Could Kathy be *self*-harming as well? Mallory couldn't thrust the thought away. The main concern was the child, not the mother.

Her last call for the day was picking up the prescription from the pharmacy. "Oh, here she is now, Mrs. C.!" The town pharmacist, Colin Watson, was leaning on the counter in conversation with a customer. His customer was standing with a rigid back to Mallory. Margery Cartwright no less.

Her cover blown, Margery was forced to turn around, looking extremely embarrassed.

Mallory went forward, hand outstretched. "Margery, how lovely to see you."

From the expression on Margery Cartwright's face she couldn't quite believe Mallory was sincere. Margery was looking very smart and scarcely a day older than the last time Mallory had seen her, but her bluish aura had dimmed.

"M-m-Mallory, dear!" Margery was reduced to stammering. "C-c-Colin was just telling me you were back."

Good old Colin, her secret admirer and Forrester's unofficial town crier, gave Mallory a big crocodile smile. Mallory gave him back nothing by way of encouragement.

A kiss on the cheek for Margery seemed more appropriate than a handshake. "You've heard Uncle Robert had a heart attack?" Mallory kept all trace of censure out of her voice.

"Yes, dear." Margery looked contrite. "The whole town knows. Robert is much loved. We would call, only—" She broke off with a heavy sigh, as though she couldn't nail down the exact reason for not paying a visit.

"If you're not in a hurry, why don't we have a cup of coffee?" Mallory suggested. "I've completed my chores. I just have to pick up a prescription." She glanced over Margery's coiffed head at Colin, who was still paying her considerable attention.

Caught out, he gave her another toothy grin.

"What do you say, Margery?"

Margery looked on the verge of scooting, but she knew it was pointless. "That would be lovely." Margery released a breath. "You know, Mallory, I think of you so often. What might have been."

Thank God it wasn't, Mallory thought.

Margery took a while mulling over hummingbird cake versus pineapple upside down cake. In the end she opted for a generous slice of the pineapple upside down cake with what looked like a half a pint of whipped cream on the side. The glassed-in display case was awash with similar treats. "Just today, mind you. I watch my diet."

"And it works, Margery." Margery's thick hair, once blonde, was now a fashionable mocha, teased and sprayed, ready to withstand cyclonic winds should they unexpectedly arise out of season. Although the pineapple upside down cake looked delicious, Mallory declined a slice. She was being very well fed by Dot, who had confessed she never fell off a diet because she never went on one.

Some minutes later Margery had arrived at the point where she looked comfortable voicing her demons. "I feel terrible about not ever seeing my little granddaughter," she confided, blinking away tears as she tore open the ubiquitous sugar substitute and poured it into her coffee.

"She's six already, Margery," Mallory couldn't help saying. "You could fix things this very day. Ivy is—"

"Oh, I don't like that name!" Margery's cheeks did a wobble of outrage. She threw up both hands like jewelled birds in flight. Fuchsia nail polish matched the flowers in her expensive printed dress. Sparkling rings, both hands, exploded with colour.

Vena amoris, Mallory thought, or vein of love. Myth

held that a vein connected the *third* finger of the hand directly with the heart. Not the fourth finger, commonly called the engagement finger.

"I understand Jessica picked it out?"

Moments of savouring, then Margery put the cake fork down with a clatter. "She *would*. Ivy. Poison ivy."

"Surely not?" Even Jessica couldn't think of something like that. Mallory grasped Margery's jewel-encrusted fingers. "Ivy is a very bright little girl, the image of Jason. Is it Kathy you hold responsible for splitting the family apart?"

Margery looked genuinely startled. "No, of course not, Mallory dear."

Her front-running theory bit the dust.

Margery finished her slice of cake as though it would be positively rude not to. "Kathy Burch, that poor little creature, is a bit on the iffy side. The father is an absolute lunatic. Probably didn't know what she was doing when she got Jason into bed. He wouldn't have known what he was doing either. They were both drunk. It would never have happened otherwise."

"Well, it *did*. Jason and Kathy are married and they have a little girl. You *must* meet her, Margery." Mallory knew she was treading where even angels would hesitate, but she felt she was being directed by an unseen hand. "Now that I'm back, I'm seeing things much more clearly. Ivy needs you. She needs her grandmother and her grandfather."

Perspiration was popping out on Margery's top lip although the coffee shop was air-conditioned. She delved in her handbag for a handkerchief perfumed with Elizabeth Taylor's enormously successful "White Diamonds." "You remember I was often called to the school to talk about Jessica's treatment of Kathy Burch." Tears stood in the bright blue eyes. "It grieves me to say it, but Jessica has a very cruel streak."

"The cruelty of children is no news to anyone, Margery. They lack understanding."

Margery nodded sagely. "But with Jessica! God knows I tried to be a good mother, yet Jessica was always so closed and so hostile. I couldn't say a thing right. If I weren't her mother I would have said she hated me, it got so bad at times. Other times she was normal enough. Not loving, never loving, but I caught glimpses of what she might have been like. The only person she was loving towards was her brother. I endured endless frustrations with my daughter, Mallory. Right through her childhood and God knows through her adolescence when she really took off. Jessica lacks the softer virtues. She's hard, so hard and so terribly unpredictable. You never knew where you were with her. God knows where she gets it from. Certainly not from me. Or her father. Jason didn't share that terrible trait, for all the rest!"

"What rest?" Mallory seized onto that, but Margery didn't answer her.

"Jessica really tormented that girl. I can't believe they get on after all those years of bullying. Who could? Jessica always was the problem, but everyone loved Jason. Jessica dominated Jason ever since they were babies. You knew we separated them at one point. Jason spent his last four years of secondary school boarding in Brisbane. But they only wanted to be back together again."

Mallory was taking note of the tremor in Margery's right hand. "So what are you saying, Margery?" She plunged in, hoping Margery would open up.

Only Margery was jumpy. She kept looking towards the door as though plotting her escape. She didn't want to be subject to any interrogation, however well meant. She bowed her lacquered head, clearly about to clam up. "Harry and I strongly disapprove of Jessica's . . ." A bitten lip and a long hesitation, then, "*Interference* in Jason's life. What's she doing working on your uncle's plantation anyway?" Margery asked in a kind of rage.

"She needed the job, Margery."

Margery's expression had turned reminiscent of Jessica's at her most fearsome. "She could have got one in Sydney or Melbourne. Jessica is *clever*." She made it sound like cleverness was a very bad thing. "Start a new life. Leave Jason alone." Margery brandished her cake fork aloft.

Several patrons glanced in their direction, their curiosity piqued. This was a small town, after all, where gossip was rife.

"Jason *and* Kathy," Mallory pointed out. "And your lovely little granddaughter."

"Yes, of course." Margery appeared reluctant to say any more. Her time limit was up. She pushed the rest of her cake resolutely away. "We do want to see our grandchild, Mallory. You must know that. Our hearts ache. But what can we do? We *don't* want to see the twins. Not the way things are."

The bit was between Mallory's teeth. She wasn't about to give up. "How bad is that? I confess I'm bewildered."

For a moment it looked as though Margery, like Kathy, was about to unburden herself big time. Only she took a deep, deep breath through her nostrils, like a show jumper about to attempt the final hurdle.

"I can't tell you the details, Mallory. Suffice to say there was a very serious falling-out. Very serious indeed. It had nothing whatsoever to do with Kathy Burch. We were terribly distressed our son had betrayed you, of course. Such a beautiful woman in every way. We had such high hopes for you and Jason. He needed someone like you. We were all set to welcome you into our family. Dear God!" She paused a moment, then carried on, clearly distressed. "The last thing I want is to exclude my little granddaughter. I'm a loving woman, Mallory. Only I don't see any other way."

"I don't mean to push this, Margery. Ivy is the innocent victim here. You would love her. She's family. Your blood. It mightn't be easy, but there is a way if you chose to take it. You *are* Ivy's grandmother. You would be such a wonderful steadying influence in her life. You know her health isn't as robust as it should be?"

Margery passed a fretful hand over her unlined forehead. "Ted Moorehouse told us Ivy had some problems. Nothing serious, just childhood ailments. Her mother is probably overanxious, bringing her to hospital all the time. She had a dreadful childhood that poor girl. As for her mother, a punching bag. The only way I can get to see my granddaughter is for the twins to break up."

Mallory's nerves went into spasm. "You're saying reconciliation is out of the question?"

"God help us, *yes.*" Margery shuddered. "I'm sorry, Mallory. I must go home. But thank you, dear. I hear you're a psychiatrist now?"

"Psychologist, Margery."

Margery reached out to touch Mallory's hand.

"You are a clever girl. I've always felt a real affection for you."

"It works both ways, Margery. I want you to know I'm here for you. I'll be staying with Uncle Robert until he's much stronger. It will take time, some months. You must come over to Moonglade for a visit. I would ensure you and Harry didn't run into anyone, except maybe . . . Ivy."

There was a sudden light in Margery's eyes. "How could you manage that?" A powerful thread of hope lifted her tone.

At that point Mallory didn't know how, but it wasn't going to prevent her from giving it her best shot. "I've spoken to Kathy. I believe—I hope—Kathy trusts me. Something could be arranged."

Margery mulled that one over. "But wouldn't the twins know? I mean with a child, one could hardly keep a meeting secret." She was close to wringing her hands.

"I'll run it past Jason," said Mallory. She supposed she could do it.

"I'm sure he still loves you," Margery exclaimed as though the door might be open for a rerun of their romance.

A moment later they were out on the street with curious looks directed at them from passers-by who knew them and their shared history. "It only takes *one* person to destroy a family," Margery spoke in so vehement an undertone it was almost a lioness's growl.

A monster in the family?

Margery Cartwright had not pointed a finger at her daughter-in-law, but at her own daughter. Alarm

bells were pealing inside Mallory's head. Big bells.
Margery was hiding a secret.

Mallory was determined to get to the bottom of all
the secrecy. Margery turned and clasped Mallory to
her bosom. "I implore you from the bottom of my
heart, Mallory. God has sent you here. You are the
one to make it happen. I must meet with my granddaughter. But be aware, Jessica is *dangerous*."

There was no need of the warning.

While her uncle was resting, Mallory walked down
from the house to the promontory. Her thoughts and
memories kept pace. A short distance from the cliff
edge she stood staring out over a sea that had turned
throughout the day from aqua in the shallows,
turquoise to cobalt, and now, at late afternoon, a
shade of indigo. So smooth was the water, it was like
glass. She could see for miles, the green off-shore
cays. It was an awesome sight. The sea more than the
sky had always suggested infinity to her. It was nearing sunset after a brilliantly hot and fine day. Sunsets
in the tropics were spectacular, each one different.
On this late afternoon the sun, a burning copper
ball, was sinking towards a horizon washed with layer
upon layer of pink, gold, lapis lazuli, grape blue, and
acid green. On the tide line two seagulls, obviously
husband and wife, were having a screaming match.
Over the water a solitary white breasted sea eagle was
soaring, showing a wingspan that had to be over two
metres. Sea eagles were solitary birds. Solitary like
her. One only saw them in pairs when they were nest-
ing. No way would sea eagles abandon their young.
Even with her loving Uncle Robert, she had found it

difficult to assuage the loneliness and longing she had felt for a *father*. A father who didn't blame her for being alive.

She was standing well back from the edge but she still had a sweeping view of their cove. Large rocks, sculptural in form, were embedded in the white sand at either end of the crescent. Growing back from the strand line were the primary colonisers, the feathery casuarinas and the pandanus with their characteristic prop roots and segmented orange fruit. Over the years the coconut palms had been bent into fantastic shapes from the cyclone-driven winds. The trees were throwing shadows on the white sand, thickly embroidered with a yellow flowering succulent. This was her idea of paradise, or the way she imagined it. She remembered Uncle Robert telling her as a child "paradise" meant *garden* in Persian.

Memories began to surge forward, like the incoming tide. Whole scenes of picnics on the beach. Swimming parties. She could remember back to the times when her mother and father had visited Moonglade.

She recalled a particular occasion when as a little girl she had stood marvelling at the burning splendour of the sinking sun. Her mother had been holding one hand, Uncle Robert the other. Oddly she had no image of her father on occasions such as that. It was always Uncle Robert and her mother. Once her mother had suffered a bout of vertigo. Uncle Robert had pulled her into his arms, cradling her head against his chest, his hand stroking her hair as tenderly as he often stroked Mallory's long hair.

Another time she had seen Uncle Robert bend to kiss the palms of her mother's hands. Her mother had not pulled away. Her whole face had been illuminated as if the sun had been shining on it.

These memories of childhood were among the most haunting. Uncle Robert had been a very special person to her mother. Yet her mother had married his brother. Even as a child, she knew Uncle Robert was by far the better man, with a capacity for loving her father totally lacked. Her father had not so much loved her mother as *owned* her. She had been his perfect possession.

The brisk sea breeze was whipping her long hair around her face. She had taken to wearing it loose. In her job she always pulled her hair back into various updated knots. For now, though, she was on holiday.

She and Uncle Robert were in a very good place at the moment. It was obvious her uncle was overjoyed to have her with him. There was a great sense of peace between them. They had fallen back into their old rhythm. They talked about the many things that interested them, just like the old days, student and mentor, books, paintings, films, and music. They listened to *their* kind of music. They shared the same tastes. Anything remotely upsetting was blocked out, never discussed. She wouldn't upset her uncle for anything in the world.

Ted Moorehouse called at the house, in his capacity as friend and doctor. Blaine was in and out of the house, but never stayed long. He was a seriously busy man. The only one who didn't make a phone call or even send an email was her father. He had ignored her many messages. He didn't give a damn about his brother or her. After all these years she still found it hard to believe there were people like him.

Mallory didn't hear anyone behind her until she heard her name spoken in a voice hoarse with emotion.

"Mallory?"

"Jason!" She turned to face him, fearing more of the same was coming up. "I'd come to think you were all avoiding me."

"Better that way." A nerve throbbed at his temple.

"*You* might feel you have to avoid me, Jason, but Kathy and Ivy don't. Do you really want to clip their wings?"

Jolted out of his melancholy, Jason reacted angrily. "What bloody wings? Kathy is as flightless as an emu. It's not a lot of fun trying to get anything into her head. She peaked in the third grade."

"And you're an intellectual giant, I suppose? Surely this isn't what being a husband is all about, Jason. It's obvious you're on an all-time personal low, but I can't help you out with that. Maybe you could try a little kindness with your wife. I don't think you realize how harsh you appear."

"Do you think I haven't tried?" Jason sounded like a man pressured beyond endurance. "Everything is a bloody great mystery to Kathy. All the Burches are stupid. You can't fight genetics."

"That family has been treated cruelly. An alcoholic and abusive husband and father. Your sister treats Kathy like an underling. You don't have to add to the pain. I can't recall you and Jess qualifying for Mensa."

"Unlike you, Dr. James. We all recognised you're smart. I don't want to argue with you. I just want to speak to you. Get some comfort. It's totally missing from my life."

"When you have a beautiful little daughter?"

Jason seemed not to have heard. "You're going to go away again, aren't you?"

"Be sure of it, Jason. Not that it's any of your business. While I'm here there's no good reason to keep your family away. You really ought to make a break from Jessica."

"Jessica is part of me. Part of my being. Don't you understand that? Part of my body and soul. *Nothing* can change that."

Such an impassioned look was on his face Mallory found herself physically backing away. That wasn't any heart-warming declaration of a brother's love for his sister. Truth be told, she was dismayed by the *strength* of his answer, the utter conviction in it. "Jason, Jessica is your *sister*, not the great love of your life. Your first thought should be your wife, not Jessica. Kathy is so vulnerable, yet you stand by while your sister insults her and calls her a silly cow."

"As well she might. Kathy is as deep as a puddle."

"What about your daughter? Jessica ranks before her too? The only love Jessica has to offer is for *you*. Even you must admit Jessica can't *share*. What did you want to speak to me about anyway?"

His answer was rough with emotion. "I saw you here."

Another woman might have burst into tears at the poignancy of his expression, only for the life of her, Mallory couldn't offer a word of comfort. Those days were long gone. What she saw was a man sticking stubbornly to a lost dream. She seized on what she saw as a God-sent opportunity. "I met up with your mother a few days ago in town. We had coffee."

"Big deal!" Jason snorted. "Jess and I made a complete break from Mum and Dad."

"So I heard. I can't understand it. Bad blood with your parents is terrible karma. You used to talk a lot about karma, remember?"

"Hippy stuff," he grunted.

"Perhaps I can help?"

Sharply he averted his gaze. "There's no way *you* can help."

She felt a prickling sensation down her spine. "Your mother said the same thing. I'm sure with goodwill on both sides, you can arrive at some sort of a reconciliation. It will make your life easier. You will have support. Your parents love you, Jason."

"Bullshit!" He cut her off.

Mallory stared at him in some confusion. "They *do* love you."

"Do they really?"

Mallory paused, perplexed. "Is Jessica at the root of the problem?" She had to be.

"They cut us out of their lives." Jason lashed back.

"Was it an argument about money? I realize it could have been difficult."

"What on earth do you mean? *Money?* I have no idea what you're banging on about, Mallory. Dad was a generous man. Don't even think you can guess."

"I can guess a lot of the friction was Jessica's fault. She makes it so hard, not only for herself but for everyone else. She makes no attempt to be pleasant or accommodating. She lacks empathy. She lacks some essential quality of the heart. She's completely indifferent to the pain she causes others. I don't have to remind you she bullied Kathy right through school. She continues to do it to this day. It may shock you, but I think Jessica could well be bipolar, probably from the onset of puberty."

"Bipolar?" A look of alarm crossed his face. "You mean she's mad?"

"Good heavens, no!" Mallory shook her head. "To be bipolar is *not* to be mad, Jason. It's a disorder that can be treated with medication and self-managed if taught the ways. A great many people don't even know they have it. Jessica's behaviour bears a lot of the hallmarks. We both know she's always had big mood swings going back to our schooldays. The manic episodes before plunging back into the dark place. Jessica should have been checked out years ago, only I'm sure your parents didn't know or even guess she could be bipolar. The good thing is she has easy access to professional help. The right medication is absolutely essential. If you love her you should urge her to seek help."

If she had imagined Jason was paying serious attention on behalf of his twin, she was far wide of the mark. "Sheer bloody speculation!" Jason spat. "You bloody shrinks are the worst, seeing mental conditions all over the place. What about you? That woman, Dr. Sarah, treated you for years after your mother was killed and your father left. Were you mental too?"

Mallory answered in the same calm manner. "I was a deeply disturbed, grieving child. I had witnessed the violent death of my mother. She died while I lived. I couldn't have done without Dr. Sarah, Jason. She offered enormous help. That was her calling. And mine. Which is my point. Jessica could benefit greatly from seeing a professional. I can give her names."

"We don't want your bloody names," Jason burst out so violently a lesser woman might have turned and run. "There's nothing wrong with Jess. I would know. She's my twin."

"Not your identical twin." Mallory stood her ground. "What does that mean?"

She locked his wild blue gaze. "If Jess is bipolar, you have a chance of being bipolar too. Less of a chance than an identical twin. Identical twins share the same DNA. You two don't."

"I'll never forgive you for that, Mallory," he said, as though bitterly betrayed. "Jess and I won't be needing any professional attention. I know my sister. I don't believe a word of this bipolar bull. Jess doesn't suffer fools gladly, that's all."

Mallory didn't hold back. "When you're feeling calmer, Jason, consider what I've been saying. I've seen with my own eyes Jessica tap dancing with rage towards a small *child*."

Jason's upraised hand chopped her off. "Ivy can be *very* naughty. She even tries *my* patience."

"I'm not one hundred percent certain you *are* a patient man," Mallory said.

The muscles of his jaw were tightly bunched. "Look, I know I've changed, but life has been hard. You have no idea how hard. Jess is super-efficient. She's not afraid of hard work, the more physical the better. I need her. The farm needs her. Kathy is useless as a wife, a mother, and a worker in the house and on the farm. If you want evidence I can show you plenty."

"Maybe between the two of you you're robbing her of all confidence. You're shockingly indifferent to her, yet you got the poor woman pregnant. You married her."

Jason's whole body stiffened. "I stepped up to the plate, didn't I?"

"You don't have a good track record, Jason."

"How would *you* know? You weren't here. At the beginning I was so bloody patient with my pathetic wife, I should have been canonised."

"No chance of that. You're awash with human failings."

"Like the rest of us," he said bitterly. "I'd better get back to work. You'll never understand."

"I'm trying to, Jason. You're walking away from the consequences of your marriage. It's a father's duty to protect his child. Your mother and father, no matter the alienation, are desperate to meet Ivy. They're good people. They could be such a help. Children need loving grandparents."

That provoked a hard laugh. "As long as Jess and I keep out of the way. Life's a bitch, ain't it?"

"Why does everything have to do with *you*? If you want to make a start on ending this extraordinary rift, you might begin by allowing your parents to see Ivy in private. I'm sure they'd be thrilled to look after her from time to time. It would give you and Kathy a break."

Jason clearly was being buffeted by waves of anger and frustration. "To do what? Have a lovey-dovey weekend away together? Can't you get it through your head? Our marriage is a disaster. I don't *love* Kathy. There's no such thing as loving to order. I didn't know I was getting Kathy pregnant even when I was doing it. It's like it happened to someone else. One drunken moment and my life was ruined. I lost you. I got Kathy Burch instead. What a consolation prize! You don't call that a disaster? We've been married for years but I haven't been able to form any sort of bond with her. I don't *know* her. I don't recognise the person she is. She'll never get herself sorted."

Mallory saw the terrible anger in him, the immense frustration. "You should have thought hard about consequences before you got her into bed. Bedding such a vulnerable creature was a breach of decency and honour."

Melancholia had descended on Jason's shoulders like dark outspread wings. "The weird thing is I don't remember getting her into bed."

Mallory's heart was beating suffocatingly hard. "You don't remember getting her into bed? You did. Ivy is here."

"I love Ivy," he cried.

"It makes me truly happy to hear it."

"You're so bloody perfect, aren't you!" His whole demeanour had turned hostile. "Heaven will surely be yours. You even look like an angel. Smile like an angel. I can't understand why Ivy's so sickly. Jess and I have scarcely had a sick day in our lives. Jess thinks Ivy's poor health could have something to do with the way Kathy took drugs."

"Drugs?" Disbelief hardened Mallory's voice. "Where's the evidence for that?" she shot back. "All you're doing is throwing something else into the equation. This is the first I've heard of Kathy Burch taking drugs. There was no talk of Kathy having a drug problem *or* a drink problem, for that matter. Forrester is a small town. Everyone knows everyone else's business. There was no evidence of drug taking, even if she was a bit promiscuous. Looking for love in all the wrong places, poor girl. Kathy revealed something I didn't know. She said Jessica was with you that night you and Kathy got drunk. Is that true?" She pinned his gaze. "Jessica, always screwing things up for you."

"Kathy *lied*," he gasped.

"What would be her reason to lie? Tell me that."

"Because she's a bloody pathological liar, that's why. Tell one lie, you can tell thousands. Anyway, she was probably hallucinating. Jess swore to me Kathy takes drugs."

Anger flared. "Good old Jess! Ever think she was running a bluff? Your sister has always had her own agenda. If Kathy takes drugs, where does she get them from? How does she pay for them? She walks around in rags. Who is her supplier? If you believe Jessica's story—which I don't—why don't you find out? It's your responsibility. But tell me, *what* part of the evening was Jessica with you?"

Jason's tormented face was filled with real confusion. "Mallory, I hardly remember. All I know is, I lost *you*."

"But you did gain a wife and daughter. You say you and Kathy can't bond. Maybe the remedy is for Jessica to get another job in another part of the world. She sticks so close to you, Jason, Kathy must feel she doesn't stand a chance."

Jason wiped the sweat from his brow with the back of his hand. "You're not listening, Mallory. You're supposed to be a *trained* listener. There's no possibility I can ever love Kathy. I love *you*. I will never be able to deal with losing you." He drew closer, taller, infinitely stronger, looming over her. No wonder women feared men's vastly superior strength. Mallory would have felt real alarm had they been in some secluded place instead of in plain view of the house.

Still she resisted the urge to step back. "Jason, that part of our lives is long *over*!"

Jason's eyes blazed with naked hate. "*You* would

never have tolerated Jessica's interference in our lives, much less put up with her on a daily basis."

Mallory jumped on the clue. "Was *that* my big appeal? In your heart, you wanted to be free of your sister?"

For an answer, Jason grabbed her upper arm, his hard calloused fingers biting into her soft flesh. "You want me to admit it? Well, it's a YES!" he hissed. "I so wanted Jess out of the picture. It's like being held captive."

Mallory's head was awhirl. "*Captive*? Explain. While you're at it, take your hand off me."

He was slow to respond, dragging his hands down the length of her arms, his fingers encircling her narrow wrists like a pair of handcuffs. "Mallory, I'm sorry."

"No, you're not." She was amazingly calm.

"Don't you remember how happy we were?" he implored. "Has it gone from your memory? Has it gone forever?"

"I remember you betrayed me, Jason. You betrayed yourself. Your family. You got Kathy pregnant. You thought you would get away with it. You didn't. There's a price we have to pay for our mistakes. Not that anyone could call your little daughter a mistake. She's precious. You seem to be throwing aside all that a decent man wants. You're throwing aside the parents who love you, a wife who would love you if you gave her half a chance. The way things are, Kathy can't blossom. She's being frozen out by your sister. You do what *Jessica* wants. She's the one with authority, though I can believe underneath you loathe her power. Any romantic thoughts of me that you still entertain need to be knocked out of your head. I now realize back then you saw me as a buffer between you and Jessica."

"You were *everything* to me," he declared.

"You mean you saw me as the woman who could seize control from Jessica. I've studied the dark side of the human psyche, Jason. The dark side is far more widespread than people imagine. If you want to be free, you have to stop Jessica from controlling your life. What I suggest for now is to allow me to arrange for your mother to meet Ivy. It would be a first step towards normality. Kathy will have no objection. Your mother no longer holds Kathy responsible for what happened in the past."

Jason reacted violently. "Will you stop enshrining Kathy as my *wife*. I can't bear to have sex with her. If she weren't such a pathetic wimp, I'd divorce her."

Mallory gave him a bright, fierce glance. "Well, it's clear you can't remain together in such a destructive marriage. If you're not having sex with your wife, who *are* you having sex with? You're a young man. How many women have you got on the go?"

Jason's rage visibly moved up several notches. His face and throat were swamped with hot blood. Even his blue eyes seemed to bulge. "Are you losing your mind or what?"

Mallory realized any movement from her could trigger a violent physical reaction. Still she spoke out. "My advice, for what it's worth, is to get rid of your sister."

Jason put both hands over his face, dragging them down to his throat. "I can hardly see or think of anyone but *you*, Mallory. You are everything I want in this world. I want to pull you into my arms right now. Hold you. Kiss you . . . kiss you . . . kiss you. I want to *feel* something. Pure desire for a woman. I want my self-respect back. It's been gone for so long. People used to like me. Now they don't. My own parents don't want to see me. I'm not a bad man. Doesn't life owe me some happiness? As for the future, what future? I had a future with you." He was overwhelmed by despair. "There's no one like you, Mallory. There never will be again. Is it any wonder I *hate* Kathy?" Now he locked his strong hands together as if he were locking them around a small defenceless throat.

Poor diminished Kathy.

A feeling of helplessness rolled over Mallory. "Kathy didn't get much of a bargain either. Hate can make bad things happen. Look into your own behaviour, Jason. You were drunk and you got swept away. I'd think long and hard too about where Jessica was on that night. She couldn't have been far away."

Jason's blue eyes burned. "Leave it. I don't remember." His glance cut off in the direction of the house, then back to her. "What's Forrester to you?"

"What he has always been, my friend."

"Friend? Like hell. The Lord Protector, eternal champion of beautiful women has spotted us. He's on his way." Jason's intense jealousy of Blaine was obvious. "No surprises there. He's always kept an eye on you, hasn't he? If you ask me he wants you himself. You're not fooling me. But you may be fooling yourself." All the life had faded from Jason's face. He turned away and left, but not before Mallory saw the murderous look in his blue eyes.

Jason's whole life had gone to hell.

"Bad time?" Blaine enquired, when he joined her.

She could feel the probe of his eyes. "Is there a good one with Jason?" She needed a moment to take a breath. She was feeling a little spent. A squadron of sea birds streaked out of the sky to dive-bomb a wave, most coming up with a wriggling small fish.

"So, what did he want?"

Mallory released a sigh. "He's a very unhappy man."

"The whole town knows that. Jason has never recovered from losing you. Then he married a woman he didn't love. His most glorious moments in life have come and gone."

"He's not yet thirty! He has to get his life together even if he and Kathy split up. I told him he has to resolve his problems on his own. I made him furious as well."

Blaine frowned. "Furious? How come?"

"I threw him off balance. I suggested Jessica might be bipolar because I seriously believe she could be. In which case, she should see a professional."

Blaine answered with a certain amount of caution. "I know she's very aggressive. There's that rapid fire speech, though I have struck her on the odd occasion when she was blessedly mild."

"Decreased activity level. She could have been entering the depressive phase. I'm prepared to say Jessica is bipolar. Medication would go a long way to stabilizing her moods. She needs help. It's available. I told Jason this."

"And the very suggestion of getting his sister help made him furious?"

"Indeed it did. I went further. As Jessica's fraternal twin, he too could have inherited the disorder to some degree, only Jason in the old days was very good natured."

"I'm not so sure of his good nature now," Blaine said, any number of concerns flooding his mind. "I can't remember when I last saw him in good spirits. So how did you end it?"

"Badly. He's convinced there's nothing wrong with her."

"Or him." Blaine's expressive voice had turned metallic. "I'm worried about keeping Jason on. Brother and sister have serious issues that need to be addressed."

"Let's leave it for now." She turned to face him, attempting a smile.

"You're spending too much time in the house. I thought you might like a night out. There's a new Thai restaurant just out of town. The Lotus Garden. Food and service are excellent. I've been there before, and I think you'd like it."

She was silent a moment. "I'm sure I would."

"Never a woman to rush into things."

"I like to take my time, Blaine. So what night are we talking?"

He made a scoffing sound. "Well, I'm not talking next month or maybe the month after. This very night, if that suits you? I could pick you up at eight?"

She nodded. "I'd like that."

"There, that wasn't so hard, was it?"

She shook her head.

Said nothing.

Nothing of her strong rush of excitement. She should be forgetting about the past, her tangled emotions, none of which was fair to him.

Chapter Four

When Mallory was dressed, she went downstairs to show herself off to her uncle. It had always given him pleasure to see her dressed up to go out. In the living room, she made a graceful full turn, inviting her uncle to admire her. "Look fantastic, don't I?" The long floaty skirt of her dress swirled out before wrapping around her slender legs.

"Ravishing!"

Is he seeing you or your mother?

Her heart stumbled painfully. "Maybe exaggerating a bit, but keep it up." She sounded playful when she felt far from it. Her father had never once in her life told her she looked pretty, let alone ravishing. He had only been gratified by her academic successes which, naturally, he took as a reflection of his brilliant self. Looking down at her uncle, she was struck yet again by the disconcerting family resemblance between the two brothers. Both were tall, lean, handsome men with dark eyes and dark hair silvered at the temples. Her distinguished father sported a well-tended beard, which he treated lovingly, from time to time stroking it like a pet, but Robert was the one who radiated humour, understanding, and comfort, especially in times of crises. Her father's response was to run.

"I couldn't be more serious." Robert grasped her hand, bringing her to a halt. "Love the dress."

"Cost a bit, but it was worth it."

He caught a pinch of the silk-chiffon fabric in a kaleidoscope of sunset colours, rubbing it between thumb and forefinger. "Truly beautiful," he repeated.

"I'm glad you like it," Mallory managed huskily. She was deeply affected by the look in his dark eyes. There was nothing new in that look. Her remarkable resemblance to her late mother had estranged her from her father, while bringing her close to her uncle. There were always reasons for the way people behaved as they did. Brushing her melancholy thoughts aside, she held the skirt wide so he could see the swirl of colours, dusky pink, turquoise, gold, citrus yellows, splashes of purple.

He stared up into her face. "I will always carry the picture of you in my heart." Though his eyes were *fixed* on her, Mallory knew he wasn't really seeing her. It spooked her. Why wouldn't it? She was a separate identity.

"Blaine should be here soon." She spoke quickly, to cover her raw feelings. Since she had lost her mother she had always had a desperate searching for identity. She had adored her mother. But she wasn't her mother. She had a total *otherness* about her. She was *herself*.

"You're sure you're okay about my leaving you?" She was battling doubts. His aura had been *grey*. It had faded fast.

"Of course I'm okay," he assured her, looking like a man totally at peace. "There's nothing at all to worry about, my darling."

Mallory placed her hands on his shoulders, staring down into his face with great tenderness. "You are and always have been more of a father to me than my absentee father. I love you, Uncle Robert."

"I love you too, Mallory," he responded. There was such fervour in his voice it trembled. He paused a moment to take a breath, then he spoke in an entirely different voice. "After I'm gone, all this is yours, Mallory. I've made a few bequests here and there, but you are, to all intents and purposes, my sole beneficiary. You have power of attorney should my health seriously deteriorate. Moonglade is yours. It will be up to you what to do with it."

Ever the scholar, lines from Christopher Marlowe sprang instantly to Mallory's mind.

I think my master means to die shortly
For he hath given me all his goods.

Suddenly she was on the verge of tears. She took her uncle's thin face between her hands. "Uncle Robert, why are you talking like this? I mean for you to be around for a long, long time."

His smile remained wonderfully serene. "I'm not given to mentioning my financial affairs, I know. But I think it's time. Not that you don't know you are the most important person in the world to me." He continued to stare into her face, into the mournful beauty of her glistening eyes.

She shivered, not wanting to invoke the image of her dead mother. Yet how could she not? Sadness was tearing her to pieces. "My mother had precious little time. She was only a handful of years older than I am now when it was all over for her."

"All over for me. All over for my poor brother. In some sad ways over for you, a little girl deprived of her mother. And in such a brutal way! Claudia bound us all together."

She saw his mind had slipped back into its habitual mode.

No changing it. She knew in her heart, her lovely, generous mother would have wanted them all to live full lives. That was the task ahead of her.

"I have such *dreams* of her!" Robert said with a young man's passion. "The dead appear to us in dreams. As a child you were always calling out for your mother. Now nearing the end of my life, more than ever Claudia walks towards me in all her beauty. I wait, hoping with all my heart she will walk into my arms, but she has always remained just that bit out of reach. Claudia was so beautiful, so vibrant, so *clever*. My brother all but crushed the life out of her. He has always been in ruthless pursuit of his own ambitions, even as a boy. One of his goals was taking Claudia from me. I loved Claudia with all my heart, so he had to take her. Simple as that. Claudia's great mistake was marrying Nigel."

"Why did you let her?" Her lack of understanding showed in her face. "Clever women do make foolish choices. I should know. And I do know my father, Uncle Robert."

"My darling, I don't think anyone knows Nigel *well*."

"I'm so sorry he hasn't contacted you," Mallory apologized.

"We'll leave him to heaven. I see you as Claudia's

great *gift* to me. I'm convinced Claudia is watching over us."

He was in a strangely exultant mood that nothing could dampen.

She greeted Blaine at the door. He looked wonderful, the utter embodiment of the old cliché: tall, dark, and handsome. She felt a powerful surge of sensation, both mental and physical. When he smiled at her, she had the mad impulse to go into his arms. The force of his eyes was enormous.

He paused suddenly, caught her wrist, dropped a light kiss on her cheek. "You look sensational."

"Thank you." She felt like putting up her hand, touching the place where he had kissed her. He hadn't kissed her for years and years. Then she would have been enraptured. "This must be as close as it comes to a date," she said.

"A first date." He was watching her, amusement and something less readable in his eyes.

She didn't lead an exciting life. She didn't have a lover, a husband, or children. It was safe and heartbreaking at one and the same time. If anyone saw her as *herself*, even her flawed self, it was Blaine. Now they were off together for the evening. Lord knows what it would bring. Even his light kiss on her cheek had generated a lot of heat.

They moved across the spacious entrance hall dominated by a gilt and japanned Chinoiserie console. Atop it was a striking Great Barrier Reef scene that added vibrant colour. Blaine, naturally, wished to say a quick hello to Robert. "He's waiting for you," Mallory said. "He's getting stronger every day."

"Having someone you love around makes all the difference in the world."

"Maybe you should give Selma another chance?" Why in sweet heaven did she keep pushing Selma at him?

He swung a wide shoulder. "Thank you, Mallory, but I already have someone else in mind."

That stopped her in her tracks. If he did have someone else in mind—that could easily be the case given he had been chased by dozens of females since his teens—she would have the devil of a time accepting it. She couldn't be robbed of Blaine. He was *her* friend, for better or worse.

The night sky was studded with a billion tightly clustered stars that were, in fact, vast distances apart. Their light splashed down on planet Earth, exceptionally luminous, as stars always are over the sea. The Milky Way streamed across the sky like a glittering celestial river. The Southern Cross, *Jirrunjoonga*, the Guiding One in the aboriginal Dreamtime, hung over the house. The brightest star, Alpha Crucis, pointed almost directly at the celestial South Pole.

Blaine was driving a BMW coupe One Series, a beautiful machine. "Some cars announce their owners," she remarked as she buckled herself in.

"On occasions such as this I leave the Range Rover at home. I'm sure you'd rather ride in this?"

"It's a great start." Already the confined space was having an additional impact on her. She couldn't remember the last time she had been so close to Blaine in a car. "A lot has happened since I was last here."

"It certainly has," he confirmed with more than a

hint of pride in the North's achievements. "Five of the country's top ten tourist destinations are in Queensland, three in the tropical North. The Whitsundays are splendid gateways to the Great Barrier Reef. Then there's the Daintree. The rainforest has the most varieties of plants per square metre on the planet. Can't forget Magnetic Island either, half national park and bird sanctuary."

Mallory knew all these places first-hand. "Captain Cook named Magnetic, as we know, because of its magnetic effect on *Endeavour*'s compass. However, plenty of people have explored the island with various instruments yet discovered no such effect."

"Including me," Blaine, a yachtsman, said matter-of-factly. "I have a new tourist development underway at Pelican Point," he said. "I could show you around sometime. No high-rise building. Low-set bungalows in landscaped grounds, maximum privacy."

"Unashamedly high end?"

"Well, yes. The North depends on its tourists. I aim to give them what they want."

"The man with the Midas touch."

He glanced across at her. "Improving the economy of our region is the top item on my agenda."

"And I do applaud you," she said, jangling her gold bracelets like a tambourine.

They arrived at the restaurant. The Lotus Garden, designed as a Thai pavilion with its waterfront views, came as a delightful surprise. This was good for the town and its steady influx of tourists.

They made quite an entrance even if it was unintentional. Neither was the sort of person who would go unnoticed. Mallory couldn't help but be conscious of the sudden buzz in the air. People were watching.

Chairs were even being pushed back to afford better viewing. Most of the tables were taken although it was a weeknight.

A stunningly beautiful Asian woman wearing a very elegant outfit showed them to their table. The young woman had greeted Blaine in Thai. He responded in the same language. As he'd mentioned, he came here often, obviously as an honoured guest.

Both of them had to pause here and there, exchanging greetings with people they knew well. No sooner had they moved on than heads bent and voices whispered comments. The whole town of Forrester would know by the morning.

"This is lovely. I *am* impressed." They were seated beside the floor-to-ceiling windows that looked out over the Coral Sea. Mallory glanced around, studying all the details, feeling the atmosphere, alive, glowing with pleasure in good food and good wine.

"I'm glad. It's nice having you here with me." He leaned towards her as he spoke.

There was a table between them but he might have been speaking directly into her ear, their faces touching. Excitement whirled through her. If Blaine ever set his mind to seducing her, just for the hell of it, she would have a battle on her hands. "Where do we start?" She picked up the beautifully presented menu, bowing her head over it.

"We'll take the March Hare's advice. Start at the beginning."

"I loved *Alice in Wonderland*," Mallory confided, with a nostalgic smile. "I identified with Alice. As a child I used to think *Wonderland* was up with the stars, not down a rabbit hole. The stars were where my mother was."

"She was very lovely."

Her expression melted as it always did at mention of her mother.

"The most beautiful woman I had ever seen," Blaine told her. "She had such an air of refinement about her, a powerful if unconscious allure. It's no surprise both brothers loved her. Any man would have fallen head over heels in love with her."

She gave a melancholy sigh. "My mother was the love of Uncle Robert's life, only in the end she chose my father."

"Robb is a dreamer. Life is never safe for dreamers. Your father knew what he wanted and went after it."

She made a small sound of distress. "Uncle Robert must have recognised what was happening right under his nose but did nothing. Perhaps he trusted his brother when he shouldn't have? Maybe he felt certain of my mother?"

"Robb was born to be disillusioned, Mallory. He's a romantic, not a realist."

"My father dazzled her. He would have been very handsome—he still is—ambitious, very proud of his cleverness, much more forceful than Uncle Robert. A domineering man. I don't like forceful men."

"So you've said. *Repeatedly.*"

She could sense his impatience with that. "Maybe I've relinquished all faith in controlling men. I don't accept it's a woman's role to submit to the alpha male."

"Well, certainly not for you," he said very dryly. "You would bring equal weight to a partnership, my dear Mallory."

"I would hope so, otherwise what's the point?"

"We're not meant to be alone." Blaine sat back,

watching the candlelight gild her high cheekbones and put gleams in her velvet-brown eyes. It pleased him she was wearing her long, thick hair loose. It created a glorious cloud around her face and curled over her bare shoulders. "I may be many things, but I'm not a controlling man. I have too much regard for others. Too much regard for women."

She looked down at his hand lying on the table; an elegant, long-fingered hand. For a fraught instant she could *feel* that hand moving slowly, caressingly over her body. His magnetism was very powerful tonight. Quickly she took a sip of water, gaining her some breathing space. "Uncle Robert gave me a few un-settled moments tonight."

"Oh?" His black brows rose.

"He spoke about his love for my mother in such a way she might have been in the room with us. It upset me. It always upsets me. Uncle Robert has spent his life loving a woman who no longer walks the earth. He said he had been going through the motions except for me. I was his sacred trust. I will inherit Moonglade except for a few bequests."

"So?" He was aware of the contents of Robert's will. "Isn't that what you expected? You're everything to Robb."

She looked away blindly. "I couldn't help thinking of a few lines from Christopher Marlowe."

"Something about a master about to die?"

"Trust you to guess. The master giving away all his goods. Uncle Robert was staring at me, Blaine, but he wasn't seeing *me* at all. He was seeing my mother. It was almost as though I were transparent. How can that be? I have to confess I had an *electric* sense of her presence. How does one stay in love with a ghost? I thought it only happened in romantic fiction."

"Usually with a very unhappy ending."

"Only it *does* happen. I'm witness to that. I read a book by a famous American writer, David Foster Wallace. The title was *All Love Stories Are Ghost Stories.* I believe it. Why did Uncle Robert mention his will tonight when I was ready to go out? We agreed he's getting stronger every day. Ted is happy with him. If he looks after himself, Uncle Robert has years to come."

"I suppose if one suffers a heart attack well into the sixties, a will is very much on one's mind. Now, I want you to relax. That's why we're here." Resolutely he picked up the menu. "Do you like it spicy?" he asked.

"If we're talking *food,* yes."

"What else could I possibly be talking about?"

She gave a low gurgle in her throat.

The sound was so appealing Blaine wanted to hear it over and over again. "Let's call a truce tonight," he said, a serious note in his voice.

She looked back at him, smiled. "It would be a release from the sparring partners. Unless *you* break it."

"So champagne to start," he suggested. "Beer goes best with Thai. I suggest Singha or Chang for later."

Thai cuisine is all about balancing flavours: spicy, sweet, salty, bitter, and sour. So close to the Great Barrier Reef there was an abundance of the world's finest seafood to create the most dynamic dishes. The restaurant was supplied with all manner of poultry, vegetables and salad ingredients, exotic fruits, fresh from local farms including, as Mallory learned,

Moonglade Plantation. The French-born, French-trained chef had made it a point of getting to know his suppliers and touring their farms.

An exuberantly Italian waiter attended them during the meal. Instead of a main course they decided to work their way through a series of delicious starters, small portions that allowed them to taste a range of the most succulent morsels the chef had to offer: chargrilled lemongrass prawns, sea scallops, crab, steamed leaf-wrapped Red Emperor, green mango, banana blossom salads. Again both chose a light dessert, a trio of sorbets, the vibrant pink of pomegranate, golden mango, white lychee, finishing with a Thai iced coffee.

Mallory was finishing her very good iced coffee when her attention, along with the rest of the room, was caught by a late-arriving couple moving into the dining room. "Speak of the devil! Surely that's Selma with a very prosperous-looking man who've just walked in?" she exclaimed. "Don't turn around."

"I'm not planning to." His reply was short.

"You've never said. Do you miss her? I mean you've known her even longer than me."

"We're still friends."

She hadn't outgrown her games after all. "Hard to be still *friends* with a woman like Selma. Jason is definitely not friendly with me. She looks very glamorous. The man with her is many years older. It's not her father."

"Time to go, Mallory, wouldn't you say?"

"Give it a minute. They're coming our way."

"You're enjoying this?" His eyes glinted.

"Of course I am. Isn't that wicked? But don't worry, I'm here as backup."

"Backup for what?"

"Selma doesn't look cured." Her tone gentled. "She was seriously in love with you."

"Love affairs are never easy, Mallory," he retaliated. "*You* ought to know that. Yours didn't work for you, either."

"There you go again, having the last word when I thought we'd called a truce."

Selma, in all her glimmering glory, and her escort arrived at their table. Blaine rose to his impressive height, but Selma was the first to speak, an aggressively confident woman. "Darling, I thought maybe I'd see you tonight." She planted a kiss on either cheek, then for good measure a third kiss, allowing her full red lips to graze the side of his mouth. "I hope you haven't forgotten the twenty-fifth?" she enquired archly, trailing her hand slowly down his white jacket sleeve.

"I have to give it a bit of thought, Selma. The twenty-fifth?" Blaine assumed surprise.

"You're joking, of course. It's my birthday. The big three-oh," she reminded him with a touch of grimness.

"Of course it is!" he responded, as though he needed no further reminder. "Every woman would wish to look like you at thirty or any age, Selma."

Indeed they would, Mallory thought. Selma looked marvellous. Her long mane of dark hair, straightened from its natural curl, gleamed like black satin. Her make-up was perfect. She wore a short silver evening dress featuring a peplum. An assortment of serious jewellery added to the dazzle. It was miles over the top for the occasion, but it created a memory that would be hard to erase.

"Thank you, darling." Selma flashed Mallory a smile full of practised charm. "And this is Mallory, of course."

Who the heck else?

"How are you, Selma? It's been a long time," Mallory responded pleasantly.

"Not easy to come back, I would think?" Something like malice flowed down Selma's glowing face.

"On the contrary, I'm delighted to be back."

Selma turned away. "I'd like you both to meet a good friend of mine from Hong Kong, Arnold Youngberg. Arnie, meet friends of mine, Mallory James and Blaine Forrester."

The two men went through the ritual of shaking hands though Mallory, so very sensitive to Blaine's reactions, could see his heart wasn't in it. Selma's companion was now openly checking her out. His glance screamed serial womaniser.

"Evening, ma'am." He bowed slightly. Mallory smiled, but did not offer her hand. She had seen his aura.

"Might we join you for a few moments?" Selma purred, taking their acquiescence for granted.

"That would have been nice, Selma." Blaine's response was suave. "But Mallory doesn't like to leave her uncle alone for long. You must have heard he suffered a recent heart attack?"

"Goodness, that's why you've come back here?" Selma, ears pricked like a pointer, visibly relaxed. Obviously the reason neutralised any possible concerns Selma might have had about Mallory's homecoming. "How long do you plan on staying?"

"An indefinite period." Mallory calmly took her vintage evening purse in hand. Selma had been eyeing it. It was just like her to have noticed it once had belonged to Coco Chanel. One didn't have to peer closely to see the conjoined *C*'s. "It's lovely to see you again, Selma. Nice to meet you, Mr. Youngberg."

"Arnie, please." Youngberg was on the short side, top heavy, dark hair receding fast, a luxuriant Genghis Khan type moustache to compensate. His tailored suit was expensive, the double-breasted jacket hiding what Mallory suspected was a football-shaped paunch. Unabashed, he continued to stare at Mallory like a man who had found a 9-carat diamond rolling around the restaurant floor.

He broke off his scrutiny to address Blaine. "Maybe we could meet up in the next few days, Forrester? Have a drink? Discuss a little business. I'm staying with Selma. You know the number."

"Of course he does." Selma trilled as if at a huge joke. "I'd really love for you to come to my little birthday party, Mallory, while you're in town."

"Thank you for the invitation, Selma, but I must decline. I want to spend as much time as possible with Uncle Robert."

"Of course you do. I understand completely," Selma retorted. "I mean we haven't seen you in well over what—six years?"

"Roughly about the time you and Blaine broke off your engagement."

"And Jason Cartwright got that Kathy Burch pregnant," Selma ripped in.

Arnie Youngberg moved with alacrity to hold Mallory's chair, pre-empting Blaine.

"Let me help you."

"Thank you."

"May I say you're one helluva of a beautiful woman?" His smile was positively wolfish.

"No, you may not."

Selma made a heroic effort to maintain her fixed smile. Selma was peeved, an awful word but it seemed to fit.

Blaine was still laughing as they made it out into the night. "That put old Arnie in his place."

"Horrible man. I'm going to test our truce by telling you he has a bad aura."

"Ah, the auras, again. Never goes away."

"'Sad, but true."

"So you still see them?" His tone was light, smooth, teasing.

"Science will hit on an explanation sooner or later and then won't you feel foolish?"

"No way!" He looked up at the glittering sky. "It's early. Care to go for a stroll?"

"It might take the edge off that remark," she said. "Besides, we have to do something after that wonderful dinner."

"I'm pleased you enjoyed it."

"I did." She turned to front the quicksilver sea. "Isn't this just heaven!"

"You wouldn't find it anywhere else."

"And you get to live here."

"There's nothing stopping *you* from making a life here," he said. "You could continue your work."

"I know." For once she didn't want to talk about her work. The beauty of the night was heightening the strange *rush* inside her. She could feel the breeze blowing off Coral Sea enveloping her body. The scent of salt and the greenness of the offshore islands was in the air. She could hear the lapping of the inrushing waves; see the froth of white lace decorating the shoreline. She had swum in those waves, dived from Blaine's yacht into a measureless blue sea.

"What are you thinking?"

"That I'm part of all this, just as you are. This is the absolute best. My heart's choice."

"And mine. There can't be too many parts of the world that are more beautiful."

"Remember when we used to go scuba diving?" she asked, dreamily. "It was you, not Uncle Robert, who introduced me to our wonderful undersea world. The kingdom of coral. As bright, as beautiful and diverse as the most beautiful flowers. I remember the clouds of dazzling little fish with colours that defied description flashing past us, swarming in great numbers into those lacey sea fans. Paradise beneath the sea!"

"Nothing to stop us doing it all again."

"That would be wonderful."

"Why wait?"

Why wait indeed. She had the oddest feeling she was undergoing an emotional, even a physical change. She had a heightened awareness of her body, warm, sleek, satiny flesh. She felt womanly, alluring. It was almost unbelievable.

"Selma seemed quite anxious to see the back of me," she said, convinced that was so. "Actually I wouldn't like to get on the wrong side of her. Maybe she has hopes the two of you can get together again?" Was she about to mess it up as usual?

"Mallory, I won't play the game." He cut her off. "You know as well as I do, there's no coming back."

"Nothing deader than a dead love, eh? What did you love about her anyway? I genuinely want to know. As I recall you were a heavy hitter when it came to Jason."

He levelled a downward glance at her. "Our plan for a truce doesn't seem to be working."

"I take full responsibility for that. But bear with me for a minute. What did she do for you to break off the engagement? I know *you* did. Obviously it was serious. That's my hunch. You're not going to tell me?"

"You weren't the only one up to your eyes in betrayal, Mallory."

"I feel almost sorry for you." She took his arm, leaning in to him a little.

"Let it go at that." Her lovely perfume was making Blaine's senses dance. He wanted to inhale it long into the night. They walked down the short flight of steps onto the broad sandy beach. They didn't need the benefit of the street lights. There was a silvery moon and the glorious glitter of stars. "Selma entertained a visitor when I was away on a business trip," he announced, abruptly.

"Don't tell me."

"I *am* telling you."

"Who was he?" She couldn't think of anyone who could measure up to Blaine.

"You just met him."

"You're kidding me!" Mallory voiced her astonishment. "You're saying Selma, while engaged to *you*, had sex with that man? I wouldn't get into bed with him under pain of death."

He gave a brief laugh. "Selma can't live without sex like she can't live without a drink. She told me later it meant absolutely *nothing*. It was just sex as a basic need. Selma is a woman of appetites."

"She looks it," Mallory said. "Selma has a considerable sexual aura."

"Anyone could see that."

"I don't have any such appetites, of course. I don't know if that's good or bad. Love must be a transcendent emotion, surely? Sex for sex's sake doesn't bring transcendence."

"But it does bring quick thrills. Lust is the name of the game for a lot of people, Mallory. Lust for money. Lust for power. Lust for sex. Sex makes the world go 'round."

"But Arnie is old enough to be her father. She seemed happy to be on his arm, yet he has a huge deficit in the looks department."

"Not in the money department. Selma will always marry money. Arnie Youngberg is a very rich man and a smart crook. One must always take money into account. I had been thinking about breaking off the engagement before I went away on my Beijing trip. Then I decided to wait until I returned. It was a sheer fluke I found out about the love-in. Selma's cleaning lady told my cleaning lady who told me en route out the door. She never did like Selma."

"How can anyone overlook cleaning ladies, or hairdressers? They hear everything."

"Selma might have hopes, but she'll never get Genghis Khan to marry her. You had to see the way he was eyeing you. I felt like punching him. He has a harem in Hong Kong on the go. He's notorious for it."

Mallory stopped short of visualizing orgies. "How disgustingly gross."

"What happened to that nice guy I met a few times? Your colleague, Norman, wasn't it?"

"You know darn well it was Niall. He's married now. Very happily, I'm pleased to say. I attended their wedding." She bent to remove her evening sandals. "I can't walk in these."

Blaine took her heels, turned to find a convenient niche in the rock wall. "They'll be safe there."

They walked on. The white sand scrunched tenderly under Mallory's feet. It was surprisingly cool once the sun was off it. The balmy sea breeze sent her long hair flowing back like a pennant.

"You look like a goddess," Blaine murmured.

That gave her a jolt of surprise. "Goddesses had lots of problems."

"Are you going to solve *your* problems?"

She stopped, gazing up at him. "I'm happy to tell you I'm looking forward, not back. Problems take a lot of working out."

"You might find the solutions quicker if you didn't wall yourself up."

"Wall myself up? What do you think I am, an Egyptian mummy? What about the truce? I knew you weren't up to it. I have a hundred good answers to your question, Blaine. Top of the list, safety, stability, being my own person. I would hate another man in my life to betray me like Jason did. We all know it happens with alarming frequency. I prize loyalty, honesty, integrity. I couldn't cope with betrayal, let alone abandonment. Abandonment has coloured my whole life. I don't want love that would hit too hard. I want the kind of love that would leave me free."

"Mightn't you have to reach out a bit further to

accomplish that? Ever spoken to another professional, maybe your Niall?"

"He's *Leila's* Niall, Blaine," she reminded him sharply. "I handle my own grief. You know how it is. Grief shapes the psyche. What good would it do for a colleague to advise me to get on with my life, put the tragic past behind me? Besides, once one starts to talk, one invariably talks too much. No one understands me but *me*, Uncle Robert, and you. Maybe you understand me *too* well. The less anyone knows about me, the better. I don't relish the fact you know my numerous flaws."

"What flaws?" He scoffed.

"The ones you've noticed and go on to talk about. Always at the edge of my consciousness is the fear of getting in over my head. To become truly involved is to make oneself extremely vulnerable. I've guarded against it for most of my life. Even for so-called soul mates there are areas of adjustment."

"So you're saying it is one thing to crave the object of one's desire and quite another to consider sharing one's *life* with that person?"

"It's elevating the risk. I've seen it happen. So have you. People move in together because they're so much in love. Nothing matters but the two of them. They don't want anyone else on earth. They want to dedicate their entire lives to one another. Love for eternity, then in no time at all, lo and behold, conflicts arise. Conflicts that ruin everything. Next thing you hear, the party's over. They've split up. It was all a mistake. The initial feelings of love and wonderment have dwindled into dislike, even hate, boredom, leaving tremendous angst on both sides. Taking a chance on happiness is taking a chance on heartbreak. Powerful sexual attraction isn't a good enough reason to get married, in my view. Passion falters with the familiar. It certainly falters when it moves into a domestic situation."

"Only true love, and there *is* such a thing, won't allow committed people to split apart. They find solutions to whatever problem comes up. My mother and father were very happy. They were both strong-minded people. Each had their say. They had their arguments, but together they found compromises. Besides, they had a head start. They came to one another deeply in love. Also, they had character, an absolute commitment to doing the right thing for the right reasons. Maybe it doesn't always work out, but what's life without risk? What's life without love? In love we might be able to find the *truth* of ourselves."

She gave a short laugh. "The truth has proved more than one person's downfall. I'm thinking of a colleague who confessed a meaningless alcohol-driven one-night stand to her husband. Shock, horror, that instantly ended what had been hitherto a happy marriage. I could have told her that. A way to protect ourselves might well be to remember some secrets are better not aired."

"So what secrets have you I don't know about?"

"I'm going to leave you wondering." She stared out to sea, visualizing in her head all the beautiful emerald cays and atolls not far offshore. "I have my work to keep me on track. I have a natural rapport with children, especially traumatized children in need of therapy. They trust me. My experiences allow me to tap into theirs. My work aside, I battle inner confusions. Why am I telling you this, when you already know?"

"Why do you so deeply resent the fact I *do* know you?"

She waved a hand. "One of my phobias, maybe? I feel I have no defence against you."

"As far as I can see, your chosen line of defence is to keep a gulf between us."

"I guess that's what it comes down to, Blaine. There are far worse things than being on one's own."

"Agreed, only loneliness is a terrible thing."

"It's not really about loneliness with me," she said truthfully. "I can handle lonely. It doesn't invade every part of me. I have my work, which becomes more and more rewarding. There's a lot to be said for one's freedom. My private life has been a kind of sanctuary. I've lived free of the pressure to mesh with a partner. There's that old Irish saying, there's always one who kisses and one who turns the cheek. Containment has allowed me to concentrate on my work. I don't want upheaval in my life, Blaine. I don't want to be dazzled."

He made a sound of disbelief. "Mallory, you would have dozens of dazzled admirers swarming around."

"Few I remember. None I dream about. No need to regard me with your amused, contemptuous eyes." She knew she was deliberately provoking him.

"Stop talking nonsense."

Only she didn't stop. "If I'm not doing so well in the marriage stakes, what about you? I accept Selma is far too risky a deal. But there are plenty more fish in the sea. There's—"

"Do please stop, Mallory," he warned, holding up a palm.

"With your looks, your superb self-confidence, and all your money you could easily—"

She didn't get any further. Blaine pulled her hard up against him, bent his dark head, and kissed her full on the mouth. Kissed her breathless. Kissed her to a standstill.

When he finally released her she had to clutch at the lapels of his jacket for support. A giddiness had overcome her. She was a dozen and more breaths short of finding her voice. "Bloody hell, Blaine," she gasped, when she did. "That's breaking all the rules."

Her heart was hammering. Her blood was racing. Blaine could break her into tiny pieces if she let him. There was something simultaneously frightening and exciting about that.

"It doesn't matter. It was worth it," Blaine declared in a hard, cool voice.

"Oh, fine. Fine. Fine. The kiss was a reprimand then?"

"If you wish to see it like that."

The arrogance of him! "So what are we supposed to do we do now?"

"Well, we have three options," he said. "We could walk on without talking. We could enjoy the stars. Or I could take you home. Your pick."

He sounded so scornful she let out a long shaky sigh. "No other solution but to go home. I'm not going to complicate my life allowing you to kiss me when you get tipped over the edge."

"Just tell me one thing," he asked, suavely. "Did you enjoy it?"

"I was completely indifferent," she said with icy disdain.

He laughed. "Now there's a lie if ever I've heard one."

"God forgive me. You can't stop, can you?"

"I say it the way I see it, Mallory. That's who I am."

"Then it's time to go home." She wasn't about to tell him she had never felt such an exquisite sensation as his mouth on hers. That would be letting the genie right out of the bottle. She turned and began to walk quickly back to the safety of the street, only he caught her up, one arm capturing her around her waist.

She swung into him, excruciatingly aware of his body against hers. "You *forced* me to choose and I did."

"Only I think I gained the advantage." There was a challenging note in his voice. "All right, we go home. But before I do, I'm going to be a perfect cad and kiss you again."

She looked up at him, eyes blazing. "Where's the satisfaction in that?"

"Mallory, I can safely say one hell of a lot. I should have done it years ago."

"Really! And when was that?" she asked, aggressively. "Before the two of us got ourselves engaged?"

"Yes, if I'd got lucky." His hand was at her back, moving sinuously down her spine.

"This is definitely a mistake. We're no courting couple."

"I'm still going to do it."

"Go right ahead," she invited. "What a daredevil!" She couldn't run away. She had to stand within his arms and endure more wild, glorious moments. She made a token attempt to resist—resistance was obligatory—only he locked her up against him, not taking the kiss by force because somehow her head was thrown back, her eyes were closed, and her lips were parted.

* * *

They never spoke a word on the journey home, though Mallory kept observing him out of the corner of her eye. He was a consummate kisser. Her body still trembled. Her ears still buzzed. She continued to feel the pressure of his mouth on hers. She'd had protection in words. There was no protection against his kisses. She didn't regret her wayward moments. Not then. She had the strong feeling, not ever.

They arrived back at the house to find it ablaze with lights. "Robert hasn't gone to bed?" Blaine was the first to speak.

The sound of his voice unlocked hers. "That's a bit odd! The house is lit up like a ship at sea. What time is it?" Anxiety had kicked in. "I told him not to wait up."

"Let's check it out," said Blaine, suddenly as anxious as she.

Although all the lights were on, the energy inside the house seemed to be running on *empty*. Neither of them spoke; both shared identical pangs of alarm. Mallory even had the extraordinary illusion she heard her mother's voice say her name very quietly: *"Mallory!"*

Blaine had moved ahead of her, convinced something was very wrong. In the living room, he found Robert James still sitting in his favourite wing-backed armchair, his dark silver-streaked head dipped onto his shoulder, his handsome face sheared of all life, of all expression. The slim volume he had been reading had slipped face down on the carpet. It was a leather-bound book of Shelley's poems.

"Robert?" Blaine very gently touched his friend's

shoulder, knowing Robert was not going to answer. Then or ever.

"No, oh no!" Behind him, Mallory's beautiful face was wracked by grief. "He's not here, is he?"

"No, Mallory."

"I knew it. Oh, God, Blaine. Grief is everywhere. We don't have to go in search of it. It finds us."

Looking down at his dear friend's still, *empty* face, Blaine thought it wrong for anyone to claim the dead looked like they had simply fallen asleep. They *didn't*. Whatever made the person, the essence, the soul, the life's star, was gone. Life did not go on forever. There was the finishing line. If man carried a soul within him, Robert James's soul had fled.

His throat constricted, he looked back at Mallory. She was standing stricken, her hands clasped together as though in prayer. "He's gone. But gone where? Gone like my mother. She spoke to me tonight. Maybe they're together. Together at last. That's what he wanted so badly."

Chapter Five

Nigel James made a supreme effort to clear his commitments. He took a flight north to attend his brother's funeral. He was accompanied by a fellow academic and acolyte, a woman called Rachael Hoffman, his current lover (probably short term like all the others) who had, needless to say, nothing of his genius. A questionable redhead, Rachael was a tall, angular woman with an interesting face and fine grey eyes.

Rachael was such a nice woman, Mallory felt like going ahead and warning her. It seemed too cruel to let Rachael discover for herself what sort of man her father was.

It was Blaine who offered expert advice. "Rachael has to find out for herself, Mallory. She's a mature woman. People rarely welcome advice. Fact of life."

For the moment Nigel James was firmly ensconced on his throne. Mallory didn't have the slightest doubt if her father were to offer Rachael marriage, the gifted Rachael would be expected to give up her much valued professorial position so she would always be on hand for him, ready and willing to genuflect at his comings and goings. As it transpired, marriage was not to be offered. Rachael had a lucky break.

The entire town turned out for the funeral service. Mourners filled the small church. Those who couldn't get in stood outside on the grounds before all moved en masse to the graveside. Mallory had barely registered the service. She had sat in the front pew with her father and Blaine, but it was Blaine who had taken her hand and held it throughout. She had clung to him, everything a blur. All their differences, so petty to her now, were set aside. Blaine was her pillar of strength that terrible day, never her father, who lacked all warmth.

As a close family friend, Blaine had delivered a moving eulogy with touches of humour to shine a light on the man who had been Robert James. Mallory had spoken as well, able through long years of practice to keep her tears at bay. Her father had declined curtly to say a few words. He hadn't shed a tear, either.

"Your father isn't taking the sad news as hard as he might," Dot offered as a quiet aside, aghast at Mallory's handsome father's detached demeanour. So like his brother and so utterly unalike.

"Life's finite, Mallory," was Nigel's gritty comment. "We're *all* dying."

Was that supposed to make her feel better? After the burial, the mayor of the town, who had had a real fondness for Robert James, gave Mallory a tight hug. His wife followed suit. It was another brilliantly fine day, too hot to be out for any length of time in the sun, yet the mourners stood uncomplainingly. Robert had been a much loved man. A man who had quietly helped a great many townspeople while trying in vain to remain anonymous.

Mallory had gathered from the garden a sheaf of her uncle's favourite roses. Robert had managed to grow certain varieties of roses successfully despite the tropical conditions. Golden Tiger was an exceptional yellow rose that could not only survive a hot climate but loved the heat. She stood above the grave, throwing not the traditional handful of clay onto the coffin, but the sheaf of dazzling yellow roses. Her voice when she spoke was clear and steady.

"'To live in hearts we leave behind/Is not to die.' Vale, my beloved Uncle Robert."

Many mourners were openly crying. Mallory did not. As always she would only allow her frozen tears to thaw when she was alone. At least a half a dozen people approached her afterwards to say that her uncle was a saint.

"Who kept his sins well hidden," her distinguished-looking father said in a bitter, judgemental tone as they walked towards the parked cars. Nigel James cut a very impressive figure, immaculately turned out in a tailored black suit with a snowy white shirt and black and silver striped tie. His strong resemblance to his late brother had turned many heads.

"My dear!" Rachael looked aghast at her very grand partner before placing a consoling hand on Mallory's shoulder. Mallory, however, turned on her father with a burning anger that startled even her. She stood, an avenging angel demanding to know what he meant.

"I'm sorry if the remark upset you, Mallory." Nigel James spoke with his customary arrogance and lack of empathy. "You have to rub the fairy dust out of your eyes so far as my dear brother was concerned."

Mallory opened and closed her hands helplessly, then she exploded, her anger was so deep and raw. "Beside Uncle Robert, Father, you're a shallow, shallow man."

Nigel James appeared quite unmoved. "A stupid, groundless accusation," he declared, but there was an odd flickering in his eyes.

Blaine put a steadying hand on Mallory's arm. "I think, sir, we might stop there." There was steel in his voice and demeanour. Blaine was not impressed by the great man.

"Your father might look like Robert, but there the resemblance ends," Blaine said, as he led Mallory away. Nigel James's behaviour in his opinion was to be strongly condemned.

"I was fortunate not growing up with him," Mallory said. "I was so lucky to have had my uncle."

Blaine, standing quietly, felt unbearably moved by the emotion in Mallory's low, melodic voice. He too would miss Robert greatly. Robb had been like an uncle to him, always there, comforting him after the loss of his father, always gentle, accommodating, ready to listen to his grand plans, often offering very good advice which he'd had the sense to heed. In silence he steered the heartbroken Mallory in the direction of the great sheltering poincianas that brought glory into the town cemetery. The trees reminded mourners that life went on, and one had little option but to go with it.

"It's a comfort to think he did open the door onto his rose garden," she said.

"And it was a beautiful gesture sending Robb's favourite roses with him on the long journey."

"To what far off place, Blaine? Do we get to experience all the wonderful things we missed out on in life when we arrive at Paradise? We all ask what life's about. What is death all about? If it's possible for spirits to do so, my mother has already taken him by the hand. *Non omnis moriar.* 'I shall not altogether die.' No one dies who lives on in our hearts. You have wonderful memories of your father. I have wonderful memories of my mother and Uncle Robert at Moonglade. I believe the air inside a house retains imprints of the people who have lived and died there. Who's to know differently? I have a deep respect for the paranormal. I know you find that unsettling, but that's the way I am. Thank you so much for being with me today, Blaine. Thank you for being so supportive. Uncle Robert did love you. There were times I did feel jealous, but I'll never go there again."

They walked across the thick emerald grass to the vehicles awaiting them, steering away from Nigel James and the too-good-for-him Rachael. Mallory's high heels were digging into the turf. Once on the concrete path she wrenched her wide-brimmed white hat off her aching head. She hadn't worn black. She wore white for Uncle Robert. White too was the colour of grief. She had only changed the trim on her hat to a black band of wide ribbon. "What was my father getting at, do you suppose?" she asked, shaking her long hair out of its elegant knot.

Blaine watched in a sensual trance as her golden mane fell around her face and over her shoulders.

The sun picked out all the gold. "I really don't know. No place to get into a family fall-out."

"I'm sorry. I momentarily saw red. Why did he come? Was it just to say that? To hint at his brother's hidden sins? Anyone would think he hated Uncle Robert. He was always ridiculing him and his writing. Always ridiculing how Uncle Robert felt about my mother."

"Jealousy *is* one of the deadly sins." Blaine lifted a hand to acknowledge a group of townspeople. Mallory spotted Jason with Kathy and Jessica flanking him like soldiers from opposing forces. It would be difficult to find two young women roughly the same age, born in the same town, so totally unalike. They might have come from two different species. All three were wearing funereal black. No sign of little Ivy. It had to be one of those days when she actually made school. Kathy gave a timid wave. The twins scorned such a demonstration. Neither knew how to count their blessings. They had been invited back to the house along with many others.

Normal practice yet it feels like a big mistake.

"You're saying my father was jealous of Uncle Robert?" Mallory picked up on Blaine's remark.

"If only because your mother loved him. The book of Shelley's poems Robert was reading bore a loving inscription from your mother."

Truth had its impact. "Was my father hinting they'd resumed their early relationship when he wasn't around?"

Blaine had given a lot of thought to that idea. "God knows, Mallory." Robert had been jubilant about something. What?

"I'm sorry Uncle Robert wasn't my father," said

Mallory, her mind now in a chaotic whirl. "We are all, all spectacularly flawed. One of Jean-Paul Sartre's fun quotes."

The wake was off with a swing. The house was overflowing with people. In the formal dining room, the mahogany table that could seat twenty-two when fully extended, as now, was laid out like a buffet: various platters, ham, chicken, smoked salmon, a great mound of tiger prawns straight from the sea. There were salads to accompany the platters, freshly baked rolls, stacked Royal Doulton plates, glasses, and silverware. On the matching mahogany sideboard were bottles of Scotch, bourbon, beer, ice in silver buckets, and glasses. At the far end a table held bottles of frosty cold nonalcoholic drinks and mineral water. It might have been a party. She could even hear cheerful voices and the occasional burst of laughter, swiftly choked off. People did tend to laugh at funerals and cry at weddings.

Many of the mourners had already piled their plates lustily, perhaps fearing an imminent world famine. Others were browsing around the offerings, some savouring a quick morsel or two. No one was going without. Next step, a nice cold drink before making for the wide sheltered porch to catch up with friends. Whose idea had it been to celebrate death? Queen Victoria?

Mallory could see her father, tall and handsome, with Rachael by his side. As usual he was holding court, the alpha male. Mallory found his manner vaguely histrionic, but people were looking at him with admiration writ large on their attentive faces.

One or two even stood open-mouthed. Her father had a considerable flair for gaining crowd admiration. He should have been a politician.

Slightly sickened she turned away. Her father had never spoken two words to her that had struck her as profound. He and Rachael were staying overnight. They had a return flight to Sydney in the morning.

The will would be read late that afternoon. There was dinner to be got through but she had asked Blaine and Gerald Templeton—Uncle Robert's friend, confidant, lawyer, and business advisor—and his wife Leila, to join them, making six at table. She wondered if she should approach her father again about the brutal remark he had passed about his own brother on the very day of Robert's funeral. The prospect horrified her even as she was desperate to know what had provoked such a remark.

A small figure came up behind Mallory. "Your uncle was a lovely man," the voice said simply. "I'll miss him. You have my deepest sympathy."

Mallory turned. Aware eyes were on them, she threw her arm protectively around the speaker's shoulders. Skin and bone. "Thank you, Kathy. Thank you for coming. Uncle Robert *was* a lovely man. I'll miss him terribly."

"We all will," said Kathy, fragile as a baby bird that had fallen out of the nest. Her short black dress had an unfortunate rusty sheen. She must have taken a pair of scissors to her thick sable hair; it was unevenly cut. Her lovely eyes, however, shone with gratitude for Mallory's support. Both young women were well aware people had turned to watch them, expecting perhaps a show of hostility from Mallory. Even the level of rumbling in the spacious room had fallen to an expectant hush. What were they expecting, a punch-up? Punch-ups were featuring at weddings. Perhaps the trend would spread to funerals.

"Is Ivy well?" Even on this sad day Mallory was anxious for news.

"She hasn't been sick for a while I'm glad to say." Kathy found a tiny smile. "Jessy tells me I'm a bad mother. I suppose I am, but I do try, Mallory. I love my little Ivy with all my heart. She's all I've got. The only one who truly loves me. I don't understand why she's so prone to sickness. I had no attention at all as a kid. I ran wild, yet I thrived."

"We'll sort it out, Kathy, I promise." Mallory gave the young woman's arm several comforting pats. "If there's an answer—and there will be—we'll find it. Have I your permission to speak to Ivy's doctor?"

"Of course you have. I'd be so grateful."

"That's all I need to know. Try not to worry too much, Kathy. I'm here for you and Ivy. We'll catch up later, I promise."

Kathy bowed her shorn dark head, exposing her vulnerable nape. "I hope so, Mallory. It's been a hard year."

The sadness of that hit Mallory like a blow. A sad year in a sad life. There were all different kinds of grief. Some children were born into a loving family and a stable home. Other children were born into lives of never-ending misery and abuse. Even without Jessica and the three-in-a marriage scenario, Kathy's marriage to Jason would have been doomed from the start. Jason didn't have the qualities Kathy needed. She had to question now just what Jason's good qualities were. Kathy was in a psychologically vulnerable state, harried to the point of doing herself harm.

The risk factors were there: the unhappy marriage, the day-to-day presence of her husband's hostile twin, the concern over Ivy's poor state of health. Dot had hinted Kathy might have suffered postpartum depression after the birth of Ivy. Was it possible Kathy, with all the stress in her life, had developed another psychiatric disorder? It couldn't be discounted, but at the gut level, Mallory wasn't convinced that Kathy would follow the path of harming her child.

She's all I've got.

Kathy drifted away aimlessly, huddled into herself like a punished child. Mallory had the strange feeling Kathy could make herself invisible if she so chose. Mallory scanned the crowd, feeling herself the object of a hard-eyed stare. Across the room stood Jessica Cartwright, looking like she was on the verge of hurling a Molotov cocktail.

Jessica Cartwright at no stage of her life had been a fun person. Now she was downright scary. She looked Mallory dead in the eye, her regular features stretched as tight as Nefertiti's mummy. Mallory nodded back sombrely. She wondered if Jason would approach her. The twins' mother and father had attended the graveside service, but Mallory didn't expect to see them at the house. She hadn't as yet been able to organise a meeting with Jason to get his permission for Ivy to meet her grandparents.

Ten minutes later, Jason, drink in hand, came to her side. His rigid jaw and the glitter in his eyes psyched out the couple who had been speaking to Mallory. They scattered like pigeons.

"I just wanted to say how sorry I am, Mallory,"

Jason mumbled through a locked jaw. "Robert was a good man."

"He was, Jason. Where would you have been without him?"

"What's to happen now?"

His future at the farm was clearly the uppermost thing in his mind. "Do you mean will you continue managing the farm?" Mallory met the bright blue eyes so fixated on her. Same eyes as Jessica. Same colour. Same setting. "Do you need to discuss it now?" She felt a degree of shock. Didn't Jason have *any* insight into how she was feeling?

"Jess wants to know." Jason predictably shifted any responsibility onto his twin.

Mallory's icy retort carried weight. "Listen, Jason, I've had enough of Jess, indeed this whole *twinship* thing. It can't be good for the soul."

Jason's face tightened. "You might think you know, Mallory, but you don't. For all your precious degree, you're way too confined in your thinking. What Jess and I need to know is where we go from here. I expect your uncle left you the whole shebang?"

Mallory glanced away from him, searching the crowd for Blaine's handsome head. He wasn't in the room. His height alone would have allowed her to see him. "Jason, I don't want to talk about this now," she said, mindful of all the curious eyes. "The will hasn't even been read."

"We all know what's in it. Robb adored his princess. 'For whosoever hath, to her shall be given, and she shall have more abundance.'"

"Yes, Jason, King James Bible."

"You always were too smart for me."

"You could say that."

Jason passed a hand over his damp forehead. "When you inherit Moonglade, is it possible you might stay on? There's a lot you can do up here, Mal. You could make a good life for yourself."

"What, start up with you again? Is that what you're saying?" she asked incredulously. "I want a life of meaning, Jason. It doesn't include you." Deliberately Mallory turned to move away. "I thought you and Jessica were anxious for me to leave?"

His shoulders hunched. "*I'm* not. Have you the slightest idea how much it upsets me seeing you? God, Mallory, we were engaged. Doesn't that mean anything to you anymore? I loved you then. I *love* you now."

Mallory didn't have the mind or the energy to tackle the situation. "Jason, stop hankering over what you can't have. Maybe that's my big attraction. You want what you can't have. Kathy looks frail. She was *such* a pretty girl."

Jason gave a shrug of cruel indifference. "My marriage is mired in disgust. Disgust for myself. Disgust for Kathy." Abruptly he broke off, his gaze moving towards the entrance hall. "I see Forrester is strongly in the picture," he muttered, not bothering to hide his jealousy. "Standing beside you at the graveside, your ever-present protector, the man with the bottomless coffers. He even cut your father out of the picture. I saw the two of you stalk off together."

"Blaine is the sort of man who is there when you need him. My father and I have always had a blighted relationship, Jason. You know that, so don't try shoving him in with the good guys. I should point out, in case it's slipped your mind, Blaine Forrester too has been very generous to you."

"God, yes." Jason racked his blond hair back with an agitated hand. "The S.O.B. is popular everywhere. No wonder he's so full of himself."

"He *isn't*, but he has good reason to be. Jason, there *is* something I need to bring up again. It's allowing your parents to see Ivy. I have no idea what caused the estrangement, but no blame should be placed on Ivy's innocent head. Will you promise me to think about it?"

"It won't work." His tone gave new meaning to the word "adamant."

Mallory had to shut down on all the speculations that had plagued her. "I'd really *appreciate* it if you would try. You have to make a move towards reconciliation. Your parents could help a lot with Ivy."

Another man might have replied he would lay down his life for his child, but Jason's attention was elsewhere. Blaine Forrester was at the forefront of his mind. "Forrester is coming this way." The expression in his blue eyes betrayed his raging jealousy far more than any words could. "I don't think he's going to allow you to disappear. Not this time."

"This isn't getting us anywhere, Jason. We'll talk again at a more appropriate time. I hope then you'll have a calm mind."

That was the lull before the storm. There was worse to come. Jessica waited for her moment to find her way to Mallory's side. Mallory was pushing a tall gladiolus deeper into its vase when she was forced to turn and confront a woman with all the disorderly elements of her personality on display. Even with her long experience of Jessica, it still came as a shock to see such aversion. Jessica Cartwright had turned into a woman it would be wise to shun.

"Tell me, without me having to beg, you're going to allow Jason to continue to run the farm?" asked Jessica, quietly strident.

Mallory chose to use her calm, professional voice, thinking some psychotic break could be about to manifest itself in the twins. "This is a wake, Jessica." People were staring over their shoulders even as they made their departure. "I've only just buried my uncle. He took pity on Jason, gave him a start. He allowed you employment at the farm as well."

Her words fell on deaf ears. Jessica was lost in the workings of her own mind. "So are you going to continue to keep us on, or are you going to shut the place down?" She threw up agitated hands. There was some odd purplish staining on some of her fingers. Mulberry juice? Plenty of mulberry trees on the estate. Didn't she at least try to wash it off?

"I wouldn't be in the least surprised," Jessica continued. "You're not really one of us. You never were."

"Who *are* you, exactly?" Mallory was not about to be provoked into a face-off. "You have a strange way of trying to get me on side, Jessica. Jason has already asked me what I intend to do. That both of you should approach me about this, today of all days, I find disturbing."

Jessica only looked baffled and enraged. "It was an *opportunity*," she said, as though that fully accounted for the confrontation. "We had to take it."

"Why not let Jason handle it then?" From long

training, Mallory was concealing her upset. "Why would you need to double up?"

Mallory's apparently calm demeanour was reducing Jessica to a splutter. She threw off such sparks of hostility they almost visibly circled her head. "Jason is a perfect fool. He still fancies himself in love with you. Banging on about you all the time. Mallory is everything that's decent, noble, and pure."

Mallory stared into the frozen blue chips that were Jessica's eyes. She was reminded of the basilisk, the mythical animal that could kill with a stare. "You can't tolerate that, Jessica?"

Colour blotched Jessica's throat and chest like a heavy rash. "Don't give me the therapist crap, the detached tone. I'm not one of your bloody patients."

"Please keep your voice down."

"What do you want me to do, *whisper*?" Jessica shot back. "Maybe a minute's silence? Who cares about all these arseholes anyway?"

A clear warning flashed into Mallory's dark eyes. "Your behaviour is an insult to the memory of my uncle. Please stop."

"*Mea culpa, mea culpa*," Jessica crowed. "You're so bloody elegant, so refined, so fuckin' beautiful we've all got to hush. I saw you give that numbskull Kathy a big hug. What the hell does she have on, a bin liner?"

"You really are a cruel woman, Jessica. Your behaviour is emptying the house." Not that it was altogether bad. Many had been reluctant to leave. The vicar was still propping up the sideboard, downing another single malt. A pastoral calling was apparently thirsty work. "You must realize you're making yourself and everyone else miserable? You and Jason are too much in one another's pockets. I urge you to make a life for yourself. Let Jason go."

For answer, Jessica moved in closer, hissing like a snake. "Who are you, Miss Marple? Sooner or later you're all going to learn Jason can't do without me."

"Do you include your parents?"

"I told you to cut the crap." Jessica was oozing spite. "I know what you're doing, the quiet, controlled tone, the focused glance, the professional *listener.* Mallory James, the bloody psychologist."

"What's the big problem with your mother?"

"That old Bible banger," Jessica snorted. "Anyone would think she's never put a foot wrong."

"Let's not make it worse, denouncing your mother."

"You and Jason wouldn't have lasted long."

"You would have thought of something to change that?"

"Too damned right! I don't need any of your therapy. I don't give a toss for it. Your lot suck, digging into lives, getting people to expose all their fears, their dirty secrets. The *truth* is I despise you. What good do you do? I'd say you damage people even more than they already are."

"Clearly you don't know a lot about the subject. By the way, Kathy told me you were there the night she and Jason got drunk or perhaps drugged?"

Colour surged from Jessica's neck into her staring face. "That's a lie! The poor little gnat isn't a normal person."

"You're actually claiming *you're* normal?"

"I don't get rotten drunk. I know how Kathy is when she drinks."

Mallory held her anger in suspension. "You've been spreading the word, haven't you, that Kathy drinks?"

"She's her father's daughter, isn't she?" Jessica was full of contempt.

"I would say as her father's long-suffering daughter, she avoids alcohol. Would it be you who engineered it, Jessica? You've always been a woman with your own agenda. Were you planning on having me find out about it? Was that your strategy? Anything to get me out of the picture? I would be sure to break the engagement. The only thing you didn't count on was Kathy's falling pregnant. So the whole plan went horribly wrong. Jason undertook to marry the mother of his child. That must have driven you nearly crazy."

Jessica only muttered, at a loss to hit back.

Blaine coming back inside the house caught sight of Mallory and Jessica Cartwright locked in tense conversation. He supposed everyone present would realize Jessica was out of control. He crossed the room in a few strides, hearing Jessica's curious bark of a laugh, accompanied by an over-the-shoulder jerk of her head.

"Here's your knight in shining armour to the rescue." Jessica gestured in Blaine's direction.

"And what are *you*, my enemy?"

"Ten out of fuckin' ten."

"Jessica, I always *knew*." She could see a vein pulsating at Jessica's temple. "You need help. Medication to control your moods. There are doctors, trained to understand your sort of problems. You could consider a short stay at a recognised clinic."

Surprisingly, Jessica laughed. "They'd never let me out." She looked Mallory full in the eyes. "I love Jason more than anyone in the world. When you ran off, he fell apart. It was my job to put him back together again."

Mallory's apparent composure was costing her a huge effort. She was so weary of the dysfunctional twins and their unsolvable problems. "Jessica, I don't want to go any further with this. You forget what day it is. People are watching. When I'm ready, I'll review the whole situation. Kathy must find life intolerable having you around all the time."

"Kathy is the whole bloody problem," Jessica gritted. "If Jason had to choose between the fuckwit he was forced to marry and me, there would be *no* contest." Her expression was one of triumph.

Weird as her claim was, it was presented not as a boast but a truth. "For God's sake, Jessica, you're Jason's *sister*. Is there something structurally wrong with your brain? You're *brother* and *sister*. You're not seeing straight anymore. Jason could well wish to be independent of you."

Jessica's mouth worked. "If you care to make a bet, you'd *lose*."

"I have my doubts about that. Jason is under enormous stress. It could be *you* who is putting him there. Shouldn't you be thinking about that?"

It wasn't the answer Jessica's ego demanded. She was nearly dancing on the spot. "You know nothing, *nothing*!"

"I don't want to know." Mallory's expression was one of extreme distaste.

"Everything okay here?" Blaine joined them. The steely toughness in his attitude stopped Jessica in her tracks. "You have a problem, Jessica?"

A smile from Jessica that was anything but friendly. "Of course not, Blaine. I was just checking with Mallory about Jason's position as manager."

Blaine had already taken in the paleness of Mallory's beautiful clear skin. "Not a good day to raise the subject."

"My apologies," she gritted, "but Jason has been in a terrible state wondering what was going to happen now."

"Sounds like *you're* the one in the state, Jessica. Mallory will let you know her plans in due course."

Jessica got hold of herself to the point she was able to accept Blaine Forrester's position of authority in the town demanded respect. "So now we wait?"

"So now *you* wait, Jessica," Mallory said, desperate to have this vengeful woman out of the house.

"No matter what happens, Jason and I stay together."

Blaine resisted the urge to get hold of Jessica and run her out the front door. Instead he made a brusque gesture towards it. "My advice to you, Jessica, is to go home and calm down. If you come with me, I'll escort you to your car."

"Don't bother!" Ugly spots of red stood out on Jessica's face. "If this is the result of asking a simple question, what chance have we got? But then Mallory has always been the princess around here."

Blaine took a deep breath, marvelling at how he hadn't objected more strenuously to Robert's plan to offer Jason Cartwright a job. But then, neither Robert nor he knew Jason would enlist the help of his twin.

"Please leave now, Jessica." Mallory's face was a pale

mask. "I'm out of patience, out of understanding. Don't come back to the farm. You may think you're indispensable to your brother, but I don't think he'd have much difficulty finding a replacement for you. There would be plenty of well-qualified people happy to join the venture."

Jessica spun violently. "You're not hearing me, are you?" There was no hint of remorse or even embarrassment on her face, rather that weird look of triumph again. "Jason and I were fused in the womb. Attack me and you attack him. Sack me and you've sacked him. It's as simple as that."

"I totally agree," Blaine snapped. "Please leave, Jessica, or I'll be forced to help you along. You've already drawn far too much attention."

"Arseholes the lot of them," said Jessica. "The dear old vicar is a right guzzler. They should launch a church enquiry into that. As for the two of you, I wish you luck!"

"Did you hear what she just said?" Blaine asked in some amazement, his gaze on Jessica's tall, thin, retreating figure.

"She calls everyone arseholes. Don't take it personally. I think she's borderline crazy."

"Why stop there? She didn't say good luck or bad. I think we can guess which. Did no one teach her manners? She could have been raised in a dingo pack."

"Dingoes would hold that one against you." Mallory was trying hard to calm down. "Margery would have tried her best, but even the most conscientious parents can't always get it right. Jessica has a whole set of psychiatric problems. I'm not sure now where we go from here. I'm not sure reconciliation within the Cartwright family is even possible. I fear for Kathy and Ivy. Both of them are victims."

"It would be a real pleasure to fire the twins," Blaine said, brow furrowed.

"But what of Kathy and Ivy? Who do they have to turn to?"

"Us." Blaine gave a simple answer. "Don't think about it today. Today is to remember someone we both loved." He stared down at her. "Are you sure you're okay?"

"I'm fine."

"I don't believe that for a single second. I don't like you alone in the house."

She gave him the shadow of a smile. "We have a formidable security system which you had installed in an amazingly short time. What is it you're expecting, a terrorist attack?"

"I'm expecting that damned fool Cartwright to keep trying to see you. There's danger in all of this."

"Don't worry," Mallory said quietly. "I can handle Jason."

"I don't see it that way. You don't have any real idea of him anymore, Mallory," he said bluntly. "I'll make sure you don't have to handle him, as you put it. If you ask me, he's a closet psychopath who actually *hates* women. Underneath it all, there could be a lot of hate for his twin."

The idea curdled Mallory's blood.

They ate in the formal dining room though no one outside Nigel James, the gourmand for all seasons, was hungry. Rare words of praise were heaped on Dot's head. The salmon roulade with crab sauce was the best he had ever tasted. The pear and ginger tart also received praise.

Mallory wasn't the only one to find Nigel James's behaviour on the bizarre side. There had been no outpouring of grief, nothing much at all, really. Rachael, decent woman that she was, was looking quietly appalled. For a man with a near-awesome reputation, Professor James wasn't showing up well. Few men showed so little emotion on the day they buried a brother, their only sibling. It beggared belief.

The will was read, and as everyone expected, Mallory was her uncle's main beneficiary, inheriting the small fortune he had accrued and all forthcoming royalties on his very popular books. Then there was Moonglade and its contents, which included many valuable paintings and objects d'art. Her undeserving father had been left a pair of magnificent, over-the-top German silver candelabra and a rare signed edition of *Dracula* by Bram Stoker.

My father and Dracula have something in common.

Blaine received a wonderful bronze model of a *cheval de course*. His solicitor Gerald Templeton and his wife, Leila, were bequeathed a George III bracket clock they had always admired. There were several other bequests. A nice little nest egg for Dot Rawlings in recognition of her dedicated service.

Sometime towards ten o'clock, Gerald Templeton with a little pre-arranged signal to his wife rose to take their leave. Mallory and Blaine walked them to their car. The newly installed external lights were on. The brightness lit up the entire front of the large house like a stage, flooding the driveway and parts of the garden. Mallory could see how any would-be burglar would be pinned to the spot.

The alarm box with a four-digit code was inside the house, hidden in a compartment behind a convex mirror. The front door was controlled by the same four-digit code. Mallory was still at the stage of feeling quite daunted by the whole set-up. She worried if she forgot or wasn't careful she could trigger the alarm, setting off an almighty din. At the same time she was glad the system was in place.

When they re-entered the house, they weren't all that surprised to hear Nigel and Rachael enjoying a spirited late-night spat.

"What you're saying, Nigel, is extremely small-minded, dare I say *mean*," Rachael was saying with considerable censure. "Your brother was an achiever. I've read his books and thoroughly enjoyed them for what they are. Good entertainment with quite a dash of erudition thrown in. I can't understand your attitude at all. And don't you think you've had enough to drink?"

"Screw you, my dear," he retorted with an ugly laugh.

"Not anymore you won't," Rachael said with burning conviction.

Blaine held Mallory back. "Sounds like your father and Rachael are having their first lover's tiff."

"God knows what would be in store for her if she stayed with him. Rachael is starting to see things in him she doesn't like. Father has the obsessive need to be the absolute centre of attention. He reacts to any form of criticism with rage. She's made the fatal mistake of taking him to task."

"Good for her."

Mallory could hardly trust herself to speak. "So what do we do now?"

"We go back outside, then we come right back in. I'll start talking in a loud voice. That should do it."

"Right."

That was the plan. When they stepped back into the entrance hall, they found Rachael powering out of the living room, making such a beeline for the staircase she skidded on the travertine tiles. When she saw them she put a hand to her heart. "Goodness, you startled me."

"Sorry!" They apologized as one.

"Your father and I have had a few words," Rachael confided, red spots of embarrassment mottling her cheeks.

"We've only just walked in." Blaine had no hesitation in telling the white lie.

Rachael appeared relieved. "Nigel can be outrageous at times. I'll say goodnight to you both. Thank you so much for having me, Mallory. See you in the morning."

"Are you all right, Rachael?" Mallory stepped forward. Rachael couldn't hide her upset, and she was a guest.

"I'm fine, dear." Rachael produced a wan smile.

"Goodnight then."

Blaine addressed Rachael. "I'll be driving you and Professor James to the airport, Rachael. Sleep well."

"Thank you. Thank you both so much."

All three knew Rachael wasn't going to sleep well at all.

"Want me to check in on your father?" Blaine asked after Rachael had disappeared along the gallery. He didn't want to leave Mallory, but he knew he had to.

"A bit steep to ask that of you. It's my job, Blaine. It's meant everything to me having you here today."

"Where else would I be?" he said, simply.

"Father has probably made his way up to bed. He never wants to talk to me. We've never had a single *true* conversation. I think just looking at me exhausts him. It's very good of you to drive him and Rachael to the airport. It's a long way."

"No problem. Something has to be done about the Cartwrights, but we don't need to think of that tonight."

An eerie feeling was creeping over Mallory. "Jason and Kathy would be better off divorcing."

"We're both ready to help Kathy and the little girl. But understand this, Mallory," he said firmly, "the Cartwright twins constitute a real threat."

Mallory answered, worriedly. "Kathy is so needy she might stick with Jason wherever he went. She might consider being with Jason is better than being on her own. Lord knows her poor mother put up with a lifetime of hell. Kathy is her mother's daughter. She's desperately low on self-esteem. It's a pity she's so fearful. Already life is overwhelming her. Then there's the question of Ivy's frequent bouts of sickness. I'm determined to look into it."

"You're no relation, Mallory," Blaine said as they walked out of the house and towards his car.

"One doesn't have to be a relative to keep one's eye on a child in a bad situation. Dr. Farnsworth and I will be onto it like a flash if Kathy presents again."

"She will," Blaine said, without hesitation. "Somehow it all fits together with the Munchausen thing."

Mallory's heart lurched. "You think so?"

"Yes." He was blunt. "You don't need this conflict in your life, Mallory. Say the word and the Cartwrights move on. Kathy has to *ask* for help, Mallory. We can't force a decision on her."

"First up, Jessica goes. Jason can stay until something is worked out. I don't want Kathy and Ivy escaping into a worse mess."

Blaine waited until Mallory had walked back into the house before he began the cruise around the central fountain. Banks of lavender-blue hydrangeas were in bloom. The extravagant mop tops glowed in the car's headlights. He couldn't shake off his feeling of deep unease. He recalled the conversation he'd had with a friend, an ex-nurse, who had suggested Kathy Cartwright might be responsible for her child's frequent illnesses.

"Everyone knows about Munchausen by proxy these days, Blaine. She always was a needy person. Such a disadvantaged upbringing! She could well have a psychological disorder."

The comment had dismayed him at the time, although he had accepted it was possible. Unquestionably Kathy Burch had made a bad marriage. It would have been better if she and Jason hadn't married, but worked out some other arrangement. It would have helped enormously if the twins hadn't fallen out so badly with their parents. The alienation had lasted. It had to be something major, something beyond the fact Jason had betrayed them and the beautiful woman he had been engaged to. Something that had brought them all to a perilous edge.

He had the definite feeling he shouldn't be leaving Mallory. Bad things were hovering around her. He was even starting to consider auras, once a huge point of contention. Robert James had spent his life keeping Mallory safe. Robert was gone. But *Blaine* was still there.

Chapter Six

Her father had not gone to bed as Mallory had supposed or, closer to the mark, hoped. Her father's lack of love for her had worn her down. She found him sitting in Uncle Robert's favourite wingback chair, which she resented. He was nursing a crystal brandy snifter overfilled with the finest cognac.

"Ah, there you are my dear." Nigel James turned his handsome, silver-streaked dark head towards her. He couldn't and wouldn't tell her she looked beautiful, so much acrimony and bitter resentment was in him. She looked flushed. He might even say, enraptured. Ah, Forrester, the local king of the heap! She was wearing her dark golden mane loose, increasing her stunning resemblance to her mother. Mallory was a very stylish creature. Just like his treacherous Claudia. "Lover boy gone?" he asked in his bitingly mocking voice.

Don't let him upset you. You're used to him by now.

Only tonight Mallory found her father's manner appallingly offensive. "I thought you'd be in bed," she murmured. He wouldn't find Rachael cuddled up waiting for him. She now had a clear sense of his vengeful, frustrated, angry mood.

"I daresay Rachael confided we had a little tiff." A sharp dismissive flip of the hand signalled his current feelings for Rachael, who had actually dared to remonstrate him. "Sanctimonious old bag took exception to the way I behaved today. Bloody cheek of the woman. What would she know? I should never have brought her."

"So why did you?"

"What?" He reared back in his chair as though she had asked a highly impertinent question.

"It had a good outcome at least," Mallory said. "Rachael saw you in your true colours, Father."

Affront altered the composition of his hard, handsome face. "You bloody well amaze me, Mallory! Who are *you* to talk about seeing people in their true colours? When did you ever see through my dear brother?"

Mallory remained standing, though little tremors were running down her legs. Was there no end to this awful day? "All I ever saw from Uncle Robert was love and endless kindness."

Two brothers.

Polar opposites.

Nigel James almost choked getting his words out. "Are you going to shut up so I can tell you the truth?"

Mallory remained outwardly calm and collected. "Please don't shout at me, Father. This isn't your house. This is *my* house, you understand? Anyway, you wouldn't know the truth if it fell out of the sky and bounced off your arrogant head. When have you ever tackled your fatherly duties? You abandoned me almost from the day my mother died. How does that make you feel about yourself? You have no heart. There's no direct line between your heart and your brain. The only person who matters to you is yourself. You can't abide the slightest criticism without flying into a rage. You demand constant admiration. No, make that adulation. Rachael is a smart woman. I believe she has broken free. My mother didn't. You crushed the life out of her before she was ever hit by that car."

Enraged, Nigel James took a last swig, then pitched the crystal goblet towards the marble fireplace now filled with ferns, not caring it shattered, seeping brandy into the Persian rug. "I know how your mother died, damn you! I don't need *you* to tell me. You, always carrying the big chip on your shoulder; you, wallowing in self-pity. You thrive off it. Self-pity drives you. Lost your mummy, did you? Can't speak about it? Do you think you're the only one to know grief? You've never considered *my* feelings. I've found no consolation anywhere. As for you! You're a woman going to waste. You'll never get a man. You'll never have a child. You're *cold* and you've got too much of a mouth on you."

Mallory's heart shrank. "Really? Then I've no idea why it's taken me this long to get it open. I can deal with *your* accusations. I haven't been able to deal with my mother's death and the manner of it, that's true. The trauma has never left me. I adored her. But I didn't have a dad who was there for me, which made my grief so much worse. I don't believe I wallow in self-pity, as you so compassionately put it. It was your criticism of Uncle Robert that did it. On the very day he was buried. He must have done something to make you hate him. You did hate him, didn't you?"

Nigel James's fine dark eyes appeared sunk in his skull. "You started this, Mallory," he glowered. "Don't ever forget that." There was a tremor in his voice. "My so honourable older brother was screwing my wife. No need to cringe like the little puritan you are. Rutting like animals. You thought your mother was a saint. She wasn't. There was no halo around *her* head."

Mallory felt the air whoosh out of her lungs. She stared at the man she called father while he stared back. Shock was overwhelming her. She moved quickly to the sofa, feeling as though she had been pierced by a poisoned dart. When she finally spoke, it was with steady denial. "I'm not going to allow you to despoil my love for my mother and my uncle. I know my mother loved Uncle Robert long before you seduced her with your power. They could well have been lovers. I do *not* believe she would have betrayed you after she became your wife." Knowing her father as well as she did, she had picked up on his motive. "You want me to believe Uncle Robert might have been my father, don't you? You're just that twisted. Not that you believe a word of it yourself. I know you and your long history of tormenting. I was only a child, but I recognised how you constantly taunted my mother. You would have taunted me, only she put herself between us. You couldn't go a day without taking a swipe at her, could you? You seethed with jealousy. Uncle Robert was my *uncle*. Only it seems important to you to upset me."

"Damn it, you think I'm lying?"

Nigel James's face was so distorted he looked like

a complete stranger to Mallory. She too was in such a state of distress she hardly knew what she was saying. "Of course you're lying. What makes you livid is the fact you don't *know* what happened between them in the last year or two when your marriage was failing. You're tortured by *doubts*."

There was no need to tell him about her doubts. Images were catapulting to mind of her mother and Uncle Robert together. There was no question they had a deeply loving relationship. They might have been lovers when they had been together, but her paranoid father would have had an eagle eye trained on them once he and her mother were married. Besides, her mother had made her own fatal choice. Robert or Nigel. She had chosen Nigel.

"What you can't abide is my mother and Uncle Robert had the sort of loving relationship you were never able to achieve. You bitterly resented that. You had to have sole sway. You're not in control of yourself anymore, *Father*," she said with heavy emphasis.

Nigel James did indeed present a grim figure, a man on the edge of violence. "How dare you!" he thundered.

"Oh, I dare. Your colossal ego has always been a problem." All the years of hurt, now she felt utter indifference.

"Stop your bloody crackpot analysing," Nigel said with great coldness.

Utterly sickened, Mallory made to rise to her feet, only he reached out, shoving her back roughly. "How dare you speak to me like that anyway?"

"I'm sure it's hard getting used to. What are you going to do, hit me?" There was no trace of fear about her. "I've faced up to much worse human beings than you, Father."

"And don't you glory in your little bit of fame," he sneered. "Whatever bit of brain you've got, you got from *me*." Arrogance was in his every word. He staggered, struggling for balance, when a man's steely voice startled them both.

"This has to stop!"

Relief blazed through Mallory. One thing she knew for certain, Blaine was there when she needed him. She ran to him, finding comfort in the powerfully reassuring arm he flung around her. "You've come back?"

"I had a hunch your father might not have gone to bed." Blaine gave Nigel James a grim look. "I thought he might be waiting to take his mood out on you. Seems I was right."

Nigel James made a considerable effort to confront the newcomer. His expression, at first blank with shock at Forrester's unexpected appearance, had altered radically. "I'm not the monster here." He glared at Blaine, lurching back to the armchair and plonking down in an ungainly fashion, foreign to such an elegant man. "The fact of the matter is, Forrester, seeing you're making it your business, my dear dead brother Robert betrayed me with my own wife, the Blessed Claudia who fell just short of being canonised. I never ever thought he would have the bloody nerve, though God knows I knew he wanted her to distraction. I took her from him, you know. Couldn't have been easier. He was *nothing* compared to me. So why don't you pity *me* for all the misery he caused? I'm the real victim here."

"Perhaps you brought it all on yourself, Professor,"

Blaine suggested. He knew his father D'Arcy and
Robert had been close. Robert had confided in his
father, telling him Claudia had been planning on
leaving her husband. She had found him too controlling. She didn't want her daughter growing up with
such a father. D'Arcy had never breached his friend's
confidence until years after Claudia's death. The
exact extent of Robert and Claudia's relationship in
the declining years of the marriage had never been
a subject for discussion. Lives could be built on well-
kept secrets. The truth could do serious damage.
Robert and Claudia could easily have resumed their
relationship as lovers at some point along the way. If
they did, that was their business. No one should look
into the corners of someone else's life.

Mallory's mouth was so dry she could hardly speak.
She was remembering how close Uncle Robert had
been to D'Arcy Forrester. What might her uncle have
told him that he passed on to his son? Blaine had
never told her a thing, though he could well be in
possession of many secrets.

Nigel James heaved up again, using the arms of
the chair for leverage. "If Claudia had it in her traitorous head she might leave me, it would never have
happened. I would never have let her go. I would
have killed her first. She married *me*. I had her for
life. How good it is to know my bastard brother is
dead!"

Mallory put out a hand to her father as he staggered past her. Despite what he was saying, pity swept
her for his diminished state. For such a supremely arrogant man to appear so pathetic!

Her father scorned her gesture, smacking her
hand away violently. His teeth were clenched so tight

it was a wonder his jaw didn't crack. "Since the day your mother was killed I've never been able to bear the sight of you," he said with appalling cruelty.

"Perhaps the problem is you're halfway insane." Blaine was just barely controlling his temper.

Nigel stared back at the younger man, the imposing height, the build, the level of fitness. Moreover, the *readiness* about him. He tried hard to draw his own body up. "Maybe you're right," he grunted. "I don't need you to drive me to the airport in the morning. Thank you so much. I'll call a taxi. Sister Mary Rachael can fend for herself."

"She won't have to." Blaine's voice was cold. "I'll arrange the taxi for you, Professor James. I'll book it for eight sharp in the morning. I know you'll be ready."

Nigel James hesitated for a moment, pulling and scratching at his beard as though a wasp had made its nest in it. "I'll never enter this house again, I promise you." As he bore past them, such was his humiliation and rage focused on both, he turned to snarl at Blaine, "What's she like in bed, eh? As bloody frigid as her mother, I bet."

For Blaine there wasn't a snowball's chance in hell of controlling his anger.

As the bitter words spewed from Nigel James's mouth, Mallory watched in astonishment as the Blaine she had always known, so very much in control, turned into another Blaine. One she had never seen. His eyes, levelled at her father, were glittering like diamonds. He looked dangerous. Her father was sneering in his habitual contemptuous way.

She had never thought to witness such a thing, but Nigel James's long legs went out from under him as he crashed to the floor. He curled up foetus-fashion, one hand cradling his jaw. "How dare you!" he howled in utter disbelief. "This is monstrous! How dare you attack me?"

Blaine was busy massaging his hand, so he took a moment to answer. He gave the man on the floor a long, disgusted look. "Normally I'm not a violent man, Professor James, but one has to draw the line."

Nigel James appeared half stupefied by recent events. "I'll bring charges," he threatened. "Let me make that clear. I'm an influential man."

"Go right ahead." Blaine moved to get an arm under the crazily hostile man, hoisting him to his feet. "Goodnight, sir. And you're wrong. You *do* have a devil inside you."

"If I do, it's a *she*-devil," Nigel James snarled. Using up what remained of his energy he stalked away, his tall figure listing pathetically to one side.

Mallory stood stricken for several minutes after her father had gone. "That *was* my father, wasn't it?" she asked, wondering if there was anything at all left to salvage from their relationship.

"I'm afraid so. I'm sorry I hit him. Then again, I'm not."

"He did bring it on himself. Such a strange thing for a man to be so handsome and brilliant, yet so deformed."

"I was almost at the gate, but I had this feeling your father was waiting for another moment to torment you. He wanted to cause pain as he feels pain. He wanted to sully your love and respect for Robert. He does appear to have a bent nature."

"No arguing with that," she sighed.

"Come and sit down, Mallory," he said. "This has been a dreadful day for you."

"You too. Did Uncle Robert ever confide something about his relationship with my mother you've never passed on to me? I know he and your father were close friends. Did your father ever say anything to you?"

Blaine's heart gave a painful jerk. He could see Nigel James's tirade had shaken her to the core. He felt shaken himself. "Mallory, your father was making a sick attempt to break your heart. Of course I knew Robb loved your mother passionately, but discussing their relationship with me was strictly off limits. I don't know everything your father said to you, but don't follow up a dead end. Your father was extremely jealous of his brother. Jealousy makes people crazy. And cruel."

"*Is* it possible Uncle Robert could have been my father?" She didn't even recognise her own voice, it sounded so unsure.

"Use your head, Mallory. How likely is that? You weren't a premature baby. You're Nigel's child. You can't brush aside the fact your mother chose Nigel. She was in thrall to *him*. Not to Robert. Your father falls into the Svengali category. He was out to torment you, throwing up any old wild accusation. Nothing is as good to sick minds as tormenting people. Robb could never have kept the fact he was your biological father from you. He wouldn't have been able to help himself. I'm equally sure you would have felt it deep in your psyche that Robert was your *father*. You *didn't*, did you?"

Mallory shook her head. "No, I didn't. There was a great bond between us, but it's true I've always missed a *father*. At seven, one is totally unprepared to lose a mother, but I lost a father too. The attachment wasn't anywhere near what I felt for my mother, but there were times he made me feel *worthy*, I suppose, of being his daughter. It was terrifying when he cut me off, a wrenching psychic separation to any child. I was his unlovable daughter."

Blaine was appalled. "When he couldn't have had a more beautiful, more sweet-tempered, more intelligent child!"

"I changed radically though, didn't I?"

"Facing grief without a mother and father would change anyone, Mallory. You didn't lose your mother after a long illness. You lost her suddenly, violently, one terrible afternoon. What you had to deal with as a seven-year-old must have been unbearable. Robert was there for you. In a way you saved Robert's life. He had directed a lot of guilt about the quality of your parents' marriage and your mother's death on himself. I know Robert believed he could have protected her. He believed he would have made a much better husband and father."

"Of course he would have, but it didn't happen. My father would have marked my mother at once, young, beautiful, impressionable; easy to separate from his less brilliant brother. My mother was brainwashed."

Blaine shrugged. "Happens all the time. Sometimes it takes years for someone to fight free. Your father couldn't resist the sick temptation to cause a flicker of doubt in your mind. His deep jealousy of Robert—even *your* love for your uncle—provoked that disgusting tirade tonight. It's not a pleasant thing to be forced to see yourself as you are. His argument with Rachael might have set him off."

"Just think of it! My own father with all his rage bottled up, ready to unleash it on me, the survivor. Of course I was the one who should have died."

"Mallory, you're in shock and you're grieving. Don't let your father win."

Mallory gave a melancholy sigh. "I wonder if he knew my mother intended to leave him?"

"According to Robb, your mother hadn't breathed a word. Had she told him, your father could well have descended into a kind of madness."

She shuddered. She could see it happening.

"I think I'll pour you a brandy," Blaine said, his eyes on her white face. "I'll have one too. We can skip the ice."

Two weeks later

It was ten o'clock in the morning. The sun had been up since 4.30, blazing out of a cobalt sky. Mallory sat on the sand staring out over a turquoise sea. The surface was shattered by a million needle points of light. Shearwaters were tipping the water, gliding and banking, almost in slow motion. To her utter delight, a pair of reef herons, one smaller than the other, landed near the sculptural rocks off to her left. She sat very quietly so as not to disturb them, but it was for naught. They saw her and gave out raucous croaks. She watched as they took to the air, tucking their wings closely against their bodies.

Reef herons were large birds with long necks, long pointed bills, and the familiar long legs. Graceful plumes adorned the necks of these birds, the breasts and backs, revealing they were into the breeding season. She knew they wouldn't dance for her like the fabulous blue cranes of the Outback, but she took great pleasure in observing them. They looked about a few brief moments like a couple of tourists taking in their surroundings, and then they took off over the water. Unlike the brolgas, they didn't unfold wide beautiful wings and tuck up their long legs. Their heads retracted and they flew off, long legs extended.

A yacht, pretty as a picture, sailed in the distance. For a moment she was back in time on another yacht, much bigger and much faster. *Matrix* belonged to Blaine. She and Uncle Robert had been invited to go sailing for the day. She was seventeen. She remembered the occasion as a halcyon voyage. She hoarded her memories like a miser hoarded his gold. Blaine had always been in her life. In those days he had been involved with Selma, though she hadn't been with them on that day. No Selma to spoil it. Had anyone asked her at that point of her life if she had a hidden crush on Blaine Forrester, she would have burst out, mortified, "Don't be ridiculous."

She would have been lying.

The sea today was incredibly calm, sheltered as it was by the Great Barrier Reef, a continuous rampart, as hard as sandstone, that ran from New Guinea, and well over a thousand miles down the coast of Queensland. There was no surf—unlike the glorious stretch of beaches, one after the other, known as the Gold Coast south of Brisbane with Surfers Paradise, Broadbeach, Mermaid Beach, Miami, Burleigh Heads, Currumbin through Tugun to Coolangatta. Mallory had surfed them all, over the years. So too the beautiful Sunshine Coast to the north of the city. Earlier in the day she had taken a long walk along the white sand, unblemished save for her footprints, making for the bend of the deserted cove with its collection of pewter-grey boulders.

Conditions were very humid, the heat a mirage. An electrical storm had been forecast for late afternoon. Storms would build up as the monsoon season began to close in. Mallory had collected a few pretty rose bubble shells and red helmets for Ivy, then revived herself with a refreshing dip. A couple of weeks had gone by since she had lost her uncle. She had broken out of the worst delirium of grief, but she missed him terribly; the whole idea of his being there for her. He had loved her so very much, but unthinkingly he had left her with problems.

Top of the list, the Cartwrights.

Jessica had obeyed orders as well she might. Word was that she was away on one of her rainforest jaunts, staying with her friends in their jungle hideout.

Though Mallory hadn't felt up to it, she had pushed herself to organise a meeting between Margery and Harry Cartwright and their grandchild and their way-too-long ignored daughter-in-law.

"I can't be there," Jason had told her firmly as though she were about to insist on his presence. She hadn't pushed it, not even bothering with a "that's a shame." It was enough to have the Cartwrights meet Ivy and her mother.

The long-postponed meeting went so well it warmed the heart. Dot had served a delicious afternoon tea, which always acted as an excellent social lubricant;

Mallory had made sure the conversation flowed with Ivy acting as her funny little sidekick. Ivy had much of the entertainer in her. Mallory had to wonder where it came from. Certainly not from her aunt Jessica.

Kathy, though she sat there smiling, for the most part remained silent. Margery Cartwright had assured Mallory beforehand she and Harry, who was rapidly losing his once fine head of hair and had grown quite paunchy—would Jason become like that?—had every intention of being kind to Kathy.

"These family arguments do no good at all."

Mallory had to admit to feelings of concern at the slight rash that bloomed on Ivy's cheeks. Even Margery made a comment.

"Mummy said it's heat rash." Ivy touched a little hand to her cheek.

It isn't.

The initial constraint had broken down quickly. This was a child the Cartwrights *knew.* Their own blood. She was the image of her father. Jessica less so, though it was Jessica who appeared to be the one most fallen from grace. It only took one member of a family to do tremendous damage.

The afternoon tea party broke up with Margery issuing an invitation to Kathy to visit them at any time and please, *please*, bring "our lovely little Ivy," she clucked in delight.

Mallory stood back, watching with satisfaction as Margery embraced her daughter-in-law upon departure. Both had tears in their eyes. Ivy's little arms did their best to gather the two even closer. Harry Cartwright had watched on with a gentle smile on his face.

* * *

Mallory waited until her body was almost dry. Her face and limbs felt gritty with salt and sand. A hand to her sea-soaked hair told her it had turned into a wild mane. She would have to shampoo it. Blaine was coming over that night. She had been leaning on him heavily these past weeks. She had asked him to stay the night. She didn't want to be on her own. She wanted Blaine with her.

She had spent quite a bit of time considering how life would be for her if she stayed. She could open a practice here in the North. She knew she could make a go of it. The big issues that affected family life were the same everywhere. It gave her great satisfaction to know she was helping Kathy and Ivy. What had started out as obligation had become a rewarding experience. She'd had short conversations with Jason, always about Ivy or the farm. She recognised from his wounded expression he hadn't shaken off his belief he was still madly in love with her.

But then love was a form of madness, wasn't it?

She was heading up the rock steps from the beach to the clifftop, breathless, broken out in a sweat, panting from exertion. In the savage heat, the effort came close to the final assault on Everest. Finally she reached the top. She heard the wail first, loud enough to make a deaf woman do a double take. Next, she sighted Kathy running like a wild creature that had escaped the confines of its cage.

"Kathy, Kathy, I'm here." She cupped her hands to shout.

It had to be admitted Kathy could act a little crazily.

Mallory began to pray, unsure there was anyone up there paying the slightest attention. Could Jessica have returned and the two had had a terrible fight?

It took a moment before Kathy could hear Mallory's shout above her own caterwauling. She changed direction, racing back towards Mallory, throwing herself into Mallory's arms, like a bigger version of Ivy. "It's . . . Ivy," she gasped. Her breath was coming in spurts like a tap under pressure. "The . . . school . . . rang. She's . . . had a . . . a seizure. She's been taken to . . . hospital. I . . . hafta . . . get there. Jason . . . has the ute."

Mallory's training kicked in. With a firm arm around Kathy's waist, she managed to keep Kathy's hysteria in check. She turned them towards the house, launching into a string of relevant questions. "Ivy's not epileptic? She hasn't experienced febrile convulsions at any previous time, say with an infection or the flu? No family history of convulsions?"

"No, no!" Kathy's hazel eyes were as huge as saucers. "Ivy's never had a fit, even when she's been sick with a high temperature," Kathy sobbed. "Oh, God, Mallory, what am I to do? If I don't have Ivy, I have no one to love or anyone to love me."

Mallory bowed to that. "Try to keep focused, Kathy," she urged. "You're not on your own, so calm down. Ivy could have caught some bug. This is the tropics, after all. Something going around at the school?"

Kathy didn't answer. She was making fidgety little movements with the fingers of both hands like she was playing an imaginary piano.

"I'll just throw some clothes on, then we'll get

going," Mallory said, not that Kathy was paying much attention. She was so psyched out she was hardly registering anything.

No time for a shower, much less a shampoo. She pulled on the first things that came to hand: a cotton shirt with a pair of culottes, sneakers on her feet. She tried to arrange her hair only it resisted so wildly, she had to leave it in a mop.

As she threw on her clothes, her mind was running through the multiple causes for a seizure in a child six and under. Six was a bit late for a febrile convulsion. Ivy may have been exposed to some chemical substance. Inhaling the strong smell of glue perhaps in an art class at school? But surely a trained teacher would have been aware of the potential dangers?

When they arrived at the hospital they found Ivy propped up in bed, looking as fragile as a porcelain doll. "I don't remember a thing," she told them in a smiley vague sort of way.

"Don't you, sweetheart?" Mallory's soft heart smote her. "Do you remember attending an art class this morning?" she asked, bending over the child.

Ivy put her curly head to one side. "Can't remember, Mally. I don't t-h-i-n-k so."

On the opposite side of the bed, Kathy took her child's hand, looking across to Mallory. "Don't bother her now, Mallory." Kathy's tone was hoarse from all the yelling.

"Of course not. But Ivy *will* remember." Did that sound like a warning? Mallory was feeling very unsettled at that point. Could Kathy lack commitment to keeping her child alive? *No.* She couldn't accept it. There was nothing deeply disturbing in Kathy's aura.

Besides, she had seen with her own eyes how much Kathy loved her daughter. So what secret was Kathy sitting on?

The seizure, they were told, had been more like a *petit mal* attack, but the school hadn't been taking any chances. Ivy Cartwright had a history of mystery illnesses. Everyone knew that. A lot of people had their theories as to why. People had always been quick to judge Kathy and her dysfunctional family.

While Kathy smothered her child in kisses, Mallory walked outside into the corridor to speak to the doctor in charge. Dr. Marisa Farnsworth wasn't at all as Mallory had pictured: tall, slim, and patrician. Marisa Farnsworth in reality was no oil painting. Well into her forties, she was a solid size 18, not fat, but with a shelf-like derriere; marmalade hair, matching brows and eyelashes. She gave an instant impression of no-nonsense competence. Apparently she was anxious to speak to Mallory because she took Mallory by the arm much in the manner of a co-conspirator. "Why don't we walk a little way?" she invited, propelling Mallory along the corridor.

Staff passed on their right, turning curious eyes on them. Mallory was aware she looked a bit on the wild side with her voluminous mane of beach hair. Even the doctor was staring at her when she thought Mallory wasn't looking.

"Have you been able to isolate a cause?" Mallory asked, catching the doctor staring.

"May I speak plainly?" Dr. Farnsworth flushed slightly.

"Plainly makes perfect sense. I wouldn't have it any other way."

Just the answer Dr. Farnsworth sought. Plus assurances. "I would like what I have to say to be kept *confidential*."

Mallory's reply was brisk. "You have my word."

"You're a child psychologist, aren't you?"

"Yes, my practice is in Brisbane."

"Dr. Moorehouse speaks very highly of you," she said as though speaking highly of someone was no easy thing to do. "He's told me you had some concerns about Ivy?"

"Ivy's parents work at Moonglade Plantation Farm. My uncle Robert owned it. Now the estate has passed to me."

"Forgive me." The good doctor showed her sympathy. "I should have offered my condolences. I only met your uncle once, at a fundraiser for the hospital. I found him a delightful man. I'm a great fan of his books. He did autograph one for me at a later date, and gave it to Ted to bring to me. I could see your uncle in his charming detective."

"I did too." Mallory smiled through the tug on her heart. "Something is troubling you, Dr. Farnsworth?"

The doctor's orange eyebrows puckered. "Marisa, please."

"Mallory. Are you thinking that Ivy could be the victim of Munchausen by proxy? Not that the country is awash with the condition."

Marisa Farnsworth groaned without any visible movement of her lips. "I'm not convinced of it, but I admit to an increasing level of concern. The disorder is always in one's mind when a mother presents a child on a frequent basis. Kathy Cartwright appears to be unstable, poor girl. I know a little of her background."

"So you think the mother might be somehow harming the child." It was a statement, not a question.

"Hard to ignore, don't you think? She fits all the criteria. It's the classic plea for attention. We have no idea at the moment what caused Ivy's seizure. From all accounts it was mild. She doesn't have a high temperature, so it wasn't febrile. She doesn't suffer from childhood migraines either, which could be a pointer to something serious."

"And she has never presented before with a seizure."

Marisa vigorously shook her head. "This is the first time. I've run an EEG, so we can rule out epilepsy. I've run blood tests. Nothing of significance we could pick up there. She's a bit anaemic, but nothing too worrying. A problem eater, I understand, which could explain a lot. She's underweight, as is her mother. Her skin tone isn't good. The mother doesn't look well either. I don't know what the child is being given—if anything at all—but I do strongly believe something is not *right*. After today it's a source of concern. If Mrs. Cartwright is making her child ill, she has to be stopped. Am I right in thinking you share my concerns? Mrs. Cartwright seems such a sad woman. You have to wonder if she's starving herself. I've never sighted the father, by the way."

The doctor was staring at Mallory with a marked glint of curiosity in her eyes. "I'll speak to him," Mallory said, with no thought of making the doctor privy to the whole story. "So what happens now?"

Marisa Farnsworth heaved such a sigh it bounced the stethoscope on her chest. "I would move quickly if I could only be sure. Terrible thing to accuse a mother of harming her child. Once I call in Child

Welfare!" She threw up her hands, leaving Mallory to judge. "No need to tell you the consequences."

"She couldn't have inhaled glue at an art class?" Mallory put forth a theory. "She says she doesn't remember. She's still dazed."

"Well yes, but goodness, the school wouldn't have anything that strong near the children. They would all be painting together. Ivy is the only one in her class affected."

"Then all we can do is keep watch," Mallory said. "I'll speak to Kathy and Jason this evening when Jason finishes work. Kathy had to call on me as Jason was out on farm business. When do you intend to let Ivy go home? Might be a good idea to keep her in today for observation."

That bothered Dr. Farnsworth. "It *was* my intention."

"Of course!" Mallory responded instantly, as clearly she was meant to do. "It's comforting to know Ivy is in such good hands."

"It seems to me Ivy Cartwright is far less familiar with loving attention than she is with frequent bouts of sickness," Dr. Farnsworth said, more than ever determined to sort it out. "I could say the same for Ivy's mother."

What chance did Ivy have of staying alive? Anxiety was becoming a real fear. The chilling aspect was the abused often carried abuse forward. Kathy Burch had been an abused child. Kathy was leading an insecure, painful life. She had discovered the way to get attention was to bring her sick child into hospital. At such times she had exhibited intense anxiety. A battery of tests had put obvious fears to rest. Serious consideration had to be given to Munchausen by proxy whether she believed in Kathy's innocence or not.

They were halfway out the door of the hospital when they encountered Blaine coming up the short flight of steps at a clip. He addressed Mallory. "I heard Ivy had a seizure at school. Is she okay?"

"Who told you?" Kathy appeared to undergo a personality switch. She sounded as though she wanted to pick a fight.

With Blaine Forrester of all people?

"She's fine, Blaine." Mallory cut Kathy off. "I've spoken to Dr. Farnsworth. Ivy's in for observation today. Kathy and I will pick her up in the morning."

"I reckon they're blaming me." Kathy continued with her bizarre belligerence.

"Not true, Kathy. Do please calm down."

"They're watchin' me, I know." Kathy was shaking all over.

"Let's go to the car," Blaine said in a detached tone.

In the parking lot Mallory helped Kathy into the passenger seat, even assisting her to put on her seat belt as if she were a child. Kathy was unravelling, morphing into a kind of sullen defensiveness which could present a bit of a problem.

"I'll just have a word with Blaine, Kathy," Mallory said, looking down into her aggrieved, tear-stained face. "Won't be long. When we get home we'll have a nice cup of tea."

"Okay," said Kathy, looking like she had the weight of the entire world on her thin shoulders.

People who don't believe in anything believe in a nice cup of tea.

"Is Kathy in any way schizophrenic?" Blaine asked. "There's a lot of talk about her, you know."

Mallory met his electric gaze. Kathy's sudden mood swing had taken her by surprise as well. "There always was talk about the Burch family. Kathy is extremely upset. Dr. Farnsworth thinks—"

"Don't tell me the Munchausen thing?" he said shortly. "Kathy's identity was shaped by her dysfunctional home life."

"People from dysfunctional families can and do remake their lives," Mallory pointed out. "*I'm* still trying to get myself together. If Jessica were around I'd say Jessica might have slipped Ivy a few drops of one of her mystery potions. She fancies herself as some kind of authority on rainforest plants and fungi. Only Jessica has an alibi. She's out of town."

"The devil she is!" he said, explosively. "I saw her in town this morning."

"What?"

Blaine made a sound of disgust. "I saw Jason's ute in town. Looked like the lovely Jessica to me. The two of them were standing beside it, Jessica jabbering away."

Mallory's mind was working overtime. "So Jessica is back. I wonder when? By the way, who told you Ivy had a seizure at school?"

"Who do you think, that old woman, Colin Watson. It's better than buying the *Bulletin*, talking to Colin."

"You seem a bit on edge." She stared into his handsome dynamic face. His whole demeanour appeared on trigger alert, ready for action. He looked magnificent.

"I can't rid myself of the idea the Cartwrights are going to cause a lot of trouble," he said forcefully.

"They're not the maddest people I've met."

"Well, Dr. James, I happen to think differently."

That didn't surprise her. She touched his arm, gently. "I promised Dr. Farnsworth I'd have a word with Jason and Ivy this afternoon when he gets home."

"Don't do it!" Blaine looked down into her face framed by her glorious mop of hair. "I don't like the way you're putting yourself in the middle of these people. They're wackos. If you're going to speak to them, I'd like to be there."

"Maybe not the best idea. Jason might clam up. He's—"

"Half off his head with jealousy. It runs in the family."

"Let me handle this on my own, Blaine. I have a lot of experience with difficult people."

"And *I* haven't?"

"Well, *you* too, of course," she said, looking up at him. "I hope Jessica doesn't take it upon herself to come back to the farm."

"She's been told to stay away," said Blaine.

"Jessica might have a personality disorder but I don't think she's stupid. She knew we meant business."

"You're darn right!" His glittering gaze softened. The way he was now looking at her made the blood rush to her cheeks.

"What?"

"Nothing." He put a hand to her hair, curled a strand around his finger. "I'm angry. Big time. Don't get me wrong. I feel sorry for Kathy. Who wouldn't? On the other hand, as Dot would say, Jessica's a sandwich short of a picnic. The whole family is on the weird side."

"Not too many families aren't. You know the song, feuding and fussin' and a-fightin'? I've seen families locked into bitter disputes. I've been grappling with my own family all my life, as you well know. Somehow we survive. I'd better get back to Kathy."

Blaine's eyes glinted. "What's she going to do, jump town?"

"She may be tempted, but not without Ivy. She loves her."

Blaine hesitated a moment. "Many stories can be told about love gone wrong," he said soberly.

"Well, I'm not planning on making any mistakes. I mean any *more* mistakes."

"Got it!" Blaine bent and before she knew it, kissed her mouth. It was a real kiss that set her heart knocking against her ribs.

Dot was waiting for them when they arrived back at Moonglade, anxious for news. "How is Ivy now?"

Mallory touched her shoulder. "She's fine, a little dazed. She's being kept in for observation. It's Kathy who has had the big shock."

"It's just that I thought she might be dead." Kathy was looking absolutely gutted, clutching her stomach with both hands like her insides were about to fall out.

"We need tea, Dot," Mallory said briskly. "Afterwards I think Kathy should stay here and have a lie-down."

"People think I'm a nutcase."

Mallory and Dot exchanged glances.

"You're in shock. Ivy is your life."

"I lose her, I lose everything. I saw the way Dr. Farnsworth was looking at me." Kathy let her anger and humiliation show. "She wants to call Children's Services. Haul me off to court."

It had to be faced. Kathy was under suspicion.

"You mustn't get yourself all upset again. No one is calling Children's Services."

"What must happen, Kathy, is you and Jason sit down with me so we can discuss what's going wrong with Ivy's health."

"But I don't know. I don't know." Kathy's hazel eyes looked bewildered, shining with fresh tears. "I don't *think* I know." She raised a hand to chew on an already chewed-over quick. "I do my best. I cut sandwiches for her lunch but she doesn't eat them. I put in a piece of fruit, a banana, a mango, or some grapes. She tells me she gives most of it away. Lots of kids are poor eaters, aren't they, Dot?"

Card-carrying child psychologist or not, Kathy had bypassed Mallory for a bona fide mother. Dot, however, was looking a mite distracted. "Why don't I get the kettle on?" she said, by way of an answer.

"Good idea." Mallory turned Kathy in the direction of the kitchen. "You're not doing much eating yourself, Kathy."

"I find it hard to choke down food, especially when fuckin' Jess is around." She clapped a hand over her mouth to staunch a further obscenity. Oddly, the F-word sounded far less shocking from Kathy than Jessica. "Sorry, Mallory," she apologized, "but I hear that word all the time. You've no idea how *good* it's been with her gone. She's so horrible to me sometimes I want to kill her. I reckon I could pull off the perfect murder."

Mallory felt a shock of alarm. "That's terrible idea, Kathy. Don't even think it. You'd go to jail for life. Where would Ivy be then?" She felt she needed a more comprehensive view of the sad young woman she had befriended. In short, Kathy, who aroused her strong sympathy, could actually be pulling the wool over her eyes. The pattern of Ivy's illnesses was now dominating her mind.

Someone was banging on the front door, making no attempt to press the button for the doorbell. Mallory, ears pinging, went to answer it. She threw open the door, only to face Jason, brow slick with sweat, blue eyes blazing, a purplish vein thrumming in his right temple.

"When was someone going to tell me Ivy had a fit at school?" He was glaring at Mallory with accusing eyes. "And where the hell is Kathy? She's not at home."

Mallory *burned* with outrage. "Whoa, there, Jason!" she said sharply, holding up a hand. "I don't answer to you, so don't pull the mad bull act with me. Take a minute to get yourself together or leave."

"Sorry, sorry." Belatedly he reined himself in. "Sorry, Mallory. I'm so bloody angry."

"No news. Come in," she said tightly, prepared to make a few allowances. "Kathy is upstairs taking a nap. She's tremendously upset."

"I bet! She's playing you, Mallory. Playing on your kind heart."

The possibility filled her with dread. "So you want

me to believe. Ivy's fine. They're keeping her in for observation."

"I *know* that," Jason burst out in high impatience. "Jess and I went to see her."

Mallory drew in a breath. "Jason, you astound me every time. Who told you, and please don't say Colin Watson."

"Actually it was good of Colin to let us know. Jess is back from the Daintree."

"When did she arrive back?" Mallory hung on his answer.

"This morning. I met up with her in town."

"By accident or arrangement?"

Jason's features tightened. "Come off it, Mallory. Jess and I keep in constant touch. She's my twin."

"Jason, I'm sure every last soul from the Almighty down is aware of that. Understand this: Jessica is not allowed back on the farm."

"But I need her, Mallory," he pleaded. "Jess is super-efficient. I can't do without her. Kathy is no bloody help at all. All she does is sleep her head off. I swear she's half comatose most of the time. And her headaches! They're her way of shutting out the world."

Mallory swallowed hard. "Jason, I beg you to listen. Your marriage is what you make of it. You haven't given it even half a chance."

"Cut the crap, Mallory," Jason groaned. "All you do is waste time defending Kathy at every turn. She's a woeful mother. She neglects Ivy. She's the sort who takes to her bed when her kid needs her. Now, why don't you wake her and tell her I'm here to take her home?"

Mallory looked up at his tormented face, wondering

if she would ever come close to knowing the full story of this unhappy marriage. "I'll do that for you, Jason, but I'd like all three of us to sit down sometime soon to have a talk about what's happening with Ivy."

Jason clutched his hands together like a prize fighter. "What does this have to do with you?"

"Remember who you're talking to, Jason," Mallory said with sharp censure. "I want to *help*. I want to be there in a professional capacity. Plus there's the trifling fact I own this estate. I want to know what's happening on it. A quiet discussion, Jason, that's all I'm asking."

"What makes you think you *can* help?" His eyes rested on every feature of her beautiful face wreathed in masses of tousled dark golden hair. He was close enough to catch the scent of her, the scent of Mallory, the combination of clean hair, clean skin, clean heart. *Purity.*

"I'm a psychologist, Jason. There are some concerns about Ivy that need to be cleared up."

"Would you like to know what Jess thinks?"

"No, I would not," Mallory said forcefully. "I'm absolutely certain your sister blames Kathy for everything that goes wrong with Ivy."

"And that surprises you?" Jason threw down the challenge. "For God's sake, Jess isn't much good at showing it, but she loves Ivy."

"Not the type of love Ivy craves. Jessica isn't any good at showing how much she loves her niece."

"Maybe not, but Jess has a real nose for what Kathy's up to."

"Meaning?" Mallory snapped, aware she was starting to lose her cool. "Look, let's go through to the

Garden Room. Would you like something to eat, drink?"

"I'm okay." Jason followed her through the house until they reached the big beautiful room filled with all manner of indoor plants and luxuriant golden canes in huge Thai pots. "I had lunch with Jess. We could have sat all day talking about what goes wrong with Ivy. Kathy as a mother is a real joke."

"Joke, am I?"

Startled, both of them turned to face the voice. Even Jason appeared swamped by embarrassment.

Kathy stood there, her hazel eyes puffy and cloudy with fitful sleep. "God, did I mess up my life when I had sex with you, Jason!" she said with bitter regret. "You're a disgrace as a husband. As for your black-hearted sister, what a bitch!"

Jason reacted with fury. "Disgrace, am I? I've never had one happy day with you. Only for Ivy, I don't remember having much in the way of sex with you."

Mallory's heart plummeted. This was incredibly nasty.

"Are you man and wife or are you not?" Mallory angrily demanded of them. "Okay, maybe not for that much longer, but you *are* Ivy's parents."

Neither Jason nor Kathy spoke, taken aback by the usually composed Mallory's fiery outburst.

"We have to find out what is happening to Ivy," Mallory said. "We have to *know*. This state of affairs can't go on. I've talked to Dr. Farnsworth—"

"She's a fat pig," Kathy said of the good doctor, her small frame throbbing with hostility. "I thought you were my friend, Mallory."

"I am your friend, Kathy. As your friend, my aim must be to help you."

"Try to get your mind into gear, Kathy," Jason sneered, running a hand through his newly close-cropped hair. "I'll take you home. You're in no fit state to talk a bit of sense."

"You really want the answer?" Shoeless, Kathy padded farther into the room. It was obvious to Mallory that Kathy was fuelled by a deep-seated anger that at long last was bubbling to the surface.

"I'd sure like one, Kathy." Mallory moved to take Kathy's painfully thin arm.

"It's bloody Jessy," Kathy said, her gaze focused on her husband. "Not me. It's bloody Jessy. She's truly evil. She's turned her back on God."

Jason stepped threateningly closer to her. "And you're stark raving mad!"

"Stand back, Jason," Mallory ordered, giving him a sharp look of warning.

"If I'm mad it's you and your freak of a twin that have driven me there." Kathy was gaining courage from Mallory's staunch presence.

"Watch your mouth," Jason warned, barely controlling his anger.

"Listen, Kathy!" Mallory shook Kathy's arm to gain her attention. "What does Jessica do?" She ignored Jason's dark mutterings. She was seeking answers.

"Brilliant!" he cried. "You're going to listen to this idiot?"

"I haven't heard your brains clanking. Kathy is my friend. I need to protect her. She's trying hard to deal with a life skewed by men doing wrong by her."

"Terrific!" Jason cried, stony faced. "Take *her* part!"

"Anyone with a heart and a mind would. I don't have your one-eyed approach to everything, Jason. Where's your moral base? The decisions you've made have been wrong. You've allowed Jessica into your married life. You've given her virtual permission to be cruel to your wife."

"A lot you know about it," he hooted. "You took off."

"I bless the day Mallory came back," Kathy declared with touching sincerity. "I've come to trust Mallory more than anyone I've ever trusted in my life."

"Ah, shut up, Kathy. Shut up and come home with me. You love drawing attention to yourself. You'll say anything to get attention."

"Not true." Kathy turned back to Mallory. "There's no use trying to talk to Jason or Jessy. Even *you* can't do that, Mallory. They're *one* mind. I'll go with Jason now. It's like Mum said, you made your bed, now you've gotta lie in it," she said, with total acceptance of the bad hand life had dealt her.

"No you don't, Kathy." Sympathy had strengthened the bonds between her and this seemingly powerless young woman. "We have one life. One shot at it. You don't have to endure an unhappy marriage. Times have changed. I'm your friend. I promise you support. I know you have it in you to stand on your own two feet given a little help. Both you and Jason are desperately unhappy in this marriage, so the only option is to end it."

Kathy shook her head, clearly not accepting that piece of advice. "I can't walk away, Mallory. Mum said I can't. We're Catholics!" She spoke as if the family was Catholic long before Christ was ever born.

"Stay here the night, Kathy," Mallory begged. "We can pick up Ivy in the morning."

Jason broke in, heatedly. "*I'll* pick her up, thank

you. I *am* Ivy's father, might I remind everyone. I have my rights, which I will enforce. Kathy will never take my child off me. She's such a nutcase she wouldn't get custody anyway. Now she can come with me."

"If I catch Jessica anywhere on this farm, you're sacked on the spot, Jason," Mallory said in a voice hard enough to crack stone.

"Excuse me!" He stared back at her, genuinely shocked.

"Have you forgotten who the owner of this estate is? I can sack you and I will. There's a total bar on Jessica. She's a bad influence on you. She's bad for Kathy and Ivy. I don't believe for one minute she loves Ivy."

"Calls her a little bitch," prompted Kathy. "Jessy doesn't love no one but him." She pointed a finger at her husband before planting a kiss on Mallory's cheek. "It's all right, Mallory," she said sweetly. "I'll go with Jason. I have the paper that says he's my husband. He's not all that bad. At least he's never hit me."

"As if I would!" Jason looked his outrage. "I don't hit women."

"*I* don't have a lot of faith in you," said Mallory, finding the whole situation increasingly dangerous.

"He doesn't hit me, Mallory," Kathy confided almost cheerfully. "Dad used to knock me and Mum and the boys flat. That's until the boys got too big, especially Declan. I was there the first time Declan clocked him. Mum and me cheered."

"He's a real bastard, your father," Jason gritted.

"What about *your* dad?" Kathy struck back. "He and your mum don't want to lay eyes on you or that ray of sunshine Jessy. What did you do? When did they catch you out? Did Jessy unhook her bra for you? Did they catch you fondling her? Makes you want to puke. Anyway, Dad wasn't all that bad when he was sober. You're the same twenty-four seven. Come on, Jason, let's go. Mallory has just lost her uncle. She doesn't need us to further upset her."

It hit her like a tsunami. "Hang on a minute. What did you say, Kathy?" She had suspected there was something improper going on between the twins. Now confirmation.

"She's talking rubbish," Jason burst out furiously, his skin stained red. "She's a total rat bag."

"I want you to stay, Kathy," said Mallory, fearful of letting Kathy go. It wasn't enough to feel compassion. She had to act.

"Thanks, Mallory, but I'll go with Jason." Kathy had made her own decision. "You're a lady. You have beautiful eyes. They *see* things other people don't. No wonder Jason loves you. I should never have come between you."

"Kathy, you didn't really."

The look Jason gave Mallory was that of a man slashed to the bone. "You were about to marry me. Now you can say *that*?"

"When are you going to stop thinking of yourself as the jilted lover?" Mallory retorted. "You brought about your own downfall; you with the assistance of your sister. You were always too close. Now it seems there's more? If there is, I promise it will destroy you."

Jason drew himself up. "Kathy's talking a load of crap," he said furiously, rounding on his wife. "Surely you can see that? She's a serial liar. She can't stop.

Anyone can see she's not normal. You can't have
forgotten she was a wild kid, no sweet little virgin."

"But I *was* a virgin," Kathy broke in, her voice aston-
ishingly gentle. "You would have known that, Jason,
if you hadn't been so drunk. I may have flirted with
the boys, but not a one of them touched me. I didn't
want to end up like Mum. Now look at me!"

Mallory's mind was reeling. "Kathy, you must stay,"
she beseeched, feeling like a traitor for having once
believed Kathy promiscuous.

"It's okay, Mallory. Truly it is." Kathy gave Mallory
a small, sad smile. "If Jessy turns up I reckon I'll
kill her."

There it was again. "You don't *mean* that, Kathy."
Even as she spoke she was aghast Kathy could be
speaking her mind. How well did she actually know
Kathy? Had she been blindsided by pity? Whatever
the reason, she was excruciatingly aware of a gathering storm.

Jason's voice was a loud bark in her ear. "You hear
that?" he yelled. "She's saying she's going to kill Jess."

"Only if she turns up," said Kathy, in an entirely
reasonable voice.

Mallory took long, shaky breaths to bring her anxiety down. "Let's have no more talk of killing, Kathy.
Society and your religious beliefs have a major problem with that. It's a great sin."

"You're as mad as a hatter," Jason shouted. "You
don't have the guts to face Jess, let alone turn a gun
on her. You wouldn't even know how to fire one."

"I never said I'd *shoot* her. I'd pick up a rock and
clobber her."

"Oh, do stop, Kathy," Mallory ordered, wondering

if all Kathy's screws were coming loose, or she was just letting off steam.

Jason groaned in disgust. "She'd never in a million years get the better of Jess."

"It's been a very upsetting day." Mallory reached out to grasp Kathy's hand. "I'm here if you need me, Kathy."

"I won't do anything stupid, Mallory. I promise."

"I'll hold you to it." Mallory moved to hug the younger woman, rubbing the frail back with her hand. Kathy had grown up with such a sense of worthlessness, it could never be eradicated.

Jason stood by, nearly apoplectic. "To say the things she's been saying, she's certifiable!"

Kathy gave a little lopsided smile. "I'm not the crazy one. But I've got lots of scars."

Jason's mouth worked before he could get his words out. "Forget the scars. All you do is talk a pack of lies."

The odd little smile remained on Kathy's face. "You know a lot about talking lies yourself, Jason. Why don't we go?" She spoke as if the two of them had a full day's work ahead of them. She put out a hand to her husband, but Jason violently rejected it as though Kathy, not his twin, was attempting to lead him on the long road to hell.

Kathy's small hand fell away.

In the few minutes it took for them to reach the bungalow, Kathy was filled with a heady recklessness the likes of which she had never experienced in her short life. She had come to the end of the line with two opposing emotions in charge: exhilaration and fear. Pathetic little moron that she had always felt herself to be, it was time to fight back. Inside the door she turned to face the cold stranger who was her husband and tormentor. "Go on, say it. Say it," she erupted. "I can see it in your face. Say what you weren't game to say in front of Mallory."

Jason took a step towards her, towering over her small, slight figure. "I don't know what you're talking about, you silly little bitch."

"At least I have the courage to face what I am." A great flood of pent-up emotion was ready for release. "What about you, big man? I'm talking all the insults, the threats, the degradation. Jessica trying to get rid of me by any means she can. I'm sick of the abuse, Jason. You're such a weakling. Being good looking hid that. I had hoped to love you. I had hoped you would come to love me. We have a child. Instead I've grown to loathe you. I'm disgusted with all the things you and your evil twin do. I despise the both of you. You're sick people, really *sick*. I haven't said anything, not to protect *you* and your bloody vampire of a sister. I've kept quiet to protect *Ivy*."

Jason stared back at her stunned. "You open your mouth and God help you," he threatened. Purple veins were standing out in his temples and in his neck.

"What will you do, *kill* me?" Kathy challenged. "You don't have to. I'm leaving, Jason. Goin' away. And I'm takin' Ivy."

He shook his head violently in an effort to clear it. "Don't make me laugh. You're stupid, Kathy. You couldn't fend for yourself. You're like your poor bloody mother. She stuck with a lifetime of abuse. She didn't protect you kids. But don't get me wrong.

I'd be delighted to see you go, but you'll never take Ivy. She belongs to me. You're not fit to be a mother. You're unstable. You have problems. You even told Mallory you would kill Jess. A rock over the head, wasn't it? Mallory looked appalled. Jess and I wouldn't have any trouble convincing a judge you need certifying."

Kathy's face lost all colour, but she didn't back down. "Here's a message for you, Jason, old son. Your sister is devoid of all goodness. You're in Jessica's power. You can't break free. You're not even trying. Mallory is a lovely person. She's my friend."

Jason was silent for a minute before he roared out his grief and shame. "You leave Mallory out of this. She's a princess, you're nothing but a skank and a klepto on the side. What was it again, lipsticks and eye cream tucked in the bag and not in the trolley?"

"That was your sister, not me."

"Hush your mouth." Strange lights in Jason's blue eyes were flickering.

"Whatta you goin' to do, wash it out with soap? Jessie was the one who broke the elephant and blamed Ivy. We all know who you believed. Your evil sister." Kathy lashed out, her huge sorrowful hazel eyes drowning in tears.

For a minute Jason stood like a man both physically and emotionally exhausted. Then, in the next second, he threw out his strong hand, slapping her hard across the face. He watched her stagger back. He watched her reach out to an armchair for support. He could see the clear red imprint of his hand on her cheek. There had been great satisfaction in landing a blow; satisfaction, immediately followed by a crushing *shame*. He had never hit a woman in his life.

He knew he was out of control. He couldn't rein himself in. He hated Kathy. He hated himself more. He wanted to slap her again, take his rage out on her, only she took to her heels, running down the hallway and into the spare bedroom, slamming the door shut.

He stood reeling for a moment before following her down the hallway calling out vehemently, "You're an idiot, you know that? You bring things on yourself. Come out, you silly little twit." He began to bang on the door with the flat of his hand. "I'm sorry. I didn't mean to hit you, but you can't say things like that about Jess and me. I won't have it. No one would believe you anyway. Come on out, or do you want me to break the bloody door down? I can and I will." He hammered it. "Divorce me if you want to. I don't *want* you. But you won't have Ivy."

No sound from inside. In the ensuing silence, he kept up the verbal attack, knowing the damage he was doing to the vulnerable woman he had been forced into marrying. Some part of him knew it was all wrong, but he couldn't seem to help himself. He was way beyond that. "You're not fit to be a mother, Kathy," he finished off, spent. "You're not fit to be anything much. Jess is sure you've been harming our child. She plans on going to the authorities. I'll go with her. You won't have Ivy. You'll never have Ivy." He thought he heard a sound such as a wounded animal might make if caught in an iron trap. He waited a moment more, not sure if he heard the sound or not. Then he turned away, filled with a deep condemnation of himself, his twin, and his pathetic wife, who stood no chance against them.

She would calm down. She had no other option.

Chapter Seven

After an excellent dinner, they moved into the cool of the loggia, where Blaine sat brooding sombrely while Mallory filled him in.

"So we're talking twincest?" he asked, with heavy calm.

It seemed important to be calm. "It's hearsay. No actual evidence. That said, incest is found in all countries, all cultures, across the entire social spectrum. There's a chance Kathy may simply have been making it up. She may even have thought she was protecting herself, hitting out at Jessica. Victims do turn on their tormentors."

"It must have given you a bad jolt."

Mallory stared away across the garden. "I'll say! My heart rocked. I've met with incest in my practice. All of us at the practice have. I feel ill every time. Then there's the fact I was engaged to Jason, for pity's sake!"

"He loved you, correction, loves you. Jason is a badly conflicted man. He's probably wanted to renounce his sister for years, but he can't. He doesn't have the moral strength."

"It's a pathological attachment."

"Now we can understand the rift in the Cartwright family. It probably started in childhood. Some sort of play, a way of giving each other pleasure. Progressed over time. One thing led to another until it became a general pattern deeply hidden, even from family. Jessica Cartwright is a walking disaster. She led Jason along the path of perdition. Jason knew it had to stop. He most probably wanted it to stop."

Mallory bit her lip. "Those two should have been in therapy. I think Margery had her intuitions the relationship wasn't normal. She did separate them, sending Jason off to boarding school."

"So Jessica was programmed to be insanely jealous of any woman who tried to usurp her."

"Without a doubt!" Mallory gave a shudder. "Jason complies with everything she wants, which doesn't mean they have crossed the Rubicon."

"You think they've only reached halfway?" Blaine asked with black humour.

Mallory sat in silence for a moment, her mind ranging over some distressing cases she had known of. "I don't have a romantic view of the world, Blaine. I've seen with my own eyes glimpses of the netherworld. It's taboo in all societies but it's not uncommon. Human beings are wired for sexual choice along the lines of proximity and similarity. Then you have those two *fatales*."

"So where does all this sexual mayhem take place?" Blaine asked, not hiding his disgust. "There's a child on the scene. If Kathy *is* telling the truth, they have to go. They can't live that life here."

"Only innocent until proven guilty, right? It could be something extremely provocative Kathy threw into the mix. Jason looked horrified."

"Horrified you found out, you mean." Blaine offered his blunt assessment.

She knew it was probably true, but she wanted so much not to believe it. "This is a very serious allegation and if Kathy's right, they're all heading for disaster. Kathy has issues, maybe more serious than we think. She spoke about wanting to *kill* Jessica. It's just wild *talk*, I know."

"You don't know, that's the thing, Mallory. The world is full of people with the potential to kill. I suppose we could *all* kill if our life or the lives of those we love are threatened. Shouting in the heat of the moment 'I could kill you' is not a declaration of intent. It's a safety valve. If anyone was going to kill anyone, I'd put my money on Jessica."

Mallory's laugh was a little too high pitched. "The name did pop into my head. Only people aren't always what they appear to be. Kathy hates Jessica. Not that anyone could blame her."

"You're seriously questioning what lies behind Kathy's helpless façade?"

"I must. Her lot is not a happy one."

"Then she's way cleverer than I can believe. Kathy wants Jessica out? She wants you to dismiss her? She has now concocted a compelling reason. Sorry, but I don't buy it. I don't wish to be unkind. I just can't see Kathy having the wit to think it out. What I do believe is she has witnessed something deeply troubling between the twins. If you pressed her maybe she would tell you the whole story."

Nausea rose in Mallory's throat. "I don't know if I could bear to hear it. Too close to home."

Blaine saw how deeply the whole business distressed her. "I can find someone to replace Jason tomorrow," he said crisply.

She leaned towards him, her expression very serious. "God, oh, God, Blaine! Why ever did Uncle Robert take Jason on? It was a horrendous decision."

"There wasn't a shred of evidence the twins were in any taboo relationship. I have to say it never crossed *my* mind."

"Nor mine." Mallory's breath caught in her throat.

"If Jason and Kathy split up, which seems inevitable, we support Kathy. I'd like to know how much Jason loves his little daughter. I had thought he did. At least from what I've seen."

"Ivy's mystery illnesses are the top priority." Mallory's tone was grave. "Kathy could benefit from a psychological analysis. I've been feeling so sorry for her maybe I've got it all wrong. The strangest things happen in life. Think how *guilty* I'd feel if it came to be established Ivy is in peril from her own mother."

"So you do have legitimate fears?" Blaine saw the worry on her face.

"I have fears, certainly, only my *intuition*, which is far from being a science, tells me it's not Kathy harming her daughter. Not unless she's a truly great actress."

"That I cannot see." Blaine's answer was bone dry. "Look, why don't we go for a walk along the promontory? It'll clear the mind. We'll get to the bottom of this, and then we can do whatever needs to be done."

* * *

There was a flurry of cooling breezes out in the garden. Heady perfumes rose like incense: frangipani, oleanders. The snowy white flowers of the gardenia glowed in the moonlight, wonderfully fragrant. The deadly daturas, the locals called devil's trumpets, dangled their highly scented eight-inch flowers. The night was surprisingly temperate for that time of year. The Wagnerian bank-up of storm clouds of late afternoon had yielded nothing, as was so often the case.

In the near distance they could see the twinkling lights from the Cartwright bungalow, partly sheltered from view by a grove of palms. No sounds carried on the wind. Only Jason and Kathy were at home. Ivy was overnight in hospital. Jessica was in her bat cave.

Are you absolutely sure?

They walked along the cliff front, filling their lungs with fresh salty air. The Coral Sea shimmered as far as the eye could see. She remembered as a bereft child thinking she could launch herself across it to the stars, her feeling of dependence on her mother was so profound. "How beautiful it is here," she murmured, as Blaine tucked her to him.

Bad things can happen in beautiful places.

She shivered at the thought.

"Cold?" Blaine asked. The night wind off the water did have a slight nip to it.

"No, just a thought. The bad ones I usually keep to myself."

"I'm here to share, Mallory. Sharing is good."

"I keep thinking bad things can happen in beautiful places," she confessed.

"A cliff is the perfect place to push someone off," he remarked very dryly.

"Can you imagine the sensation of falling?" She

shuddered. "A doctor friend once told me if it's from a considerable height you're dead before you hit the ground."

"I don't think I'll test it out."

"It's a wonder no one through the years has fallen off Moonglade's cliff," she said.

He looked down at her. "Robert never told you?"

"Told me what?"

"Someone did. But that was nearly a century ago. A ten-year-old girl by the name of Gabriella de Campo, the daughter of the Italian family working the sugar farm. The story goes she and a group of children were playing a game, apparently unsupervised. A lot of running around, I suppose. During the game, Gabriella found herself too near the edge of the cliff, took fright, and fell off."

"How terrible!" Mallory had no difficulty visualizing the scene.

"Robert probably didn't tell you because he thought it would upset you."

She accepted that. "The tragedies fate metes out to the undeserving when so many of the bad guys get away. It could well be Gabriella's thin cries I hear in the night. I couldn't count the number of times over the years I've heard cries on the wind that sound human."

"Birds," Blaine said. "You've got too much imagination, Dr. James."

"A vivid imagination is normal for me, Blaine. According to one of my great heroes, Albert Einstein, the true sign of intelligence is not knowledge, it's imagination. 'Logic will take you from A to B. Imagination will take you everywhere.' Except into the void."

"And the void is?" he asked quietly, putting his arm around her shoulder.

"Where we're all heading."

"First we have to live the life we've got, as fully as we can. Life is a miracle."

"I know," she said softly. "I love it here at Moonglade."

"It's yours now," he said. "Wouldn't you find it hard to leave?"

It would be a thousand times harder to leave *him*. She was ready to admit it. "Here with you, I have a feeling I'm becoming more of myself or more the person I was meant to be. Belonging was what I've always longed for. What I've lived with is an inescapable *aloneness* for all Uncle Robert was wonderful to me. Security is very important to a child. I grew up a displaced person."

Blaine turned her to him, staring down into her upturned starlit face. His hand moved to grasp a handful of her wonderful thick hair. He tugged gently, tilting her head back, exposing her long neck. "I ache for you," he said.

Under the cover of the casuarinas, with their whorls of minute foliage and pendulous branches, Jason squatted in great discomfort. The darkness around him was absolute. Even in the moon's radiance it would have been hard to spot him. He was wearing dark clothing with a hoodie pulled down over his blond head. Hadn't he known if he stayed long enough he would witness something like this? He had seen Forrester's Range Rover come up the drive around seven p.m. Hours later, when he had checked, it was still there. Was the bastard staying the night?

There was only one way to find out. He had to set up a vigil. Now his constant checking had paid off, except he wanted to yell and scream abuse. He knew he was cracking up but he couldn't seem to help it. He had told himself over and over that in time things would get better, his screwed-up life would improve. That didn't happen. Life was getting too much for him to handle. God, he wasn't yet thirty and he was about ready to pack it in.

The moon was so bright, the air was luminous. He *hated* what he was watching, yet perversely he couldn't look away. There was his beautiful Mallory offering herself up to Blaine Forrester. Bodies asking questions, bodies seeking answers. Forrester had his. He was kissing her as though he *owned* her. He had *his* Mallory pressed against him. Hard, so *hard*. He had never seen anything like it. Mallory was responding in a way she had never done with him. Not ever. Not once. No passionate kisses had he ever received from Mallory.

Jess was the needy, passionate one. Poor violently improper Jess. He loved her and he loathed her. The more he loathed what they did, and the less he was able to get out of it. He was desperate to free himself of the wicked gratification and go into the light. Mallory was *light*, the *goodness* of her was inspiring to him. He had been able to overcome his shameful addiction while he was with Mallory. Then she left him to his fate. God, how often had he wished his twin had been a brother? A million times, ten million times? What was the weakness in him that Jess wore him down every time?

"You traitorous bitch, Mallory," he muttered, strong hands clenched tight, teeth grinding in impotent rage. Only he loved her just the same. He had thought of his feelings for her as Pure Love, when he knew in his heart women were the root of all evil. Men did well to fear them. Wild chattering was issuing from his mouth. He pressed his fist against it. It was like having the heart ripped out of his body seeing Mallory surrender like that. Boundless grief. There were real tears—tears of hatred—standing in his eyes and running down his cheeks, unchecked. He didn't have a bloody handkerchief anyway. He was furiously, murderously humiliated. Mallory should have been his. She would have saved him. She was the Light. He was desperate for the Light. What was his purpose in life without Mallory? He didn't have one. Mallory had been so nearly his salvation, only Kathy got in the way.

He had snapped when they arrived back at the bungalow, totally pissed off with Kathy. He had torn strips off her, heading after her and calling insults outside her locked door. He couldn't believe Kathy had actually shown some guts, though she had looked terrible, deathly pale.

Gradually his heartbeat had calmed. He started to wonder what the hell had gotten into him, apart from his screwed-up life. Kathy wasn't responsible for it. Not really. Kathy was a victim. It was he who had to fight out of this terrible situation they were in. Despite all Jess had claimed—vehement as usual and so bloody convincing—he wasn't all that sure Kathy was harming their child. If Kathy loved anyone, it was Ivy.

He had knocked on the door a few hours later begging Kathy to come out and get something to eat. He had prepared a ham salad. He had apologized for his behaviour but she had ignored him. Hours later again she was still locked away in the bedroom. It made it easy for him to exit the bungalow, quietly and unseen.

Mosquitoes were making a feast of him. He flailed at them wildly. He shuffled back an inch or two, his shoes crunching up dried leaves and fallen twigs. A giddiness was in his head. Could they have heard? Bloody hell, Forrester had. Just his luck.

He couldn't cope with Forrester right now. Forrester was the big man. Worse, he couldn't cope with Mallory's knowing he had been spying on them. Was there no end to the humiliation? He suddenly saw with appalling clarity he was a pathetic bastard. The knowledge gutted him. What had he turned into? When had it all started?

He knew exactly when it had started. Was it even a medical condition? Genetics? They were programmed to be of one mind? Only he truly believed it wouldn't have started, only for Jess. Jess had taken him down the dark tunnel. Catastrophe didn't always happen overnight. In his case it had been a long progression. . . .

Jess barged into his room where he was lying on his bed leafing through one of his father's boating magazines. She was crying fiercely. He could see it wouldn't be long before she was out of control. She had been like this for at least a year since they had turned twelve, the violent mood swings, her stomach-turning spitefulness. She was sobbing her heart out, hiccupping with the force of it, while she denounced their mother as a Judas, a cruel bitch, who had accused her

*of turning into a hateful person and bullying the kids
at school. He had wanted to say she did, but he just
couldn't. His love for his twin was all consuming.*

*She had thrown herself on top of him, thrashing
wildly, then unbelievably she had turned temptress.
She had begun moaning into his mouth he was the
only one she loved. She had stunned him. He couldn't
fight her off. His head was spinning. It had shocked
him her kissing him on the mouth, her body on top of
him grinding into his penis. It was shocking but so
exciting. It was almost as natural as breathing. Him
and Jess. She started to pull at her clothes, exposing her
delicately pink-tipped breasts. They were white as milk,
unlike her tanned limbs, that were twining snake-like
around his. He didn't stop her. Why didn't he stop
her? He was shamefully aware of the tumescence in
his adolescent body. Why didn't he stop her? To this
day he didn't know.*

Blaine's hearing was eerily good. His head
snapped in the direction of the rustling sounds in the
underbrush. His voice cracked out, "Who's there?
Come out." Without hesitation he moved off in the
direction of the bungalow that was nearly obscured
by the trees. "Wait here," he called to Mallory over his
shoulder. It was an order. The weeping casuarinas
were perfect cover for any stalker. There was only one
stalker that came to mind. Jason, who was living such
a tangled and tainted life.

Near bent in two Jason fled in a running crouch,
screened from view by the thick swirl of acacias. Now
he knew how it felt to hit rock bottom. His eyes
were so filled with tears he could hardly see a thing.

Once people had liked him, even respected him. Not anymore. He had become an outcast. All of his own making.

Mallory opened her mouth. Shut it again. She knew full well who was spying on them but she was concerned by what Blaine might do. She knew he had a daunting temper when aroused. She ran after him. "Let it go, Blaine," she implored. "If it was someone, they've vanished into the night."

"More like back to the bungalow." Blaine wasn't about to be easily persuaded. "No need for you to worry. I'll go over and check exactly who's at home."

"Oh, *don't*. Please don't. It would only stir up more trouble. Let's go back to the house." She grabbed onto his unyielding arm, but it was clear he wanted to investigate further.

"Mallory, you know someone was watching us, most likely that lunatic, Jason. Chances are both he and Jessica are psychotic."

She was pitching all her strength, but it was as nothing. "Forget them. Remember *me*. I've had enough for today, Blaine. I beg you. Let's go back."

Abruptly Blaine left off. "Jason has to be dealt with."

"Absolutely. In the morning."

"This is *not* acceptable, Mallory." There was steel in his voice. "I'll back off now as it upsets you, but I'll be having a little chat with Cartwright tomorrow. He's making himself very unwelcome. If what his wife claims is true, nothing will change the path the twins have so perilously embarked on. God only knows what the consequences will be."

The answers to all Mallory's questions were falling like a dead weight into place.

***

Later that night, they came together in a great tumult of emotion. It was proof if they ever needed it of the powerful chemistry between them. Moonlight streamed into Mallory's bedroom through the wide open French doors, roaming the walls, haloing the ceiling. Even the air, laced with the fresh salty scent of the sea, was alive with spangles.

There was something incredibly erotic about their shared nakedness; bone on bone, the texture of skin on skin, musculature rippling and coming into play as they turned and twisted this way and that, touching, kissing, exploring every crevice, every contour, with each passing moment, fanning the flames. Her hair fell around them, thick, heavy, and lustrous as sparks ignited. At the same time she felt a tremendous languor. If they hadn't been lying on her plush, high bed she surely would have sunk to the ground.

My God! My God!

Sensations piled up. Spasms that had begun as tiny began to build in strength, causing her back to jerk up off the bed, building towards a climax so powerful she had little hope of controlling the pace. Her eyes were shut tight against all her inner tremors, her fingers digging into the flesh of his broad shoulders.

"Mallory!"

His voice was ragged with desire crying out for release. Their lovemaking had become a kind of frenzy, with no barriers. She had no option but to go with it, her body fused to his in the darkness, her long, slender legs wrapped tightly around him. She was his. Heart, body, and spirit. It seemed crazy now she had resisted him for so long. She had no idea tears were streaming down her face.

Afterwards, she slept deeply and dreamlessly within the curve of Blaine's arm and shoulder. It wasn't until hours later that she arrived at a luminal state between sleep and waking. A huge pair of hazel eyes in a lifeless, bone-white face were staring down at her, wrenching her completely out of her sleep.

Her warm blood turned to ice. Her involuntary little cry was thin with dread. She would never become accustomed to the images she saw, images that were part of her and her psyche. All her life she had been dreaming of the ghost of her mother. There *were* ghosts. She was convinced of it.

She sat up, full of a tearing sadness. Dreams, she knew, were powerful intuitions trying to fight their way to the surface. Her hand moved blindly to Blaine. His breathing was quiet and steady. He was lying on his side, one hand curled over her lower body. He was there. She needed him. Now more than ever.

"Blaine, wake up!" She was aware of the trembling in her limbs.

He didn't mumble in his sleep, or turn away. He snapped to attention like a soldier. "Mallory, what is it?" He sat up, fully alert.

"I heard something."

"What?" He strained his ears. Heard nothing.

"A cry for help." Mallory was close to tears. Her intuitions had steered her successfully through life. She had to follow them.

Blaine suppressed all urges to tell her she'd been dreaming. His attention was drawn to the quality of the air in the room. It should have been warm, yet it was so cold his skin was reacting to a sharp drop in temperature.

"It was a woman's cry," she said.

"Mallory, it must have been a bird."

She drew in a long sibilant breath. "It wasn't a bird." She could feel her heart banging against her rib cage like it wanted to escape. "Believe me."

"Right, I'll check." Blaine was out of the bed, quickly pulling on clothes. He was there for her no matter what. Too much grief had fallen over Mallory's life. "That blasted alarm system can be a pain, but if anyone came close to the house it would have gone off. You stay here."

"No." Mallory too was out of the bed, searching for something easy to pull over her head. "I felt the cry in my *soul.*" Swiftly she knotted her hair, reaching for the first footwear to hand.

Blaine was well aware he was humouring her, but Mallory was such a highly sensitive creature he was prepared to let her have her head.

"What time is it?" Her voice was muffled as she pulled a kaftan over her head.

"God knows. Can't be all that far from dawn." He glanced out at the lightening sky. He too was experiencing foreboding. Something was wrong. Either that or he was galvanized by Mallory's mood.

Downstairs, he deactivated the security system. They went out into the night, moving in accord along the face of the cliff. Their path was accompanied by the sound of a billion chirping insects. The moonlight was ultra-bright, cutting a silver swathe from the sea to the stars. Blaine played his torch into the shrouded parts of the heavily scented garden.

"Down on the beach," Mallory said, as though she possessed knowledge he didn't. "The steps will be fine. There's plenty of light."

Alarm bells were ringing in Blaine's head. "What are we looking for, Mallory?"

"Someone is down there," she said, with certainty.

Who, exactly, he wondered, but made no attempt to ask. His job was to protect her. She might have been following marks on a map, so totally involved was she with getting to her destination. Indeed it seemed to him her manic energy couldn't be contained. There had to be some explanation for this. What was she doing guiding him through this illuminated night?

The powerful beam of the torch lit the rock steps. Both of them held firm to the iron handrail. Certainly Mallory knew things he didn't. Mallory had powers he had to consider he might well lack. They reached the strand line, moving through the stands of pandanus. Mallory with her kaftan flowing around her resembled a goddess following a spectral image. A few feet head of him, she stopped short, standing as though transfixed. He watched as her hands rose prayerfully to her mouth. He too came to a halt, feeling out of his depth. What was going on here? God knows what truth was going to burst on him. He heard Mallory's stricken gasp.

"Blaine, over here."

He had excellent night vision, and besides that, the moon was very bright. Still he could see nothing. All he could see was Mallory moving like a wraith into the patch of darkness beneath the cliff's overhang.

"Blaine!" she called again, her voice so raw it broke his heart. "It's Kathy."

A fierce dread drove him on.

Mallory was down on her knees, chanting over and over, "Kathy, Kathy, Kathy, I'm so sorry."

Blaine's heart was flailing about in his chest. He had seen death, but this was too much to cope with. He moved to get a clearer view of the small broken body. A hideous indignity. The skull had been split on the rocks. The pool of blood around it was as black as ink. Kathy was lying on her stomach, one leg drawn up, the other at an odd angle. Her head was turned to the side, her cheek pressed into the sand. They could see dark runnels down her chin and on her pitifully thin neck. Her right hand was lying beseechingly palm up. The fingers of the other hand were wedged under a rock.

He sank down on his knees, beside Mallory, waiting for his heart to settle and his stomach to stop lurching. There was a sudden haziness to his vision. Here was little Kathy Cartwright.

The night that had been so beautiful mutated into something terrible.

"Where is God in all this?" Mallory asked raggedly, overwhelmed by despair. "Where does He get to when He's needed? Kathy, what chance did you ever have? Broken and never mended. I'll carry the memory of this for the rest of my life."

"Don't, Mallory, don't." Blaine brought her gently to her feet, keeping a tight hold on her. "I'll take care of this."

* * *

The police, paramedics, and a doctor, once alerted, were on the scene in a remarkably short space of time. The yellow and black helicopter to Mallory's blurry eyes resembled a mechanical bumblebee. It was almost full daylight.

"Did Kathy plan it?" Mallory asked sadly.

"She couldn't cope," was all Blaine could find to say. He too felt drained.

Sometime later at the house, the officer in charge told them Kathy Cartwright had left a note in a bedroom of the bungalow. He had spoken to her distraught husband, who had refused a minister, a cup of strong tea, a stiff drink, or the comfort of friends at the big house. He had thought that a bit odd but made no comment.

"Suicide, poor thing," he murmured with gentle respect. The battling Burches were well known in the town. Everyone knew Kathy Burch Cartwright and her tragic story. It was a suicide just waiting to happen.

There was the expected autopsy. Another violation, to Mallory's mind. Neither alcohol nor drugs were found in Kathy Cartwright's blood, only the remains of a light meal in her stomach. Mallory hoped that would put the record straight. The childlike handwriting on the suicide note was confirmed as hers. The body was released. Kathy Cartwright had committed suicide. A great many were saddened. Few were surprised.

The funeral was a grim affair, made all the more so because it happened on a dazzlingly blue and gold day. Kathy Cartwright would never live through

another such day. Her burly, handsome brothers,
Declan and Sean, turned up as bodyguards flanking
their mother, who may or may not have been intox-
icated.

Mallory let her eyes rest on the woman the whole
town had once sympathized with, the battered wife
who couldn't or wouldn't break away from her abusive husband. Kathy's mother looked like hell, as well
she might, wearing a dress that was too small. What
make-up she had applied had gone for a slide down
her face in the heat, pooling around her jawline. She
was still a pretty woman. No sign of the father, not that
anyone cared. Danny Burch had been steadily dying
of alcoholism, gallstones, cirrhosis, haemorrhoids,
lung cancer, take your pick, for the past twenty years.
Against all the odds he had survived, even if everyone
had mentally buried him.

The Cartwrights attended at the church and at the
graveside, with the exception of Ivy. Ivy's immediate
situation had been resolved. She was living with her
paternal grandparents and had been left in the
care of their housekeeper for a few hours. It was an
astounding sight to see Jessica Cartwright at the
gravesite in floods of tears. Jessica at her best was a
good-looking woman, but she appeared to have lost
all ability to make herself attractive.

"It's my fault," she kept crying, tugging at her
blonde hair. It wasn't clear whether she was trying to
tame it or pull it out by the roots.

"Now you don't see that every day," Blaine said in
disgust.

"She should stow the forgiveness thing."

"Or get bound over for breaking the peace. Grief

manifests itself in many different ways, but this is *bizarre*. Sure she's not possessed?"

"Jessica considers herself quite sane."

Jessica was still crying out like a lost soul seeking redemption.

Blaine was sickened by what he believed were antics, not a demonstration of remorse. He wasn't the only one. Mourners were standing about, shaking their heads with disbelief.

The parish priest got on with the prayers for the dead with unholy haste. For once Jason didn't console his twin. Once when she took his arm he shook her off, then moved away a few steps. Her father continued to pretend his son and his daughter didn't exist. Their mother, overdressed for a country funeral, the pretty skin of her face showing red and white blotches, appeared blind and deaf to the commotion. Like Blaine, Mallory couldn't shake her belief Jessica was putting on an act. Jessica was glad her sister-in-law was dead and out of the way.

It was time for them all to take the sombre walk back to their parked vehicles. But such is the unexpectedness of life that it didn't happen. Declan Burch, puce in the face, thick necked, barrel-chested, turned into a roaring volcano, belching lava. Declan, who rejoiced in the nickname of "Bull" Burch, started to unleash an eardrum-shattering scream of obscenities at Jason, who after an initial shocked stop-start, chose to ignore him, white with anger. Jason started to visibly lengthen his stride but Declan was on the war path. Moving very fast for a man of his size, he grabbed Jason from behind, raining expletives more suited to

a high-security jail for the worst prisoners than a quiet
country cemetery. He spun Jason around, in a shuddering fury.

"You bastard! You mean bastard," he shouted,
looking terrifyingly intimidating. "I know all about
you and your sick sister."

"Sweet Jesus!" Blaine groaned. "Where is it all
going to end? I'll have to break it up."

"No, let Declan have his way." Mallory, who hitherto had considered herself a peacemaker, now
found herself condoning violence. She was feeling a
measure of violence herself.

Blaine started to remonstrate before he too was
struck by the same thought. He couldn't have
stopped what was about to happen anyway. Declan
Burch was determined to be heard and heeded, a
brother aching with loss. Both men were over six feet,
Jason very lean and fit, but the much bulkier Declan
was a man on a mission. He swung a punch that delivered some of his pent-up grief and rage with a good
dollop of self-guilt thrown in. Jason reeled back,
straightened up, and then danced forward with a
counterpunch.

Declan didn't appear to feel it. He didn't whimper.
His mother and brother, previously grief stricken,
were now locked into manic mode, egging Declan on
like ringside supporters. Declan swung another mighty
punch. This time it felled Jason like a tree brought
down by a champion axeman.

Jessica, whose tantrums were legendary, threw herself dramatically over her brother's prone body. It was
then that Blaine judged it time to move. The parish
priest, with a horrified expression, was standing well
back, wringing his hands and possibly pleading for

divine intervention. He couldn't have seen anything like it before or since he had entered the priesthood.

"They ought to put Jessica away. She's off the wall." Blaine closed in on Declan, getting a powerful restraining grip on his arm. "Don't hit him again, Declan," he warned, a metallic glint in his voice. "He's not worth it."

"I want to hit him. I want to pulverize him," Declan confirmed quite unnecessarily, working the muscles of his powerful shoulders. "I want to run over him with a bulldozer." His surprisingly beautiful eyes were filled with tears. "I want to kill him. If you can't shut that stupid bitch up, Mr. Forrester, I'll have a go."

"Get up, Jessica." It was Harry Cartwright who finally took charge. He pulled his distraught daughter to her feet. "Get up, girl, and stop that racket." It was clear he meant business.

Jessica, still sobbing wildly, was hoisted to her feet, where she stood bobbing back and forth in her black patent leather pumps. Her mascara had dissolved into brackish tears that formed panda eyes and ran in dark streaks down her cheeks.

Her father turned away in parental sorrow and disgust. "My wife and I are so saddened by this, Declan. Please accept out most sincere condolences."

Declan swung his head dazedly from side to side as though Jason's punch had only just caught up with him. "My poor little sister deserved better. How did this dreadful thing happen? I'll tell you, those two bloody sicko murderers." Declan was readying for a return bout.

Blaine wasted no time getting Harry Cartwright's attention. "Get the two of them away from here, Harry. I'll take Declan to his car."

"Right you are."

For a moment Declan looked like he wanted to head-butt Jessica's father. "They're not going to get away with it," he threw back over a massive shoulder, with ringing hear-hears from his younger brother, who was hard-pressed to restrain his own broken heart, and also that of his highly vocal mother.

"They won't. They have to live with it." Mallory caught up, ranging herself beside Blaine.

Declan turned his large, handsome head towards her. "You meant a lot to Kathy, Miss James. You were kind to her. You always were, going way back. My poor little sister! This was always waiting for her like some bloody Greek tragedy, it is."

In the distance, Jessica Cartwright was still wailing as though she didn't have a clue how to turn the sound system off. It might have been comical only it was all too, too terrible.

"I don't want Jessica Cartwright to set foot on Moonglade ever again." It was much later that dreadful day. "I don't want Jason, either. Their cruelty to Kathy was appalling. *I* should have done more. I should have acted sooner. I should have acted on my instincts."

"Mallory, you *did* act." Mallory, being Mallory, was beating herself up. "It's impossible to help everyone. You did everything you could. Focus on that. You were very kind to Kathy."

"So why do I feel up to my neck in guilt? I should have tried harder. I've known all along nothing good was going to come of the whole situation."

"Difficult when you're trying to cope with Robert's death and your father's appalling behaviour."

"I've stopped wasting time on my father," she said bleakly, but without bitterness. "He won't change. We can be sure Jason will leave Ivy with his parents. They love her. She'll be safe in their hands. Maybe he'll come back for her later on. Who knows?"

"Kathy chose to end her own life, Mallory. The rumours about what she did to Ivy are all around town. Kathy couldn't forgive herself. She took the final step."

"For all that and the circumstantial evidence against her, I can't accept she harmed Ivy, Blaine. I just *can't*. Ivy was her everything. Kathy was *driven* to suicide. Harried to her death, yet she made a promise to me. She told me she wouldn't let me down."

"Her promise would have receded into the background in the light of Jessica's threats," Blaine said. "You have to face it, Mallory. Jason too could have threatened to take Ivy from her. He would never own up to it. Not now. They ganged up on her. Kathy was unstable. She didn't stand a chance. Suicides get to a point where they can't feel anything but their own pain. That happened to Kathy."

Life continued, sweeping everyone along with it. Some chose to jump off the merry-go-round, most didn't. Days ran into each other, always accompanied by swirling undercurrents that locked Mallory *into* doubts, not out.

Mallory couldn't hold with the collective wisdom. She knew in her soul Kathy had not deliberately harmed her daughter though she hadn't a hope of proving it. Instead she lived with the extraordinary belief that Kathy was not fully dead. She was still with them weeping at her fate, though her crying was no more than whisperings in Mallory's ears; whisperings that rose above the hullabaloo of the wind. Whisperings she heard in the dark.

Friends and neighbours called at the house, the Cartwrights several times with a beautifully dressed if naturally subdued Ivy. Ivy had gained weight in a very short time. Her skin tone had acquired its natural bloom. Ivy was to remain in the custody of her grandparents, who clearly loved her. Indeed, she appeared to have given them a new lease on life. Ivy to all appearances was thriving. Only what was going on underneath? Memories were hidden away in the whorls and recesses of the brain. Sadly Ivy's greatly improved health was taken as clear evidence Kathy Cartwright had been harming her child.

One afternoon when Mallory was alone, she had a visit from Selma Loxton-Palmer. It came as no surprise. Selma wanted to know what was going on with her and Blaine. Selma, she correctly intuited, had not given up hope of winning Blaine back. Mallory was in the Moonglade library at the time, looking up tropical poisons, in particular those very difficult to detect. She had been having nightmares involving strange fungi growing up through the mounds and mounds of decaying leaves and debris on the rainforest floor. In the aftermath of such dreams she had even thought of talking to one of the aboriginal women living in the area. Nothing much they didn't know about their own country. They had lived in harmony with it for at least 40,000 years.

She was working her way methodically through all the berries; amazing quandongs, electric blue in colour, dropped to the ground with red leaves nearby. There were red quandongs as well, both edible. Now the native walnuts. Possibilities there. They bore no relation to real walnuts. There was for instance a poison walnut, commonly seen on the ground in undisturbed rainforests. It was a highly poisonous plant. In fact, there were dozens and dozens of poisonous plants in the rainforest, and they were only the ones as yet identified. The seeds of the striped cucumber were highly toxic. Jessica Cartwright was widely considered something of an authority on tropical plants.

Food for thought there.

Dot charged into the library at such a cracking pace a Category 5 cyclone might have been forecast to hit the town by nightfall. "Selma Loxton-Palmer is at the front door. She brought flowers. I'll put them in a vase."

Mallory's focus was destroyed. She looked up from a photograph of bright orange fruit split to reveal small mounds of sticky seeds. One taste could kill. On the opposite page was a picture of some weird-looking toadstools poking their heads through millions of fallen needles that had accumulated on the rain-forest floor. The scene resembled the site of her night-mares. Towering over the area was a giant strangler fig with thick soaring prop roots like the buttresses on Notre Dame in Paris.

"Thanks, Dot." Mallory placed a bookmark between

the pages. "You can bet your life she's here on a mission."

"I reckon!" Dot paid a lot of attention to Mallory's well-being. "She'll have heard on the grapevine you and Mr. Forrester are close."

"We've always been close, Dot."

"It's an open secret you're much *closer.*"

"Dot, you're a holy terror." Mallory sighed.

"Of course I am. I'll make coffee."

"Nothing a good cup of coffee can't fix. We'll be in the Garden Room. Give us ten minutes."

"Will do. Probably she wants to know when you're going back to Brisbane."

"And would I be interested in selling the estate to Daddy?"

Dot chortled. "They know you're sitting on a gold mine, I reckon. At least she didn't arrive with her pet Chihuahua, a fluffy little thing. I saw it in town once. It was looking out of her bag with its teeth bared."

Selma looked wonderfully vibrant in a dress of strongly contrasting primary colours. It was said around town Selma was never seen in the same outfit twice. Putting forward the air of friendship, she gave Mallory a brilliant smile that didn't have a lot going for it in the way of staying power. "Truly awful the things that have been happening," she said, staring about her as one might in a museum.

Such an embarrassment of riches, Selma was actually thinking, sinking gracefully into a wicker armchair. "So this is the Garden Room?" It was easy to see why. Such a plethora of ferns and palms! Giant ferns were even hanging from the high ceilings. One almost expected to see monkeys swinging to and fro. There had to be a fortune inside the house. She'd never seen anything like it. Way too much clutter of course: paintings, objects, furnishings, tall Oriental vases and screens. The late Robert James had collected far too many things, in her opinion. If she had ever needed to, she could easily have become a top interior designer. She had *style*. One either had it or one didn't.

"Poor little Kathy Burch slipping out of life like that." Selma's eyes came back to rest on Mallory. "Though slipping is scarcely the right word. She didn't go over by accident. She *jumped*, for God's sake! Imagine it, jumping off a cliff. *Your* cliff. One hates to speak ill of the dead, but it wasn't terribly considerate of her. I suppose she was past it by then. Poor girl had more than her share of misfortune. At least the child is being well looked after, so Blaine tells me."

Mallory didn't react. She had the certainty Blaine hadn't told Selma anything. "If you don't mind, Selma, I'd rather not talk about it. I didn't know Kathy long, but I became very fond of her. I was stunned by her death. Has your friend gone back to Hong Kong?" Deliberately Mallory changed the subject.

Selma's eyes slewed back to her. "Matter of fact he has. He wanted to meet up with Blaine but events got in the way. I have to say Moonglade—the house, indeed the entire estate—is very beautiful in an old colonial style. A bit Somerset Maugham–ish maybe? If I shut my eyes we could almost be in Malaysia."

"You've read a lot of Somerset Maugham?" Mallory was instantly taken back to the time when Uncle

Robert, the writer, had told her Maugham had once said, "There are three rules for writing a novel, but unfortunately no one knows what they are."

Selma waved a vague hand in response. "I'm sure I did but I'm no good remembering titles."

"*The Painted Veil, The Razor's Edge, The Sun Also Rises,*" Mallory prompted, throwing in Hemingway for good measure.

"All three," said Selma, who vaguely remembered seeing a movie called *The Painted Veil* with their own Naomi Watts in it. "*The Painted Veil* is one of my all-time personal favourites," she said, with nary a twinge at the fib. "I don't suppose under the circumstances you would want to settle here? I suppose nobody could, given what has happened. Besides, you have your career."

"I haven't made any decision as yet, Selma." Mallory broke off as Dot wheeled in the afternoon tea trolley. It was set with a Coalport coffee set and a three-tiered matching plate, holding delicate little sandwiches and mini-cupcakes, enough for six greedy people.

"You must want to become settled." Selma was astounded by the lavish offerings. It was really, really bad for the figure to eat cake. "Black, thank you. No sugar."

Dot poured. Selma leaned forward, taking her exquisite coffee cup in hand. She planned to upend it later, to examine the company mark. Aynsley, Coalport, Rosenthal? She had never seen the pattern before, emerald and gold with a small bouquet of mixed flowers on the central white background. Quite lovely!

Mallory accepted her cup of coffee from Dot. A little

cream. One sugar. Dot knew it by heart. "I am settled," Mallory remarked after Dot had retreated. Probably to settle behind the door.

Selma's beautifully arched brows rose. "Really? I must have got things wrong. Blaine told me . . ." She paused theatrically, one hand hovering over the three-tiered plate. Selma had fully intended declining the cake, but now she appeared to have second thoughts. "These look delicious. Your Mrs. Rawlings must be a good cook. No wonder she's so overweight." She was being kind. Personally Selma thought Dot Rawlings was built like a mini-fridge. "Perhaps I'll just have a taste, like the French. Couldn't be too many calories?" She laughed lightly.

"You were saying, Blaine told you?" Mallory crisply prompted, irritated by Selma's remark about Dot.

"Well he does tell me everything," Selma confided, giving Mallory a steady burning look. "That's the beauty of being such close friends."

"Is this before or after your dramatic split?" Mallory asked.

That unexpected salvo caused Selma to blink so rapidly, one of her long eyelashes landed in her eye. "We still *talk*, Mallory. In fact we talk all the time. Heavens, we've known one another since forever. Longer than you. We *were* engaged." She made it sound as if their split weren't permanent. "I know Blaine would love to buy the estate." She fired another little dart at Mallory; it fell wide of its mark. "I expect you already know that. But he has so much on his plate, even for him. Daddy is very interested. Moonglade wouldn't be everyone's cup of tea, of course. There's Kathy Burch's unfortunate header off the cliff. The house is rather spooky, isn't it?

I believe some child fell off the cliff many long years ago. You could be sure Daddy would offer top price."

And Daddy would knock it down.

"What kind of price are we talking, Selma?" Mallory feigned interest in the answer. "You're obviously here as an agent of sorts for your father."

Selma, a morsel of cake in her mouth, couldn't speak for the moment.

Mallory decided to cut speculation short. "I'll never sell Moonglade, Selma. It's in my blood. Uncle Robert left it to me as a sacred trust, if you like."

Selma was seriously taken aback. "It's common knowledge you're making a name for yourself in your field in Brisbane. There can be no big future for you in a small coastal town. What is it you do again?"

"Quantum physics," Mallory said. "Quantum theory explains how matter acts both as a particle and a wave. Understanding the structure of atoms, even molecules. You would have studied that at school, physics, chemistry, maybe biology?"

"But I thought you were a psychologist, a child psychologist?" Selma shifted her taut bottom around in her chair.

"That too. I'm a born academic."

"Like your father. Surely that's not how you want to spend the rest of your life?" Selma's laugh suggested incredulity and pity rolled into one.

"I'd find it difficult being a lady of leisure," Mallory retorted. It was well known Selma Loxton-Palmer had never worked a day in her life. She didn't have to. At twenty-one years of age she had inherited a small fortune from her paternal grandmother, and her father had handed her over a portfolio of blue chip stock.

Selma still lived at home with her parents, but in a house so large her wing was entirely self-contained.

Selma apparently found Mallory's remark not at all to her liking. She all but leapt up from her chair, consulting her yellow-gold Bulgari watch. "Goodness, is that the time?" she cried. "I have a dinner party tonight. I just hope Blaine manages to get there. He was always the life of the party. Nowadays he works too hard. He's been very busy on his latest project. I have to say it's coming along splendidly and it creates so many jobs. Daddy thinks the world of him. I'd have invited you to dinner as well, Mallory, but I understand you're in mourning and won't be able to make it."

Mallory rose unhurriedly to her feet. "You always know the right thing to say, Selma. It was good of you to call in. Thank you so much for the lovely flowers. Let me walk you to the door."

At the front door Selma bypassed an air-kiss, settling for a pat on the shoulder. "Now you think about what I said. Daddy would do the right thing by you."

"Goodbye, now, Selma." Mallory spoke as pleasantly as she could. "If you're going to call your father later in the day, you might tell him I'm *not* selling."

Chapter Eight

Blaine had been away two long days, visiting his mother, Rowena, in Melbourne. Rowena had moved there some years after her husband's death when the family home was sold. Her own family was in Melbourne. Her two sisters had been instrumental in the move. Rowena had greatly mourned her husband, killed so prematurely. Her sisters rightly considered that she had needed a complete change of scene. Blaine had agreed. He saw his mother frequently, with the usual phone calls and emails to keep in close touch.

He arrived, apologetic—with no need—right on dinner time, filling Mallory in on all the news from Melbourne, which was good. Mallory greeted him with a kiss and a glass of champagne. She hadn't been perturbed by anything Selma had to say during her visit. She didn't plan on making mention of it.

Dot slotted the news in as she set out dessert, a lime and ginger crème brûlée. She had been told to leave the dishes. She was meeting up with old friends who were in town. Mallory had booked a room for her in the same motel so Dot wouldn't have to worry about driving home. A treasure like Dot had to be looked after.

"So the burning question of the hour. What did Selma have to say?" Blaine later asked. They were dining in the breakfast room just off the kitchen, which made things easier. French doors led out onto the spacious terrace, bathed in a golden light, awash with tropical scents from the garden, with the stands of creamy frangipani providing the top notes.

"Nothing newsworthy. Courtesy call like everybody else." Mallory cracked the caramelized top of the brûlée with a spoon.

"Not Selma." He gave her a quick smile. "Selma always has an agenda. I love that dress."

She glanced down at herself. "Thank you. As you can see, handprinted with our glorious rainforest butterfly, the blue Ulysses. I bought it locally."

"I guessed that." The material clung lightly, fluidly to her body, but he was very aware of the contours beneath.

"Selma wanted to know if I intended selling."

"Cheek of her!" Blaine said, wry amusement on his handsome face. "Go on. There has to be more. Her father would have sent her."

"Of course. She did bring flowers. It was a nice thought. I don't think she liked the house much."

"No, she wouldn't. I think you could call Selma a minimalist."

"Like Uncle Robert, I'm anything but a minimalist."

"My position as well. Knowing Selma as I do, what she really wanted to find out was just how serious *we* are."

"I didn't tell her."

"What! You didn't tell her I'm the most wonderful man you've ever known?"

She let her dark eyes rest on him. "I didn't want to upset her."

"When it's all around town?"

She stretched out the eye contact. "*Is* it?"

"Some of the brokers are even placing bets."

"Which wouldn't surprise me." She had to laugh. "What Selma really wanted to find out is, what's going to happen next?"

"Don't we all."

Mallory stared across the table at the man who had become the centre point of her life. "I wish we could travel back in time," she sighed.

"What year would you stop?" He caught her fingers across the table.

"Before we got ourselves engaged to the wrong people. What do you suppose we were doing?"

"Letting too many years go by." Blaine increased the pressure on her slender fingers.

"My fault."

"If you expect me to say it wasn't, I'm not going to."

"That's a comfort!"

"I'll comfort you later," he said.

There was a definite pattern to her dreams. They were always about Kathy. She told herself countless millions of deeply spiritual people believed in an afterlife, believed in the spirits. Kathy wasn't at peace. As a result, Kathy wasn't giving her any peace. Her subconscious had been preoccupied with working through her dreams, trying to identify their significance so she could deal with whatever was required of her.

She did worry Blaine might tire of the whole business. What tormented her, clearly tormented him.

"The dream again?" Blaine woke almost on cue.

"It won't let me alone."

He felt powerless, which didn't suit him at all. This whole business was proving beyond his limited comprehension of the spirit world. He couldn't seem to help Mallory. All he could do was *be* there. "You've come through some very bad experiences. You're coping well."

"I hope so." She moved her body to fit his. "I hate worrying you. Just give me a little time to get my mind into gear."

"We can deal with it, Mallory, whatever it is," he said quietly, stroking her hair away from her face.

She knew he was trying hard to come to grips with what was happening to her. She tried to explain. "It isn't my imagination running riot with messages from another world. It's not like that. I can't explain why these dreams come to me. Aren't the living and the dead as *one* if the soul lives on? The major religions are based on an afterlife. The ancient Egyptians lived for the afterlife. The great pharaohs built their burial chambers stocked for the afterlife. Can we really discount the existence of ghosts, the spirits of people who suffered great violence in this life? I don't believe the way I am is something to worry about. It's *natural* to me. Whether it's a gift or not I don't know, but my perceptions have worked for me as a psychologist."

"So what do you believe now?"

"I believe Kathy can't go *home*, wherever *home* is, until her soul is freed."

"So what is it she wants you to do?" Blaine's eyes

were drawn to the French doors. The sheer curtains were doing some kind of weird dance when there was scarcely a breeze. By now he knew better than to look for a reason.

"I don't yet know," Mallory sighed. "All I do know is she's desperate to have me heed her message."

"Then hopefully we can *all* move on?" He would give anything for that to happen. Kathy Cartwright, though dead, was still a dominant figure. A dead woman was begging Mallory for help. It was all too weird. Yet it made sense to Mallory. All he could do was keep the faith. It was Mallory who had divined Kathy was lying dead at the base of the cliff. How had she known? There was no easy answer.

"Will we make our home here at Moonglade?" she asked. "Or would you prefer somewhere new?"

His reply came strongly. "Mallory, we stay *here*. You love it. I love it. It's a safe haven."

"It was for Uncle Robert. He has moved on. There is no desperate ghost here. Uncle Robert is happy. It's completely different with Kathy. She was in so much pain that she took her own life. That level of agony and hopelessness doesn't disappear overnight. It leaves a residual."

Blaine didn't answer because he didn't have an answer. "I can't walk your path, Mallory. I don't have the same belief in ghosts, even an afterlife, that you have. I'm a rationalist. But if the ghost of poor little Kathy is still hanging around, I'm certain she's not going to hurt us."

"She only wants help."

"So do I." He shaped her satiny shoulder, allowing his hand to slip down to her breast.

All further discussion was put on hold.

* * *

The following afternoon, Mallory received a frantic phone call from Margery Cartwright. "It's Ivy." Margery sounded badly shaken. "We haven't been able to get a word out of her since we brought her home from school. She's mute with misery. She's not the same little girl. She's switched off."

It was bound to happen. In the weeks following Kathy's death, weeks of deceptive calm, Margery had taken Mallory's advice, keeping Ivy at home to be schooled. Margery had collected all necessary books from the school along with a schedule of what the class would be doing in the weeks ahead. Margery Cartwright was quite capable of keeping Ivy up to date with her lessons. Now this!

Mallory knew instinctively one of the children at the school had taken it upon his- or herself to tell Ivy exactly how her mother had died. No doubt in graphic detail accompanied by actions and sound effects. Children could be very cruel.

A distraught Margery greeted her in the driveway. "I feel so guilty!" She took Mallory's arm, compelling her up the short flight of front steps to the house. "Ivy could have stayed home for the rest of the year. It was too soon to go back."

"Someone was bound to tell her, Margery."

"*I* ought to have told her, instead I only told her Mummy has gone to heaven. The same old thing. I didn't think Ivy could possibly handle what had really happened."

Well, she knows now.

"Where is Ivy?" Mallory asked.

"She's in her bedroom. I can't get her to come out.

I can't possibly drag her out. She isn't eating either. The girl who told her, Emma Munroe, must be a very mean child." Margery's voice hardened. "I'd like to give her mother a piece of my mind."

"Where's Harry?" Mallory asked. She supposed Emma's mother would be appalled.

"He has appointments he can't change. He's as distressed as I am. Brian Munroe is a nice young man. I always thought his wife was too."

"I'm sure they are, Margery. Children constantly surprise us. I'll go up, shall I?"

"Oh, *please*," Margery exhorted. "I'm just so grateful you're here."

Mallory made her way up the stairs. The layout of the house was well known to her. She stopped outside Ivy's door, tapped gently on it. No little voice answered her. She called the child's name again and then slowly opened the door to a spacious room decorated with pretty chintzes and a lovely wallpaper featuring flowers and birds. Mercifully, the door hadn't been locked. Margery had shown presence of mind and extracted the key in case Ivy took it into her head to lock everyone out.

Ivy was lying rigid on the full-sized bed, face to the wall, her knees drawn up against her stomach, arms folded tight around her like she was holding herself together. Somehow it was reminiscent of her mother.

"Ivy?" Mallory spoke very gently. "It's only me, Mally. I didn't want you to be alone. May I come and sit on your bed?"

Ivy's voice was little more than a whisper. "Yes, Mally."

Mallory's heart melted. She skirted the end of the bed, sitting down by Ivy's side. She waited a moment before gathering the child into her arms.

"Where's Mummy?" Ivy asked, tears starting to pour down her face. "Where is she?"

Mallory gently lowered her head over the child's, rubbing her back. "I know this is a very sad time for you, Ivy. My mother died when I was about your age, so I know. Your mummy died too, Ivy. You know that. She had become very sad. A great many people have these sad feelings, and though they try very hard, those feelings won't go away. It's important you remember Mummy loved you with all her heart. You were the most important person in the world to her. Only she wasn't strong enough to live with her pain. That means she was finding it harder and harder to feel happy."

"I know why!" Ivy drew back in a sudden fit of anger. "Daddy didn't love her. He doesn't love me. Aunt Jessy hated Mummy. She hates me." The child spat like a cat. "Mummy said life wasn't worth living with Aunty Jessy around."

The truth and nothing but the truth.

Mallory looked around for a box of tissues. She saw one and handed it to Ivy. "Here you are, love. Wipe your face now. That's a good girl. No matter how much Mummy tried, she needed help. We all need help at different times. Never be afraid to ask for help. You must learn early to talk about the things that are troubling you. Your grandparents love you."

"I know, but they're not Mummy," Ivy said mournfully, making full use of the pink tissues. "I don't really know them yet. Emma, one of the kids in my class, said Mummy gave me poison to drink. That's why I was sick all the time."

Mallory looked at the child with grave, steady eyes. "Children make things up, Ivy. Things they might remember ever after with shame. Emma could have got herself into a lot of trouble with her parents. I'm sure they were shocked and mortified. But tell me, what did you usually drink?"

"Mummy gave me milk with Milo. It always tastes nice. Aunt Jessy was the one who gave me nasty drinks, especially the purple one, the blackcurrant juice. She used to stand and watch me drink it so I wouldn't spit it out. Some days Mummy put lemonade with it to make it taste better. Mummy loved me."

"Of course she did, Ivy." Mallory hugged the child. "You were her sun, moon, and stars . She's not here now, but she would want you to have a good life, wouldn't she? She wouldn't want you to be unhappy. She wanted you to grow up with good feelings. She knew your grandparents would look after you. They love you."

"So where's Daddy?" Ivy's blue eyes were blazing. "Why doesn't he come to see me? I don't want to see Aunt Jessy. I'd scream the place down. You have to promise me Aunt Jessy won't come here, Mally."

"Aunt Jessy *won't* be coming, Ivy. I won't allow it. Your grandparents won't allow it. Above all they want you to feel loved and settled. As for your father, you have to remember he is very sad too."

Ivy's expression said plainly she didn't believe it. "He never took much notice of me, until he got mad. The only one he took any notice of was Aunt Jessy. He loves *her* all right."

"She is his sister, Ivy." Mallory felt she had to point that out. "His twin."

"I'm glad I'm not a twin," Ivy said in a disgusted voice. "It's scary. Daddy and Aunt Jessy won't miss

Mummy. I bet they don't even care she died." This time there was outrage on Ivy's small face.

"They do care, Ivy, in their own way," Mallory said. "Not your way. Not my way. Not your grandparents' way, but they have their own feelings and their own problems."

"I hope they die too," Ivy said, the picture of wrath. "I don't want to go back to school. Not ever. Emma *was* telling lies just like you said. Mummy would never hurt me."

"Of course not. She loved you. I don't think there'll be a problem with your staying home for a while longer, but you have to keep up with your lessons."

"I hate lessons," Ivy said mulishly.

"You're smart. Put your mind to it. Keep saying, 'I'm going to do this for Mummy.' She believed in you. I do too, Ivy. So do your grandparents. When your father is feeling better he will want to see you."

"Do I have to go home with him and look after him?" Tears of anguish spurted.

"No, Ivy. It's his job to look after you," Mallory said gently. "We just have to wait until the time is right."

Ivy blew her nose loudly. "Mummy said Daddy's not normal. What does that mean?"

"Normal means behaving well with the people around us, Ivy. Take school. Children are expected to do what you're told by your teachers. You're expected to pay attention in class. You don't call out to one another. Ignore the teacher. Jump up and walk around the classroom."

"That's not normal, right? Daddy wasn't kind to Mummy. Aunt Jessy used to snarl at her like Mrs. Finlay's pit bull terrier. Mrs. Finlay isn't supposed to have it, you know. A couple of times it got out and

bit a chunk out of Mr. Finlay when he tried to get it
back. Some of the kids are nasty to my friend, Wally,
and make fun of him, but I like him."

"Bullying is bad, Ivy. It's something to be ashamed
of. Bullying is cowardly. Wally might be a little slow
with his lessons, but he's probably very good at something else."

"Yes, he is," said Ivy, wisely nodding her head. "Wally
can draw. He draws the most beautiful frogs. His baby
frogs are adorable."

Her presence had definitely calmed Ivy. Mallory
stayed for an hour, encouraging Ivy to confide in her,
drawing out all her worrying thoughts. What was
saving Ivy, very mature for her age, was the fact she
had already developed a thick skin. At the tender age
of six, Ivy was far less fragile than her mother had been.
*Having an aunt like Jessica Cartwright would toughen
any kid up.*

"We must go downstairs now to see Nanna," Mallory said eventually, holding out a hand. "Don't worry
about going back to school for the moment, Ivy. If
you work hard, you won't fall behind. I'm counting
on you to do that."

"I'll try real hard for you and Mummy." Ivy made a
solemn promise. "Can I come over to Moonglade to
see you?"

"Of course you can. Nanna will arrange it."

"Nanna can't cook fairy cakes like Mrs. R.," Ivy said
regretfully, then brightened. "But she's pretty good
with sausages and rissoles. Nanna always smells lovely.
I smell lovely too. And I have lovely clothes. Nanna

and Poppa love me, don't they?" Ivy raised her bright blue eyes.

"Yes, they do, Ivy."

"I see Mummy, you know."

"Do you?" Mallory asked gently, unsurprised.

"I don't speak about it, but I do. I don't want to frighten Nanna. And you know what?"

"I think I do, Ivy," Mallory said. "She sees you."

Ivy's little face shone. "I knew you'd know, Mally, 'cause you're a skycrist. Did you see your mummy after she went to heaven?"

Mallory squeezed Ivy's hand. "For you and for me, Ivy and for countless others, our mothers will never die. They're alive inside our hearts and our heads."

"Isn't that lovely!"

Mallory had the feeling this little girl would be one of those fortunate individuals who would go through life with a controlling hand on the rudder. But Ivy would need ongoing counselling. It would be absolutely necessary. She was very grateful she was well placed to do it.

Downstairs again, Ivy ran to her anxiously waiting grandmother. "Mally says it's all right. We can go over to Moonglade when we want to, Nanna. I'll get Mrs. R. to write down her recipe for fairy cakes. Is that okay?"

Margery Cartwright's anxious expression turned to a shaky smile of relief. She found Mallory's eyes over Ivy's head. They were alight with gratitude. "Of course it is, sweetheart."

"From now on I'm going to ask everyone to call me Evie," the little girl announced. "It's got a nice sound to it. Everyone must call me Evie from now on. Mummy never liked Ivy. She said I came by it by way of Aunt Jessy. Mummy will be happy with Evie." The little girl turned to look directly at Mallory. "What do *you* say, Mally?"

Mallory had recovered from her surprise. "If that's what you want, Evie, it is. I'm sure Nanna agrees."

So Ivy became Evie, increasingly Eve, with no fuss whatever.

She knew she had died. Or her body had died, but that was okay. She didn't need it anymore. She was doing just fine without it. She wasn't lonely. There were others drifting around with her, the ones, like her, who had reasons to keep them connected to the other life. She didn't know exactly what dimension they were in. She didn't care. Care had left her. She had never experienced anything like this wondrous state of calm. She had never been surrounded by an aura, a smoky white substance that framed her and all her airborne companions.

She didn't think they were angels No one had wings. It wasn't important to be an angel anyway. They all wore similar garments as misty as the clouds they were floating around in. All of them were waiting, waiting for something to happen to send them onwards. None of them had voices, yet they all knew what the others were thinking. All of them had stories. Stories of what had happened to them when they were living, breathing human beings.

Now they were souls in transit. They all had questions that needed answers. That was essential before they could move to the next level. She had to have Mallory's help. She had to make Mallory understand. Mallory had greater powers than she knew.

* * *

The dreams kept coming as visions. She always woke with the visions clear in her mind; Kathy dressed in a long white transparency to cover her nakedness. Kathy who drew closer and closer, bending over her, until their faces were almost touching.

At that point with a great lurch of her heart Mallory always woke up. Her dreams were too compelling not to have *real* purpose. Her job was to find out what that was. Blaine, her great strength and solace, lent calm to her, in body and mind. Blaine was always *there* for her. He was her psychological escape hatch.

As he was leaving the house the following morning, Mallory mentioned a plan she had in an offhand way that she knew wouldn't fool him for a minute. "I think I'll take a look around the bungalow today."

"Instigate a thorough search, don't you mean? Couldn't it wait until I get home?"

"You think I'll take off without you?"

"I surely do. We'll both go over this evening. It's as I told you. There's nothing there, Mallory. We could let the foreman and his wife have the bungalow. What do you think?"

"Best to wait until things settle. Kathy's suicide has unnerved the whole town."

"God, yes!" he agreed. "Quite a few are feeling guilty about how they treated Kathy in the past. Wouldn't you think Jason would have the decency to come home? And why do you suppose we're all finding it easy to call Ivy, Evie?" His tone had changed to wry amusement.

"It suits her better. Besides, I think being called Ivy reminded our newly christened Evie of bad things."

"Like what?" Concern darkened his dynamic face.

"Secrets. Things shoved to the back of her mind. God knows what she saw or heard. It's quite extraordinary how children can suppress memories that frighten them. They hide them well away. I've seen too much of it, the bad things children suppress. But sometimes fragments come back in dreams."

"That poor kid! God knows what she had to deal with."

"She's tough," Mallory said, with pride and affection.

"She'll have to be. Rumour has it the twins are staying with Jessica's hippy friends, the Volkers."

Mallory had a sudden vision of greyish white fungi lighting the forest floor. "Jessica had purple stains on her fingers at Uncle Robert's wake."

"Maybe soap's a luxury at Jessica's place," Blaine said.

"A violent purple stain." Mallory wasn't distracted. "Like mulberries, but much harder to clean off, apparently. Jessica is supposed to be something of an authority on rainforest plants. The Volkers too."

"What are you getting at?" Blaine stared down at her.

"It wasn't Kathy who was making Evie sick."

"You're saying Jessica is behind all the illness both Evie and Kathy experienced? Much as I dislike Jessica Cartwright, I have difficulty accepting she harmed her own niece."

"I've reviewed the whole situation. Jessica has monstrous traits."

"But *why* would she do it? What could she hope to

achieve? She wanted Evie out of the way? I'd have trouble with that."

"I believe Jessica wanted *Kathy* out of the way. Haven't you ever heard of good old-fashioned wickedness? Jessica got rid of me."

"For which we should both go down on our knees. This is all conjecture, Mallory. You're making quantum leaps."

"I realize it's only conjecture, but Kathy won't let me rest."

Blaine remained a man out of his depth. "Kathy's dead, Mallory. Her short, unhappy life is over. Robert's dying and then Kathy's suicide coming on top of it would unsettle the strongest nerves."

Mallory shook her head. "My nerves are fine. You mustn't think they aren't. I have to see this through."

"And nothing and no one on earth is going to stop you?"

Her mouth tilted up. "*Your* job is to stay on side while I put the wrongs right."

He held her by the shoulders, shook her gently. "Just remember I won't allow you to make yourself a buffer between this world and the next." It was the only response he *could* make.

"I'm on the side of Light, Blaine," she explained, smiling up at him. "So off to work."

"I want to stay at home," he muttered.

"You can't stay at home." Her whisper was a little ragged.

"Why not?" He slid his arms around her.

"Don't tempt me."

The hot blood was rushing. She could feel herself catching fire. In another second she'd forget they both had work to do. Resolutely she put her hands against his chest, pushing him away. "Off you go."

He caught hold of her again. Kissed her. "I'll be back. Meanwhile try to keep out of trouble, if you possibly can."

The rain, patchy at dawn, increased throughout the morning. Mallory waited for a break. Storm clouds had spread massive dark wings over the plantation. From time to time radiant white light split the bruised sky, robbing the world of colour. When the rain came, it poured hail, firing down like silver bullets on the house, the gardens, and the lawns. The break didn't come until around lunch, though she suspected the blue canals that cut through the waterlogged grey skies wouldn't last for long.

She made herself a sandwich and a cup of coffee, after which she intended to go over to the bungalow. Blaine had rung mid-morning, fully suspecting she wouldn't wait for his return that evening. He knew her sleuthing instincts. They spoke for a few moments before he had to go, but she didn't reveal her intentions. She knew he wouldn't be back until 6.30 p.m. at the earliest. She couldn't wait that long.

A raincoat with a hood served the purpose. She didn't bother about an umbrella. If the wind picked up, it could blow an umbrella inside out.

It was truly amazing how the plant life, the flowers, the trees, the very leaves, responded prolifically to the rain. Native lilies were shooting up everywhere and all the nectar-eating birds, the honey eaters, and the brilliantly plumaged lorikeets were out revelling in the stormy weather. The very air vibrated with the whirr of wings. Nature was signalling the big Wet was coming. On the banks of the tropical rivers the "salties," the saltwater crocodiles, would nest, building mounds of vegetation in which to lay their eggs. Unfortunately, the male crocodile took great delight in eating its young.

No fatherly feelings there.

She hadn't heard a word from her father. She didn't expect to. There was too much angst between them.

The first thing she noticed was the front door was unlocked. She had thought they had all the keys, but someone had obviously been inside. She overcame a reluctance to go in. Had Blaine had forgotten to lock the door? It didn't seem likely.

Not for the first time she thought she would buy a couple of large dogs. State-of-the-art security was one thing; she liked the idea of guard dogs. Two German shepherds to keep one another company. They were splendid animals and very protective.

She was aware her heartbeat had picked up substantially. One would have thought she'd been on a three-kilometre run. She put her head cautiously around the door, calling out, "Hello, anyone there?"

Do ghosts hang around in the daytime?

Her voice left no echo. She might not have called out at all. Yet nothing could have been louder than the *silence*.

What am I going to do if someone answers?

She marshalled resolve. She stepped across the threshold, feeling as though she had stepped across the portal to another world. She threw off her wet raincoat, shaking raindrops from her hair. The air was chill. She had become used to that. The chill overcame the heat and high humidity. The air vibrated not with hostility but with a kind of psychic pain. Sweltering only a minute before, now *this*. Inside, the bungalow was preternaturally quiet, except for the wind moaning outside and rattling a few windows.

Gathering her wits, she began to move around, feeling she wasn't alone. It was a feeling she had experienced many, many times before. She had come to think of it as a split in reality, showing her not one but *two* worlds. If she was accompanied by a presence, she knew it wasn't going to harm her. The answer would be here.

The rain was coming down in sheets, turning the world an opaque grey. She turned on a few lights. She didn't recognise any of the furniture. There was nothing surprising about that. The interior was casually furnished, with a new open plan layout. The kitchen was set galley style along one wall with bar stools tucked under the black granite-topped bench. A sturdy pine dining table with four chairs around it had been positioned near the window. Comfortable seating was in the way of a large sofa and two matching armchairs, all facing the television. A tall bookcase held colourful paperbacks, half as many hardbacks, autobiographies, garden books, cookbooks, and some very good pieces of local pottery. It was the first time she had been inside the bungalow since Uncle Robert had had it transformed from the old country cottage to a modern dwelling. Uncle Robert had been a very kind and generous man. Only he had visited the terrible twins upon her.

The hallway led to the bedrooms and the bathroom.

Modernizing changes had been made there as well. The main bedroom now boasted a small en suite. Across the hall was the family bathroom. Jessica had her own apartment in town, but where did she sleep when she stayed over? From all accounts Jessica had stayed over a lot. The hall light wasn't working, turning the corridor into a murky underworld. She moved quickly into the main bedroom, switching on the light as she entered. Again she had the sensation someone had swished in with her. Another puff of cold air brushed her nape. She never had been able to do anything about her operatic imagination. "Supernormal intuitions" a colleague had once claimed she had. The way such knowledge gathered in her even she found strange. Was a presence with her?

A double bed, Asian chest at the bottom of it; two bedside tables with pale green shades on the lamps, to match the pale green and cream bedspread and the curtains at the windows. A large print of Van Gogh's *Vase with Fifteen Sunflowers*. She had seen the original in the National Gallery in London, so much more than a portrait of flowers, more floral sculptures wrought by the world's greatest jeweller. There was a niche for books. She would have a look at them after she finished going through the house.

In one of the spare bedrooms were twin single beds with a Queen Anne chintz for bedspreads, cushions, and curtains, a small cupboard holding a lamp separating them. In the other was a single bed with a charming wallpaper of yellow daffodils growing under sun-dappled trees and a sunshine yellow quilt. This was Evie's room. Both rooms were the same size, different only in the furnishings. No secretaires with secret compartments, no desks, bookcases only.

The family bathroom was attractively tiled in blue
and white, and had a bath and a shower cubicle, long
counter with two porcelain washbasins, medicine
chest above it. Everything was clean and tidy.

She would make her start here. The cabinet yielded
the usual contents. She shifted things about, looking
at all the labels: shampoo, conditioner, eye drops,
Listerine, moisturizing lotion, antiseptic cream, a still-
packaged tube of toothpaste, and a four-pack of soap.
Two small bottles with the labels removed, one with a
dark blue glass, the other purple. Nail polish? The
bottles were the right size. She knew dark colours
were in fashion, only she couldn't recall ever seeing
either Kathy or Jessica wearing nail polish. For one
thing Kathy's nails had been bitten down to the quick.
It had to be Jessica's nail lacquers when she was out
on a Goth evening.

Mallory was shutting the cabinet door when there
was a sudden shrill scream in her ear that drenched
her in an icy sweat. Ice was cold. It could also *burn*.

*Take the bottles with you, Mallory. Take them. You
must. Gather them up. Don't leave them.*

*It was important she get through. Floating from
side to side, she half circled the living woman. Only
she could feel herself dimming. She couldn't always
retain the brightness. Daylight drained her.*

For the next forty minutes Mallory searched the
bungalow thoroughly: wardrobes, bookcases, fanning
books in case something was lodged between the
pages. There was a collection of books, fiction and
non-fiction: very surprisingly a well-worn copy of
Nabokov's *Lolita*, a stack of romance paperbacks—

poor love-starved Kathy—books on the Great Barrier
Reef, the Daintree, the Queensland Rainforest,
Australian native plants. No books on poisons. Sev-
eral very tattered books dating from the 1940s on
tropical diseases and preventive medicines by Queens-
land's own Sir Raphael Cilento, father of Diane
Cilento, the famous actress who had been married to
Sean Connery.

The pantry was next. There were poisons inside
every pantry. A toxic substance would have shown up
in the blood tests that had been run on the then
malnourished Evie. She had been found to be defi-
cient in the C vitamin, some B vitamins, and calcium,
but not the D vitamin with Queensland's abundant
sunshine.

Ingestion of anything under the kitchen sink
would have resulted in dire consequences and been
easily identifiable. The interior of the fridge smelled
slightly rank, the culprit a half block of cheese
turning mouldy. She pulled it out to dispose of it.
Tomatoes, a cucumber, a couple of avocadoes, and a
lettuce in the crisper, two large bottles of soft drink
on the inside door, and at the back of one of the
shelves a bottle of blackcurrant syrup, a rich source
of vitamin C.

She was about to leave with the most likely harm-
less blackcurrant juice stowed in a plastic bag she
found in a kitchen drawer when she experienced a
ringing in her ear that caused her to stop and shake
her head from side to side. The sound was like a bell
rung under water. She couldn't ignore it. It was
making her so dizzy she felt like she might fall to the
floor. Even her skull was tingling. She tried to steady
herself, breathing in deeply. Without knowing or

understanding why, she felt compelled to go back to the bathroom.

With barrel after barrel of rainwater cascading over the roof, the bathroom was engulfed in gloom. She didn't stop to snap on the light. There was just enough illumination. She glanced in the mirror above the washbasin. She looked extremely tense. A woman on a mission. Quickly she withdrew the nail lacquers from the medicine cabinet, setting them down on the counter. She picked up the purple one, remembering the purple stains on Jessica's hands, holding it shoulder high and shaking it vigorously.

The contents couldn't be nail polish. They were sloshing liquid. She uncapped a bottle with some caution, sniffing the contents, finding the small brush used to apply varnish had been completely removed, if it had ever been there. There was no label to tell her what the bottles had once contained. She placed her forefinger over the top, allowing a dribble of the glistening purplish contents to come out. She touched the finger to her mouth, tasting the concoction—whatever it was—with the tip of her tongue. Actually it didn't taste all that bad. Fruity, but extremely tart so that her tongue puckered. A fruit juice concentrate in a tiny bottle? What could be weirder than that? It had to be a concentrate. Perhaps a very powerful one. It would be palatable enough in a glass of cold water with a teaspoon or so of sugar. She put the cap back on, stowing the two small bottles in the bag. Quickly she left the room.

Good, Mallory, good. In the gloom she was able to circle Mallory more quickly, closing in on her, with

always that unbridgeable space between them. She had
willed Mallory to heed her. She knew Mallory was able
to sense her. It was a communion most living beings
would find incomprehensible. Not Mallory. Mallory
heard voices no one else could. Mallory saw things no
one else could. She continued to see her mother through
all the long years. Her own little daughter saw her but
it would only be for a very short time. Then the
window would close. She draped the edge of her
transparency over Mallory's shoulder. Mallory could
do what she could no longer do. Mallory would act
as her earthly agent.

The shrill sound inside her head mercifully had
stopped, but the tension inside her body wasn't abat-
ing. As she closed the bungalow door Mallory felt
the same swishing sensation as before. Someone had
come in with her. Someone was leaving with her. She
didn't feel fear. But she did feel curiously weak.
What's real and what's not real?
My idol, Einstein, didn't know.
Do spirits frequent the border regions of black holes?
She didn't have an answer.
The rain was accompanied by flashes of incandes-
cent lightning and drum rolls of thunder. It swept in
from the sea like an army on the march. The enraged
wind had picked up to the point when it was howling
like a wild beast from the jungle threatening to pounce.
The air smelled green, green, green, oozing with
ozone. No fresher scent than the scent of rain. So
great was the wind's force, Mallory had a job making
the journey back to the house without being blown
off her feet.

Finally she was back at the house, closing the front door behind her, locking it in case the beast tried to get in. Nothing had come in with her. She was quite alone. She wasn't frightened of the storm, fierce as it was. She had lived through countless tropical storms. She had lived through cyclones. The house had always stood firm though she remembered many a tree being blown over, palm trees stripped of their great fronds, blossoms in multiple colours thickly carpeting the soaked lawns. She remembered with great sadness Blaine's father had lost his life in the aftermath of a great cyclonic storm. Even in paradise there were dangers.

Once the storm passed, the phone rang. Mallory ran to it quickly. No one answered a phone in an electrical storm; consequently no one in the town made phone calls at such times unless it was an emergency. As it turned out, it pretty much was.

"It's not over yet." Blaine made short work of giving her the news. "Everything is going to hell in a wheelbarrow. Declan Burch went after Jason again. He heard on the grapevine Jason was up in the Daintree. So he took after him. I've just had a call from the police. Declan has been arrested for assault and Jessica has disappeared."

"God, I thought I could only take one catastrophe at a time," Mallory groaned. "Knowing Jessica, why would she disappear? I would have thought she would have insisted on accompanying Jason to hospital, to sit by his bed, stroking his hand. I assume he's been taken to hospital?"

"He has," Blaine confirmed, not sounding at all sympathetic. "He took a beating but Declan isn't in great shape either. Declan did manage to break Jason's nose, blacken his eyes, and knock a couple of his teeth out."

Mallory was running on empty. "Considering what Declan could have done, it's not all that bad. He could have killed him. So where *is* Jessica? She must be having a major episode of some kind."

"According to Carl Volker, he broke up the fight by firing off his rifle—I hope he's got a licence for it—Jessica simply took off, heading for the jungle. Sergeant Dailey's understanding is Jason and Jessica had a huge argument."

"About what?"

"Can't help you there. Carl Volker said they'd never heard Jessica in a full-blown rant before. He thought she could have been on something. Apparently she was out of control."

"So Jessica takes drugs?"

"I really don't know what Jessica Cartwright takes," said Blaine, his tone grim. "If she does, the Volkers are probably her suppliers."

"Or she cooks them up herself. Is anyone going into the jungle to fetch her?"

"Well, she's in no danger," Blaine said. He didn't really care. "She knows the area well. She's done nothing wrong but display a degree of crackpottedness even Volker noticed. He said he would go after her and bring her back."

"I take it the Cartwrights have been told?" Mallory asked, wondering if that might miraculously prompt a reconciliation.

"They have. It's about time this family feud was

over," Blaine said tersely. "I bet you went over to the bungalow?"

"How do you know?"

"Just a wild guess."

"Nothing there, as you said."

Except a couple of little bottles containing unknown substances.

Chapter Nine

She thought it might help if she visited Jason in the hospital. He might tell her something useful. When she arrived, she found Jason barely recognisable. Indeed he looked so bad Mallory had to turn away with a sick gulp. Beyond the injuries that would take time to mend, two of his once perfect teeth would need replacing. Jason had been gutted in more ways than one.

"I never expected to see you here, Mallory." He stared up at her through rainbow-coloured, badly swollen eyelids. "I didn't start out a bastard, did I?" he asked with more than a hint of self-pity.

"You didn't, but you certainly allowed yourself to be derailed. And you've paid the price."

"I'll be paying the rest of my life. That bastard Burch knocked my bloody teeth out, did you see? I've always had good teeth."

"Indeed you did, Jason. Good enough to sell toothpaste. You'll need crowns." The lesson had been brutal but Jason had had it coming.

"What the hell does it matter? My life has gone to hell."

"*You* still have a life," Mallory reminded him grimly.

"Look, I'm not bringing any charges against Burch," he said, with a show of magnanimity. "I guess I had it coming."

"Hard to disagree."

"All right, I did." His blue eyes looked wild. "He's a bit of a mess too."

"Have you seen your parents?"

His head pressed back into the pillow. "I've seen Mum." He grimaced painfully. "The old man doesn't want to lay eyes on me."

"So what are you going to do? You'll be discharged later on in the day, I believe."

Jason made fevered eye contact. "Can I ask a great favour of you, Mallory? Can I go back to the bungalow until at least the worst of the bruises fade? Mum and I have agreed she'll keep Ivy until I'm able to get my life in order."

Part of her felt pity. Part of her felt a stunned amazement. She knew Blaine would be far from happy if she said yes. Where was the justification?

"Have you heard from Jessica?"

Jason spoke with an uncharacteristic anger towards his twin. "I want Jess out of my life. All she's done is screw it up."

"She's been doing that for most of your life, Jason, yet you still kept returning to her."

"I can't seem to get away." He blew air slowly through his swollen lips. "Once Jess gets her claws into you, she won't let go. You wouldn't understand. I guess most people wouldn't."

"You're dead right!" Mallory felt ill she had ever

become involved with Jason. "I had no idea about you and Jessica, Jason. I never thought such a thing remotely possible. I just hope to God you weren't with Jessica when we were engaged," she said, her stomach churning.

He rid her of her fears. "I wasn't. I swear. You were everything to me. Please forgive me, Mallory. You were a miracle. The answer to my prayers."

"I can't forgive you for all you've done, Jason. I never will."

"That's because you don't *understand*," he cried. "You with all your training, your insights into human nature, and you still don't understand. Jess and I were entwined in the womb. Is it so unnatural to be bonded to your twin? We did make pacts to disentangle."

"You mean *you* made a pact to get out of a hellish situation, but Jessica wouldn't let you go."

"She loves me, Mallory," he pleaded. "We're two peas in a pod. We didn't ask we be like this."

"You weren't like this until Jessica seduced you into it," Mallory flashed back. "You've suffered for it. You're still suffering and the suffering will go on until you fight your way clear."

"Call it mind control, Mallory," he said, sounding utterly miserable. "Nothing changes. Love. Hate. Fear. Jealousy."

"Taboo makes it all the more delectable, is that it? The excitement of the *wrongness*. Sex, the drug of choice. Then the shame. And you are ashamed, aren't you? You want to stop. You *must* stop. Heaven is watching, Jason."

Jason put up a hand to cover his battered face.

"Heaven? Where the hell is that? Whatever is between Jess and me, *it just is.*"

Mallory could only feel sorrow. "One hell of a sick shock for your parents."

Jason lifted a hand. "I would have given anything for our secret not to be discovered. But it was. I want you to know I loved *you*, Mallory. I was true to you. I wanted marriage. I wanted children. It felt so good being with you. You're so strong. I would have been anything you wanted me to be. I was desperate for my life to change."

Mallory shook her head in disbelief. "So you got Kathy Burch pregnant. You figured that was the way to go?"

Jason put his badly bruised hands together. The knuckles were a red mess. "It took a long time for me to remember, Mallory, but it was all Jess's doing. I knew deep down she was there somewhere on the night. Since you spoke to me that time, I've been pounding my brain trying to remember. Then I started to get flashes. I tried to talk to Jess about it, but she denied everything. Then when I tackled her at the Volkers place, she reacted like a savage. She actually attacked me, screaming abuse. Right in front of my eyes Jess flipped. She drugged us, Kathy and me. Jess had it all planned."

"Of course she did," Mallory said with a calm that covered tremendous upset. "At least you got her to finally admit it?"

"Sure." He jabbed the air. "Jess has done a lot of things."

"Oh?"

"A lot of things," he repeated, not about to say any more.

"Do me a favour here, Jason. Did that include doping your child?"

That remark roused him. He drew a breath so harsh blood trickled from under his taped up nose. "She would *never* do that. Ivy is my daughter. Jess is her aunt."

"Some aunt! You just said it. Jess is capable of anything."

Jason flew to his twin's defence. "It was poor messed-up Kathy. Jess didn't count on Kathy getting pregnant. Kathy was just a means to an end, to get rid of *you*. You were the big danger. Kathy harmed our child. It's common knowledge. All determined."

"Only I don't buy it. Right now Jessica is *my* suspect."

"Then you're mad! Too stubborn for your own good. Kathy was under a helluva lot of stress."

"She'd endured a lifetime of abuse, as we all knew. She wasn't strong and she wasn't getting any help. There are many factors that go towards pushing a vulnerable person to their death; being unloved and unwanted, being treated with contempt, being locked into a situation that must have shocked her. She caught you out, didn't she?"

Jason tried to raise his head off the pillow, let it fall back with a groan. "Doesn't this smack of *your* jealousy of Jess?" he asked, astounding her. "So Jess has a predilection for causing trouble, but she would never hurt Ivy."

"That's Evie, by the way," Mallory corrected. "Ivy that was, wishes to be known henceforth as Evie."

"Ivy's a pretty enough name."

Mallory let that go. "So is Jessica hiding out, or is she out there collecting poisonous fungi while raging at the trees?"

Jason's battered body spoke of outrage. "I don't know where Jess is and I wouldn't tell you if I did. You can be sure of one thing. Jess knows how to look after herself. Kathy had a rendezvous with death, Mallory. Maybe from when she was a kid. It's hard to even remember her now. I can't even summon up her face."

Mallory stood up, sick to her stomach. "You'd remember had you seen her broken body at the base of the cliffs, Jason. You're a pitiful excuse for a man. I was the one who found her. Not you or your appallingly cruel sister. Cruelty always was infinitely more pleasurable to Jessica than kindness."

"Finding Kathy must have been awful for you, Mallory," he said, in a choked voice. "But think about it. Had Kathy lived she would have been charged with that Munchausen thing. Jess explained it all to me. Kathy was guilty. I know you liked the poor little pinhead, but she was a tormented creature."

"As are you." Mallory spoke with icy contempt. "As is your sister. Your torment isn't over. I wouldn't like to be either of you. There is such a thing as karmic justice. You have a week to recuperate at the bungalow, Jason. Be in no doubt that if Jessica turns up, both of you will be moved on by the police."

"Why would you need the police?" Jason was back to sneering. "You've got the great Lord Protector Forrester there to hold your hand. Forrester has always wanted you, even when he was engaged to that stuck-up Selma. Forrester always gets what he wants. He was dead set against me. That's because he wanted *you*. He just had to wait."

"It was you spying on us that night we were walking along the cliff front?" Mallory asked.

"What night?" He sniffed back blood.

Mallory passed him tissues that were quickly soaked. "It *was* you, Jason. Perhaps I should change my mind about allowing you the use of the bungalow."

Jason's head fell back on the pillows. He looked a total disaster. "Do it for old times' sake, Mallory. Did you have any *real* feelings for me?" he asked, with the strangest look on his face. "You never wanted sex."

"How glad I am of that fact. I did have considerable affection for you, Jason. I thought it was love. It wasn't. Our marriage would have gone ahead as planned."

"Only Jess didn't want it." He spoke as though Jess always knew best. "Jess can't share, I'm afraid."

On the drive into town, Mallory considered how Blaine might react to her hospital visit. She could call into his offices, although there was a possibility he could be over at the Pelican Point project. She decided not to ring ahead, in case he put her on the spot and asked how her visit with Jason went. She could feel a build-up of tension playing havoc with her body. Was she as easily swayed as her uncle, trying to ease Jason's lot?

There was a parking spot right outside the pharmacy. As chance would have it, her admirer, eagle-eyed Colin Watson, spied her and gave her an enthusiastic wave. She and Colin had become buddies without any contribution from her. As a concession she returned the wave, and then headed off to the Forrester Enterprises building, which also housed the district's legal fraternity.

The receptionist, Susan, an attractive young woman, gave her a bright smile, telling her Mr. Forrester was in. She would ring through. She seemed very pleased to see Mallory. Mallory knew rumour was running rife around town. There could very well be a serious romance afoot. She suspected the whole office was abuzz with it.

Blaine's spacious office had all the trappings of success. Floor to ceiling mahogany cabinets, furnishings, lighting, two very fine Oriental area rugs positioned over the pale beige carpet, one very fine tropical landscape dominating the far wall. He picked up the phone to organise coffee. He didn't retreat behind his impressive desk. He gestured towards one of the leather armchairs in the seating area. A glass-topped coffee table stood in front of the sofa.

"So how did your visit with Jason go?" he asked smoothly, bending to kiss her cheek.

"You're psychic. There, I've proved it." She leaned back.

"Not psychic. I know *you*, Mallory." His tone was light, laconic.

"I thought I might get something out of him," she said, her dark eyes hooded.

"Like what?"

"News of Jessica maybe?"

"I'm going to have to take your word for it, Mallory."

"He's very beaten up," she remarked.

Blaine gave a hard laugh. "Declan doesn't look too crash hot either. Kathy had to bear the dead weight of her dysfunctional family all her life. They moved much too late to help her. They have to live with that now." He broke off at a tap on the door. "That'll be the coffee."

Mallory poured. She passed a cup to Blaine, dwelling

on the elegant shape of his hands. She loved those hands on her face, on her body. No one had ever touched her like Blaine. His touch was tender, demanding, passionate, and always deeply loving.

"So what is it you have to tell me?" Blaine sat back, his eyes moving with great pleasure over her. Today she was wearing a simple white dress that was absorbing adjacent colours. It reminded him of a Vermeer painting. "I hope it's not anything to cause me alarm. Like promising Jason he can recuperate at the farm?"

Mallory took a long sip at her coffee. "Very good coffee. Rich and strong."

"Let's get back to Cartwright," he responded, giving her a searching look.

"He looked so pitiful."

Blaine put his coffee cup down so hard it rattled in the saucer. "Just tell me."

Mallory's heart started to trip hammer. "I told him he could stay on for a week to recuperate. Any sign of Jessica and they'd both be out."

Blaine shook his head in disbelief. "I simply can't have that worry on my mind. I don't want the Cartwrights anywhere near you. Robb's good intentions backfired, remember? It could be exactly the same for you."

"He can't convalesce at home. His father won't have it. His mother has been to see him."

"Well, mothers are mothers," said Blaine. "I'll attend to this." He sounded absolutely unyielding.

"And let you find him a nice dry jail cell?"

Blaine ignored her remark. "I'll arrange accommodations for him. I'll even have food brought in, in case he's too sensitive to show his battered face."

"Where?" she asked.

"No need for you to know," he returned, his tone crisp. "Jason can stay there until he feels ready to move on. I'll even have him picked up at the hospital and taken there."

"I have to be thankful," she said.

"Yes, you do. End of story."

In the heart of town people were walking to and fro, in and out of shops and down the main street. The baking heat was bouncing off the concrete and glinting off the chrome on the line-up of vehicles, mostly sports utility vehicles. Mallory was in her car, seat belt on, ready to turn on the engine, when someone opened the passenger door and darted in beside her, bringing a strong whiff of body odour overlaid by an odd cloying smell like decaying leaves.

Her heart seized up as if she'd received an electric shock. Events were careening out of control.

"Well I'll be darned, the very woman I want to see." Jessica with her blinding orange aura was clearly relishing the fright she had given Mallory. "How are you, Princess? I've been stalking you, by the way. I'm very good at it."

"Get out of my car, Jessica." Mallory issued the blunt order.

"But I've only just arrived." Jessica spoke like a woman who had successfully pulled off a hijacking. It was apparent she had been living rough. She indicated with a downward flick of her eyes the dark wooden handle of what looked like a hunting knife standing upright in her scuffed leather bag. "Drive on if you would please."

"Why would I do that?" Mallory knew she couldn't show any fear. "Am I supposed to be afraid of you?"

Jessica's head went rigid, like a snake about to strike. "If you've got half a fuckin' brain, yes."

Again Mallory showed no reaction. "I'm not going anywhere, Jessica. Get out of this car before I blare the horn. That will get people running."

For answer Jessica slid the knife out of her bag. Mahogany handle, high quality steel blade about six or seven inches long. A curve to it. A knife to cut through flesh, sinew, right to the bone. In one deft movement she made an exploratory jab into Mallory's side. Blood spurted.

"Aaah!" Mallory's heart did a complete somersault in her chest. She considered screaming for help, only her mouth was so dry her tongue was sticking to its roof. The point had sliced through the fabric of her dress and the side of her bra before piercing her skin. She bit down hard on the inside of her lip, determined not to let another cry escape her. Psychopaths loved inflicting pain. But Mallory was her mother's daughter, fierce and brave.

"Unpleasant being at close quarters with a knife, don't you think?" Jessica said with manic calm. "Do what I'm telling you and you won't get hurt. I need to go back to the bungalow."

"What for?" Mallory managed to speak as though Jessica, with her feet firmly planted on the slippery slope to madness, had something of interest to tell her.

"You have to be fuckin' kidding me?" Jessica snorted. "There's something of mine I have to pick up."

"Can I ask you what?" Mallory spoke each word

slowly and distinctly, praying for someone to approach her car.

"No. Drive on, girlie girl. I won't tell you again."

She pulled out fast without showing an indicator, without even looking. She hoped with all her might some outraged driver might signal a protest with a furious honk on the horn. They were even welcome to crash into her car.

No one did.

Her mind was working overtime. Once at the bungalow she planned on making her escape. The door leading into the hallway, she knew from her search, had a lock. The family bathroom also had a lock on the door. She had her mobile with her. She could ring Blaine, or she could ring through to the farm. That would be quicker, providing someone was there and they were not all out in the field. The CD was playing Callas in her prime. Bellini's *Casta Diva*.

"Turn that squawking off," Jessica roared, as though the glorious sound was battering her tender eardrums.

Mallory obeyed.

"So you've been to see Jason. How is he?" Jessica asked almost normally now they had moved off and Callas had been silenced.

Adrenaline was pumping into Mallory, deadening the pain in her side. She was surprised by the amount of blood, but she was able to match Jessica's weirdly conversational tone. "Why don't you go see him yourself, Jessica? I could drop you off. If you weren't all that long, I could wait."

"Think I'm a bloody fool, do you?" Jessica blasted. "I know what you're up to. The minute I'm out of the car you'd take off."

"Why should I?" Mallory's nerve held. "Wouldn't you like to see Jason? I could come in with you if that would make you feel easier. I'm letting him have the bungalow while he recuperates."

"Are you?" Jessica turned mad bright blue eyes on her. The pupils were so visibly enlarged they had almost taken over the irises.

Drugs.

Jessica is as high as a kite.

"Jason needs a friend right now."

"He doesn't need a friend like you," Jessica snarled. "He has *me*."

"So shouldn't you be there?" Mallory sounded entirely reasonable. "He wants to see you."

Jessica shrank back against the seat, shining weapon in hand. She was moving it around experimentally, sideways, back and forth. She was handling it like an expert. Mallory had an idea the knife had probably belonged to Jessica's father. It looked like a trophy of some sort. Jessica hadn't put on her seat belt. Mallory wasn't about to remind her. People under the influence of drugs were capable of anything.

Jessica's eyes were flashing a lurid blue. "He said so?"

"Indeed he did." Mallory spoke in a calm reassuring voice. It was extremely important she convey calm. Jessica in her manic state would relish any show of fear from her.

"Liar!" Jessica turned on her, clutching fingers locked around the handle of the knife.

Mallory was aghast but kept remarkably stoic. *Is this the way my life is going to end?* she thought. *In violence, like my mother?* Never make plans. God laughed at

man's plans. One deep stab was all it would take. The
world gone. Her dreams gone.

"How I wish you'd never come back, Mallory," Jessica said. "You've brought this all on yourself."

The air conditioning was running at 22 degrees
Celsius, yet sweat was dripping from Jessica's forehead and her nose, and her body odour was sickeningly strong. "Now, stop dickering about," she shouted.
"I'm not that little slut, Kathy, God rest her pathetic
little soul. I know what you're up to. By the way, there's
blood all over your arm and your lovely white dress.
Now ain't that a shame."

"I'm sure you don't mean to do this, Jessica. You're
clearly distressed. I've known you since schooldays.
Can't you tell me what's wrong? Jason is very upset he
hasn't seen you."

"You're not lying to me?" Jessica stared at her in
puzzlement.

"We can sort this out. Jason loves you." Mallory
managed to sound deeply earnest. After all, it was
true, perverted love or not. "I'd say more than anyone
else in this world."

Jessica nodded vigorously. "Yes, he does. I have his
heart and his body. You were *nothing*." That thought
seemed to cheer her immensely. "Jason has always
done what I've told him."

"Not too late to take the turn-off for the hospital,"
Mallory suggested.

Jessica shook her head. Her tone was back to
weirdly flat. "We'll go to the bungalow first, then
you're of further use. You can drive me back to the
hospital."

"I'll be pleased to." Mallory prayed silently.
Dear God, deliver me.

* * *

Blaine was expecting an important interstate business call to come through. No way did he anticipate having the local pharmacist on the line instead, claiming the call was urgent.

"What can I do for you, Colin?" Blaine asked crisply, wondering what the hell the man wanted.

"This is, well, a hunch, a bad feeling, Mr. Forrester." Colin's tone was muffled like some character in a spy movie. "I can say that because my hunches generally play out."

"Get to it, Colin." Blaine's tone was brusque.

Colin obliged. "I waved to Dr. James as she got out of her car. She'd been parked outside the pharmacy. When she came back, the thing that alerted me and what I thought I should tell you is Jessica Cartwright jumped in the car beside her. Then Dr. James took off."

"*What?*" Blaine was so startled his voice thundered down the line.

Colin held the phone away from his ear. "Dr. James didn't look happy. Not angry exactly, sort of more disgusted. Jessica Cartwright is a bit of a rat bag, isn't she? They sat for a moment or two, talking, arguing, I think, and then Dr. James drove off. I've had my eye on Jessica Cartwright for quite a while. In my humble opinion there's something wrong with that woman. She's on drugs. I thought you'd want to know."

Blaine shoved back his chair so hard it shot against the back wall. "I do want to know, Colin. Thank you. You've done the right thing calling me."

"Take care," said Colin, thinking he had earned himself a nice little stockpile of brownie points from the Big Man in town. Apart from that he genuinely wanted the beautiful Dr. James kept safe. She had his unbending devotion. He could say a little prayer, he thought. Then immediately did so.

Blaine made short work of quitting the building. He was convinced, like Colin Watson, that Mallory could be in danger. By the time he reached the Range Rover he had already rung the police, getting them involved. He needed Mallory and Jessica Cartwright found quickly. They were travelling in Mallory's Mercedes. He gave the registration number from memory. The police would put out an alert. He couldn't bear to think of Mallory alone with that unhinged woman, even though he knew Mallory would keep her head. Mallory was strong and she was a trained clinician. Even so, Jessica Cartwright had the advantage, being entirely without boundaries. As far as he was concerned, Jessica Cartwright was barking mad.

The feeling of powerlessness was near to overwhelming. Where would they go? Not to the hospital. He was fairly sure of that. Back to the bungalow? If Mallory's hunch was the bottles of nail varnish or whatever contained some toxic substance, Jessica might very well try to retrieve them. Mallory, stalling for time, might have promised to help her.

He put through a call to the foreman at the farm. He hit the steering wheel hard when he was told to leave a message. This was one trauma too far. Mallory had prevented him from doing what he had wanted to do about the Cartwrights. Now he was tortured by the idea Jessica Cartwright was out to do Mallory harm.

Worst of all, he shared Watson's opinion Jessica used drugs. No one could say with certainty how anyone might act under their influence. Jessica Cartwright had crossed many forbidden lines.

He switched on the ignition of the Range Rover. It responded at once, the engine powerful and refined. He lit out of town at twice his normal speed, flying down Poinciana Road, for once blind to its beauty, heading for Moonglade Estate. Terrible anxieties were moving from his head to his heart. He was thinking of all the bad things that had happened to Mallory. They had come so close to making everything in their lives right. Their shared life was what he fervently desired.

It was the longest drive she had ever made. Her mobile rang several times.

"No way you're going to answer that, girlie," Jessica warned. "Don't try turning into the main entrance either. Take the fork that leads to the bungalow."

Mallory drove another couple of hundred yards, taking a left turn along a farm track. A minute later she parked the Mercedes where Jessica directed. Not in the big open garage, but on the front lawn less than two feet from the front steps. Her side was throbbing. She could feel the sticky blood all over her dress, her arm, and her leg. It had even run into her shoe. She didn't want to look down. She had to ignore the blood. She felt quite woozy, but she forced herself to stay focused.

"Come along," Jessica urged. "I need a few of my books. I have a great interest in aboriginal medicine. The rainforest is filled with native plants with powerful medicinal properties. I really should have been a scientist."

"I'm sure you would have been a very good one," Mallory said, managing to sound admiring.

"That's true." Jessica spoke like a normal person, which she undoubtedly was not. It was like a switch being thrown on and off in her head. Normal or what passed for normal one minute, manic the next.

The bungalow was waiting. Densely shadowed by mature trees, it looked something out of *Grimm's Fairy Tales.* The ultimate haunted cottage. No one was around. It was very *quiet.* Not even the prolific bird life was astir. A smouldering sun caused Jessica's face and throat to glisten with sweat. She made no attempt to wipe off. Indeed she didn't even appear to notice it.

"This fuckin' place is cursed," she muttered, bulldozing Mallory up the steps in front of her. Both of them were of a similar height and weight, but Mallory had the certainty Jessica could overpower her with her manic strength. Jessica was very strong physically, very weak psychologically.

"Go on. Go in," Jessica breathed in her ear, shoving the key at her.

Mallory unlocked the door, pushing it open. As before, she felt a *presence* swish in with her. She didn't understand it, but she *felt* it. Many people possessed powers they had never asked for and chose to shut down.

"Lock the door," Jessica barked.

Mallory made a business of obeying. When Jessica

momentarily turned away, she swiftly unlocked it. Her experience of inanimate objects was they had a life of their own. Her heart tightened as she waited for the lock to click back loudly. Miracle of miracles, it didn't.

Jessica had crossed with great purpose to the bookcase. She stood a moment then began pulling out one book after the other, tossing them this way and that to land on the floor. "Sit down, Princess. Just you and me. Relax." Another manic giggle. "I won't be a minute, then we can go to the hospital."

Keen to appear dutiful, Mallory pulled out a chair and sat down, head bent, hands clasped on the table, the picture of compliance, with adrenaline buzzing in her veins.

Satisfied with her body language, Jessica moved off down the hallway.

Mallory had one chance and she knew it. She was on her feet, adrenaline kicking in like a boot to the back. It gave her a much sharper sense of reality. She could throw open the door and start running. She was a good sprinter. Jessica probably was too. Her actions could invite a plunging knife but she would have a chance at finding help. What wouldn't she give to have Blaine within reach! To have him hold out his arms to her. Save her. She had to save herself. For *him*.

Jessica came flying back into the living area, her features distorted by rage. "Caught ya!" She came at Mallory like the wind. "You're not going anywhere yet, girlie. Sit right back down again." She caught Mallory hard by the shoulder, forcing her down into a chair. "You've been here, haven't you? You've searched the place. What were you looking for?" Another little knife jab, this time to the upper shoulder.

It was imperative to obey, or get sliced to ribbons. This was a woman well into the process of disintegration. Teeth clenched Mallory said, "I've been inside once. I wasn't looking for anything in particular. I just wanted to check on the place. It won't be standing empty, you know."

Jessica's mad eyes lit up. "You're lying again."

"Why would I lie? What's the point?" Mallory tried a shrug, fighting to distance herself from the pain. It could be done.

Jessica stared at her, a cold rage on her face. "You better not be lying."

Mallory showed no change of expression. "This place belongs to me, Jessica. Have you forgotten that?"

"Then who else has been here?" Jessica appeared disconcerted by Mallory's calm demeanour.

Mallory frowned, as if trying to think. "Possibly a nosey farm worker could have taken a peek inside. That could well be the case. The bungalow wasn't locked when I came over."

"Maybe we should just ask them?" Jessica said, with her weird menacing smile. "That'll settle it."

Mallory stood up as though happy to oblige. "Okay."

Again Jessica seemed surprised by Mallory's capitulation, but then she did her about-face. "You're lying, aren't you? I don't trust you. I never did trust you. You were in the medicine cabinet."

Mallory prepared herself for what was to come. Jessica was sweating profusely, while she was bleeding but chock-full of adrenaline. "Whatever for?"

"This is a joke!" In a plunging movement Jessica stabbed the knife through the air, an oddly jerky movement like a robot. She was getting fiercer by the minute.

"What are you going to do, kill me?" Mallory challenged.

Jessica gave her incongruous bark of a laugh. "How could I do such a thing to the town's princess? Lady la-di-da-di da. I could have put a drop of poison on the edge of this knife for all you know. Just a few drops. They could already have entered your bloodstream. I know a lot about our rainforest plants and their toxins. I've learned a lot from the aboriginal people."

"You wouldn't want to spend the rest of your life locked up in a jail. You wouldn't see Jason then. He might not visit. Why don't we go?" She made a move towards the door.

"We go when you tell me the truth."

Her head was swimming. She was having a little difficulty breathing. "Jessica, I am telling you the truth," she said, sounding as weary of all the questions as possible.

Jessica's nostrils flared. "The little bottles in the medicine cabinet, where are they?"

The weight of dread was in Mallory's chest. "Are you telling me you're worried about bottles of nail varnish?" How she spoke so scornfully she would never know. "I'm supposed to have pinched a couple of bottles of nail varnish? What's a bottle of nail varnish worth these days? A few dollars?" Her blood was rising. There was a copper taste in her mouth.

Jessica's eyes flickered. She backed away. "People lie all the time. I *know* you're lying."

Courage was now part of her. This was either the day of her death. Or it wasn't.

"Jessica, I'm *not* lying." She sounded convincing even to her own ears. "What's so important about the nail varnish anyway?"

"You tell me." Jessica came close to hiss into her face. Her breath was so bad, involuntarily Mallory drew back her head.

All the destructive elements in Jessica's nature had been let loose. Instinctively Mallory raised her hands in a defensive position before her face. She knew her hands would be the first to be badly wounded. She continued to watch Jessica with extreme concentration. She took several quick breaths, trying to moisten her parched mouth with her tongue. She was ready to put up a fight. She felt unaccountably powerful, primed to counter the first thrust.

Only nothing happened.

For a moment Mallory could make no sense of it. Her brain couldn't be working properly. Jessica was standing rigid. In fact, the two of them were posed like a couple of statues. What Mallory became *most* aware of was a strange turbulence in the air. She felt air whooshing out of her like sand running through an hourglass. She had to stay conscious when all she wanted to do was sink to her knees, then fall to the floor.

Jessica had turned into a stone carving. She was staring in mounting horror at the front door as though some fearsome figure had suddenly materialized. Her voice, when it came, was barely audible. "What *are* you?"

The terror and incredulity in her voice caused the hairs on Mallory's nape to stand on end. The turbulence was growing denser, gathering into a column of smoke, not grey, but as white as the thick clouds one saw from the porthole of a plane. The column appeared to be forming a shape. Mallory felt she could very well be losing her mind. There was no draft, no smouldering smell of smoke. She had not been advised of any burn-off on the farm.

There wasn't a *living* soul in the bungalow but the two of them. Beads of sweat were running into her eyes, burning them. She had no idea what was going on. She was moving out of reality, a consequence of blood loss and multiple shocks. She stared across at Jessica while slowly inching forward.

Jessica's words had been reduced to an incoherent babble. She continued to stand frozen, as if she hadn't the power to move away.

"Look . . . loo . . . loo . . ." It sounded as though her tongue had grown too big for her mouth. Next minute Jessica started to flail the shining steel hunting knife at thin air. Her head was swinging violently from side to side.

Mallory knew illusions weren't readily explained. Yet people had witnessed impossible things become possible. There was a loud humming in her ears. Maybe she was about to pass out. Now the cloud was hovering over *her* head as if it were somehow animated. She felt propelled outside of herself. She lunged forward in blind faith.

Her bloodied right hand shot out to connect hard with Jessica's knife hand. She was on the point of following up her surprise attack, only she had managed to knock the weapon from Jessica's slackened grasp. The bloodstained knife spun madly across the floor. Mallory sprang after it, defying weakness and pain. She fully expected Jessica to come after her, both of them on the floor, grappling for the weapon. Her limbs felt heavy yet she was able to get a hand on the knife, bracing herself for whatever was to come. She had no intention of letting herself be knifed to death by a madwoman. Besides, she had the advantage of *outside* help.

It took her many seconds to realize Jessica hadn't come after her. Indeed, Jessica had shown no reaction to the loss of her weapon. Unseen terrors had a powerfully fierce hold on her.

"What's she doin'?"

The fear and bewilderment in Jessica's voice curdled Mallory's blood. Strong vibrations were sending her own body into little spasms. She had a sudden image of Kathy's broken body lying at the foot of the cliff. Could it be Kathy's *soul* floating above her? The white illumination, some organised intelligence, was still there. A profound sense of unreality had set in. She fought against pitching over. Her whole body was gluey with blood, her once beautiful white dress stuck to her, an unrecoverable mess.

"Can't you see, she's coming for me." Jessica began to flail her arms violently. She was attempting to hit through something invisible to the naked eye. "Go way. Go way."

Whatever Jessica saw, Mallory did not.

Even in her woozy state, Mallory heard, above Jessica's keening, the unmistakable sound of vehicles speeding down the side of the house. Now they rounded the front of the bungalow, coming to a halt near the stairs.

Deliverance.

Brakes, the bark of shouted orders. She caught the blurred reflection of spinning blue lights. Doors slammed. Hard thump of boots on the timber steps.

The voices were more resounding. Urgent. One voice she heard above the rest. She would recognise Blaine's voice anywhere. She felt such relief her body regained some strength. Thank God!

She forced herself to stand upright while Jessica continued to fill the room with her tortured cries.

Jessica Cartwright has crossed the line.

A moment later Blaine kicked in the front door so forcefully it was a wonder the whole building didn't fall down. The door hit the wall so hard it bounced back, slamming into one of the policemen, who fell back a pace, winded. Jessica's wailing was making the windows rattle. Following Blaine were two uniformed police officers, big burly men. Even then Jessica seemed unable to cease her crazed wailing. The two policemen, unbelievably, had to struggle to hold the thin woman upright by the arms. From the expression on their faces, they might have been expecting Jessica's head to do a 360-degree turn.

Blaine moved like lightning to where Mallory was standing. He felt such a profound relief he was light-headed, but fighting a tremendous anger. "God, Mallory," he exclaimed, in such a fury of anger against Jessica Cartwright, it burned like acid in his throat. "You're bleeding all over." The sight of her in this terrible state shocked him to the core. "We need an ambulance right away." He half turned back to where the police were holding the shuddering Jessica. She was a pathetic sight, shivering all over as though she were freezing while sweat dripped off her nose and ran in runnels down into the neckline of her blouse. In the face of authority she had turned pitifully submissive.

"No ambulance." Mallory placed a staying hand on Blaine's arm. "I'm okay. Just a few nicks." In reality her head was spinning, but Blaine was there. That was all that mattered.

"Nicks?" Blaine looked like he was ready to explode. Swiftly he began to examine her wounds. Mercifully, they appeared much worse than they really were. He took her very, very, carefully into his arms, her blood soaking into his clothing. It was of no importance. The only thing of importance was Mallory was alive, and relatively unharmed.

"You can take me to the hospital," she said. "Grab something so I won't bleed all over the car. The police will attend to Jessica."

"She needs to be committed," Blaine muttered, reaching for a throw-over off the back of a sofa and placing it gently around her.

There was to be a final reckoning. Jessica Cartwright's mental state was precarious. It had happened in escalating degrees, fuelled by her mental disorder, her life of transgression, and her increasing habit of drug taking. Was she now beyond recovery? Time and the right treatment would tell.

Exactly who Jessica had been talking to was left to Mallory to ponder. Was it Kathy's spirit that had caused such fear and panic? Or was Kathy a drug-induced hallucination? But what of her? There was no hallucinogenic drug in her system, yet she had reacted very strangely too. She had seen things that had never been there. Then again, what did anyone really know about the place they inhabited or when portals opened and then closed? If there was a Divine Being, miracles happened, small miracles and wondrous miracles.

There is Life.

There is Life Beyond.

Epilogue

Two years later

Mallory walked out onto the veranda where Blaine's mother, Rowena, was feeding her six-month-old grandson, Robert D'Arcy Forrester, the pride and joy of the family. Since the arrival of her grandson, Rowena had been a frequent guest to Moonglade. Indeed, having a grandson to love appeared to have given Rowena a new lease on life. It was a situation that worked supremely well. Mallory had grown very fond of her mother-in-law, and although Rowena and honorary aunt Dot had the occasional difference of opinion on what was best for Robbie, they too got on well.

It was sobering news Mallory had to deliver.

Rowena looked up with a welcoming smile that quickly faded. "Everything okay, dear?" she asked in concern. "You look pale."

Mallory sank into the wicker armchair near to Rowena with Robbie sleeping peacefully in his grandmother's arms. She turned to Rowena, briefing her. "I've had some . . . tragic news."

"News?" Rowena's still-beautiful face took on an expression of alarm. Although years had passed since the tragic death of her husband, Rowena still feared the worst.

Mallory hastened to reassure her. "No, no, no! Nothing for you to worry about, Rowena, only lament. That was Margery Cartwright on the phone. She's tremendously upset. Jessica died from a drug overdose last night. You know she'd been committed to a psychiatric hospital in Brisbane for treatment under the Mental Health Act."

"For her attack on you?"

"Yes. From all accounts she was a model patient. In fact, she showed such sensational progress she was released a year later. Jessica is . . . *was* clever. She could have fooled the most experienced psychiatrist. It was hoped she had been rehabilitated, but she couldn't kick the habit. The fatal blow was when Jason went off to God knows where. Margery has no idea. I don't think she *wants* to know. Jessica would have been totally lost without her twin. She had assumed they would always be together. Instead it ended in raw estrangement. Jason abandoned her. He loved her and he hated her. An overdose could have been Jessica's way out."

"Oh! I am so, so sorry," Rowena murmured. "Although I hardly knew the girl, I can never forget the grief she caused. As for her threatening you! Anything could have happened."

"I had help, Rowena," Mallory said. "I had my beloved Blaine." She had never spoken to anyone outside her husband about her belief Kathy's spirit had been with her that terrible day. She had worked tirelessly to clear Kathy's name. The two small bottles she had found at the bungalow did indeed contain toxic substances of plant origin that had significant physiological effects. Kathy had done nothing to harm her daughter. The town had had to confront that. Kathy had gone, as all spirits had to go once cleared.

Rowena wasn't concealing her joy. "Blaine adores you," she said. "I've never seen a man so happy. Now to be blessed with Robert D'Arcy." Rowena bent to kiss the top of her grandson's head with its feathery blond curls. "You know Margery and I used to be friends."

"You can be friends again. Why don't you consider spending six months with us and six months with your sisters, Rowena," Mallory suggested.

Rowena blushed with pleasure. "Heavens, dear, you don't want me moving in with you."

As saddened as she felt, Mallory laughed. "You've seen the size of Moonglade, Rowena. It's a *family* home. Blaine and I have discussed it. We would be delighted to have you stay with us for much longer."

"Are you sure?" Rowena looked like she was about to burst into song.

"Absolutely sure." Mallory smiled.

"Then I would love to!"

"Look, I'm calling in on Margery tomorrow," Mallory revealed. "She feels very comfortable with me. I have a few little things for young Evie too. Come with me. Dot can mind Bubby."

"What a treasure you've got in Dot," Rowena declared, beaming as her little grandson woke up. "I couldn't be happier you and Blaine have built such a *good* life, Mallory."

"Amen to that." Didn't she celebrate her blessings every day of her life? She would celebrate their continuance. New life was growing in her. Maybe a little sister for Robbie? Another boy? Did it matter so long as their much wanted baby arrived safely in the world trailing their clouds of glory? She would make her announcement tonight over dinner. They were having friends dine with them. But first she would tell her darling husband. She couldn't wait. They both wanted a big *family*.

Out in the garden a whole chorale of birdsong rang out like some wonderful staged performance. The birds couldn't have been more than thirty feet away, their song spreading and soaring as if over speakers. Competing with the birdsong they heard their two collies, Prince and Blaze, barking excitedly. Next they heard Blaine's thrilling voice calling from the door, "Mallory, darling. Mallory. Where are you?"

Mallory stood up eagerly.

"Go to him. Go to him," said Rowena with a smile, turning her attention back to her gurgling grandson. She had never seen a more beautiful baby.

Mallory went. She would have to give Blaine the serious news, which she knew he would receive with a minimum of fuss. He had always maintained Jessica Cartwright would never pull herself together. At the same time he would take her, his wife, in his strong protective arms and empathize with her. She knew she would never have to manage alone as long as she had Blaine.

"Oh, there you are!" They met up in the living room. Blaine, in a blaze of energy, surged towards her, one arm drawing her into him as he dropped a kiss on her cheek. "One extra for dinner if that's okay. Guy Gibson is in town. He's at a loose end so I invited him."

"No problem. I like Guy." Mallory leaned against her husband, her body with total trust in his. They were two sides of one physical being so far as she was concerned.

"Love you," Blaine murmured, in a low intimate voice.

"Love you." However lightly their bodies touched, desire ran deep.

"I've got time for a cup of coffee," he muttered into her hair, "then I have to get back on site."

She pulled away, smiling. "Coffee coming up. Rowena is on the veranda with our precious boy. I'll bring it out."

"Great!" He bounded away.

No matter how hard he worked, the long hours, Blaine never showed the slightest fatigue. He was a powerhouse. *Her* powerhouse.

Together they bloomed.

Be sure to look for Margaret Way's titles
published in Lyrical e-book format:

HER AUSTRALIAN HERO

HIS AUSTRALIAN HEIRESS

available at your favorite e-tailer.

Now, turn the page for an excerpt of

HER AUSTRALIAN HERO

by Margaret Way!

Alex walked quickly, even though the day was a scorcher with high humidity. A white-hot sun flared out of a sky that was bluer than any sea. The very air sparkled with heat. It sprang up from the rich volcanic soil, beating at her body, burning through the thick soles of her runners. If there were such a thing as spontaneous combustion, she thought she might go up in flames. She could feel the flush on her skin, but trusted in her daily routine of applying the most effective sunscreen on the market. Glancing down at herself, she noted the sweat marks on the red singlet she wore with a pair of denim shorts. These were her everyday work clothes. Once upon a time in the city she had been something of a clothes horse. Not now. She was back on the farm, and far too busy.

She had been out longer than she intended amid the green colonnades. R2E2, their second most popular mango variety, was bearing a bumper crop. The trees were laden with large, greenish yellow fruit that would quickly turn a deep orange with a lovely reddish blush. The heat had set the sugars, guaranteeing the fruit would be delicious.

The air over the entire plantation was saturated with a soporific fruity fragrance that made some susceptible people drowsy to the point of falling asleep. Everyone had heard of the term "going troppo." Another name for it was "mango madness." It happened before the onset of the Wet. There were no distinct seasons in the tropics, only the Wet and the Dry. She had always thought the name R2E2 was like something out of *Star Wars*, but the fruit had actually taken its prosaic name from the its row and position in the field at Queensland's Bowen Research Station.

She had kept her meeting with the plantation foreman, Joe Silvagni, brief. They needed to set the date of the mechanical pruning that followed on the harvest. No relaxing post-harvest. There was always something that had to be done.

Alex and Joe worked in harmony, which was essential to the smooth running of the plantation. Harvest was a stressful time. There was always the fear of battering storms, hail, flood, early onset of the monsoon. Their top-quality bumper crop would be on the shelves from this coming November through February. It was estimated North Queensland and the Northern Territory would send to market eight million trays, with each tray packed to contain at least twenty large mangoes. Her own favourite and that of the entire country was Kensington Pride. KP had a unique flavour. The drawback was it was an irregular bearer with a relatively low yield. The September harvest had been disappointing, but there was always next year.

It was she who had given Joe the job, sacking the previous foreman, Bob Ralston, her father's appointee and a known slacker. She had endured quite an argument with her father about replacing Ralston. The good news was, in little over a year, Joe had proved himself. He saw all the things that needed to be done without waiting on orders from her or Connor. She and her father were meeting up with Rafe later in the day. Rafe's privately owned Jabiru Macadamia Plantation was one of the biggest in the world. Australia was the world's largest producer of the native Queensland nut, the "bush tucker" the aborigines called *bauple*. Not that the macadamia plantation that processed the delicious nuts through their various stages was Rafe's sole business interest. Rafe was an entrepreneur, just like his forebears who had ventured north from the colonised southern states, into the wild frontier that was Northern Australia.

Rafe Rutherford! Lord of the valley.

Some men cast a long shadow. Rafe Rutherford was one of them. She could scarcely remember a day when Rafe hadn't figured in it somewhere, whether in reality or in the caverns of her wounded heart. He had been hers and her brother Kelvin's idol when they were kids. The two of them had looked on him as the big brother they never had. Even their one-eyed father, Connor, could see past his adored son and heir to Rafe and the outstanding qualities he had in abundance. Their gentle mother, Rose Anne, had always had a great fondness for Rafe. In a strange way he still reigned supreme with her, if he only knew it, but their once idyllic childhood relationship had undergone a catastrophic seismic shift. That had begun twelve years before on the fatal day when Kelvin had been lost to them. At fourteen, Kelvin Ross had been

destined never to grow old. Gone these many long
years. Dead.

> *Past touch and sight and sound*
> *Not further to be found*
> *How hopeless under ground*
> *Falls the remorseful day.*

Kelvin *really* was gone, though she talked to him
often, even if it was only in whispers. At the tender
age of twelve she had been crippled by an overwhelming sense of guilt. She had continued to live.
Kelvin had not. She knew better than anyone that if
her father had to lose one of his children he wouldn't
have agonized over his decision. He would have
chosen Kelvin to live. Kelvin was his finest achieve-
ment, the apple of his eye. It should have been a
daughter who died, not a son. The whole community
knew it, though not one word was uttered in public.
Everything was said behind closed doors. Kelvin
Ross's death was a tragedy that lived in the collective memory of the town.

Rafe had always been extremely protective of her
and her mother. Only she hadn't wanted that. She
wanted it for her vulnerable, grief-stricken mother.
Not for her. She shunned pity. Especially from her
idol. Kelvin's death had stripped her of so many of
her finer feelings. Guilt was her due. Death had been
waiting for Kelvin that fateful day. She had sensed it
without knowing why.

The close bonds between the Rutherfords and the
O'Farrells, her mother's family, went back genera-
tions. The two families had pioneered Capricornia.
Both families had greatly increased their wealth during

the Queensland gold rushes of the late nineteenth and early twentieth centuries. Gold mining had transformed the landscape of the State of Queensland. Gold had financed the building of Lavender Hill. The O'Farrell estate boasted one of the most beautiful colonial mansions in the state, so called because the house built in the eighteen sixties was surrounded by glorious lavender-blue jacarandas that protected the mansion like shields.

It was her O'Farrell grandfather who had deeded the estate to their daughter, Rose Anne, their only child. The estate included the house and the thriving sugar and burgeoning mango plantation. Her grandparents were returning to Ireland. Out of the blue, her grandfather had inherited a grand country house in the Irish Midlands. It came along with a minor title on the unexpected death of a cousin who had been shot dead in the wilds of Africa by an ivory poacher. A case of being in the wrong place at the wrong time.

Her grandparents had confidently expected her mother would return with them to Ireland. Instead Rose Anne had shocked them by announcing she was going to marry Connor Ross, a young man they had considered highly unsuitable. Deaf to all advice, the normally dutiful Rose Anne had stood firm. She was madly in love. She refused to give up the handsome Connor Ross. Seeing no other option, her parents had deeded Lavender Hill to her as a magnificent wedding present.

So that, then, was the way it was.

A sigh welled up from deep in Alexandra's breast. She still heard her mother's voice, just as she heard Kelvin's. She thought of them as silver bells pealing softly in her head. She had fought hard to block out her grief, though the scars remained. She got on with life. There was no other option. These days the great irony was her father couldn't manage without her.

By the time she was in sight of the house, her head felt woozy from the heat and the thick, pungent air. Her heart was hitting against her chest. Everything was starting to look *white*. There was no breeze to ruffle the feathery leaves of the compound's jacarandas that were on the cusp of bursting into an ecstasy of lavender-blue bloom. No shrieks from the legions of brilliantly coloured parrots feeding on the wealth of nectar-bearing flowers. A solitary hawk hovered above her head. It was waiting to pounce on some tasty bit of prey. She was so looking forward to the bliss of a cold shower before she started back to the office to go over the books.

Things were looking up. She had found four new markets. Two domestic. Two overseas. Her father had allowed her to take over the business side of the plantation in double-quick time. Over the years he had taken many unnecessary risks that had led to the plantation's financial difficulties. Under her stewardship things had made a marked improvement.

She had intended entering the house via the kitchen even if she risked running into Hazel Pidgeon—a surprisingly morose creature for one endowed with such a benign name. Mrs. Pidgeon was the woman Sasha had hired to run the house and do all the work. To be fair, she did it well.

Connor had married Sasha a scant ten months after her mother died. It by no means shocked the town. They were used to Connor Ross's ways. Except the glamorous Sasha, whom he had met on a trip to Sydney, was said to be years younger than him.

Connor Ross wasn't yet fifty and still a big, handsome man. Many women in the town thought so but were too canny to get caught up in his macho aura. They all remembered his treatment of Rose Anne, Alex's mother.

In the end, in no mood to contend with the house-keeper's seemingly permanent scowl, she walked around the side of the house, making for the front door. She didn't live here anymore. She had been virtually ejected from her mother's house. It had taken a couple of weeks to move into the Lodge on the extensive grounds. One of the few times she had allowed Rafe to help her. She and Sasha didn't get on and never would. Her father had gone along with the plan. That still didn't stop her from entering the house, invited or not. No one would stand in her way. Certainly not Sasha, a woman who Alex guessed had been on the make from her teens. She knew she had all the fight her beautiful mother had not. She had plenty of grit, but her heart was barred. She was herself, yet not herself for years now. She wasn't happy and she wasn't sad. She was *busy*.

She heard voices. Her heart flipped. The male voice was Rafe's. She would know it amid a hundred raised male voices. Sasha was cooing like a turtledove. Sasha thought it a secret known only to her that she was madly attracted to Rafe, but then so were most of the women in the town, married or not. Rafe was the alpha male. The utter embodiment of tall, dark, and handsome. He put life into every woman's beating heart. Not that Rafe cared about any such thing.

It was too late to turn back. Sasha had spotted her. No doubt Sasha's big blue eyes would be rejoicing in Alex's somewhat grubby appearance.

"Sandy! Sandy!" Sasha lifted a slender arm in greeting as Alex knew she was bound to do. Unfortunately it was all an act. An outsider might have been forgiven for thinking them bosom buddies. She swallowed down her irritation. This "Sandy" thing was a game. No one, but no one, had ever called her Sandy, yet Sasha had hit on it from their very first meeting.

Petite of stature, Sasha had taken her hand sweetly, before making a point of standing on tiptoe to kiss her cheek. That hadn't been necessary; Sasha had been wearing very high heels at the time. Her brand-new stepmother had laughed delightedly, her eyes sparkling with mischief. Sasha and her father had been married in a registry office in Sydney, so the marriage had been a fait accompli before anyone knew, including her. From that moment on, Sasha made it plain she was the new mistress of Lavender Hill.

Alex mounted the front steps, appearing calm and self-possessed.

Rafe rose to his impressive six-three. "Hi, Alex."

She had to wonder if there was ever to be an end to his hold on her. Was it even possible? His mere presence called up tumult. She gave him a faintly bitter smile. "Hi, Rafe." Their eyes locked. She wished she could cut the live current that surged through her body, but she couldn't. The force was too strong. Embarrassed, she became aware her damp singlet was clinging to her. She wasn't wearing a bra. She didn't have much of a bust in any case, but what was there was good enough. "You'll have to excuse me," she said, anxious to bypass the area where he and Sasha were seated companionably at the white wicker table. Its glass top was covered by a pristine white linen-and-lace cloth, embroidered at the centre and around the edges. Matching small napkins. Obviously from the trolley that stood a short way off, they had been enjoying what appeared to be a lavish high tea any tea expert would die for. Her mother's favourite Wedgwood tea service, Wild Strawberry, was on show. There was a silver three-tier cake stand holding what remained of a selection of delicious finger sandwiches—she spotted crab and cucumber—an assortment of pretty little cupcakes, and the obligatory scones. Mrs. Pidgeon had surpassed herself.

"Do stay and join us for a few minutes," Sasha urged. For some reason she was beating a tattoo on her teacup with her long, painted fingernails. An inferior piece of bone china might have cracked. "Take the weight off your feet. I'll ring for fresh tea."

How she hated these games! Never an offer of a cup of tea and a chat when they were alone together. "Please don't bother, Sasha. I need to take a shower."

"Of course, dear." Sasha smiled her understanding. "You do look terribly hot and bothered, I must say."

She was well aware of that. "That's probably because it's sweltering out there." Alex turned her head briefly to address Rafe. "You're a bit early for the meeting, aren't you?" As usual it popped out like a challenge. If she weren't careful, one of these days Rafe might react and put her firmly in her place.

"As you can see, I invited Rafe over for afternoon tea beforehand," Sasha cut in, as if she at least knew how to do the decent neighbourly thing. She was watching them with the utmost care, her light blue eyes darting from Alex to Rafe as though she believed some of the things she had heard from Connor were true. No one would question that Rafe and Alex were extremely aware of one another, even if there were no big smiles, much less hugs. Sasha couldn't recognise exactly what it was that simmered between them. Memories, she supposed. Heart-stopping moments. The death of Kelvin.

"Dad is out there somewhere," Alex found herself saying aloud, almost inviting Rafe to respond. There was an odd prickling at her nape and between her shoulder blades; an acute and uncomfortable sense of what could go wrong in life. "He's on his quad bike. I just hope he's wearing a helmet."

"He'd be very foolish not to." Rafe matched her tone with a quick frown. "Quad bikes put riders at risk. They're so unstable at speed, as we all know." He realized it was quite possible Connor wasn't wearing a helmet. Connor was a foolhardy man. Poor Kelvin had inherited his father's gung-ho attitude. He knew Alex would be thinking the same.

Alex!

As usual, whenever they met she stood alert, braced on her lovely long legs, resolute to keep him at a distance. He knew she had long since convinced herself that was the way to go. Certainly she hadn't unburdened herself to him for many long years. She had chosen to do it hard. It was a kind of self-punishment, he had always thought. Sometimes when he got angry—his anger was becoming more frequent these days—he thought of it as her ecstasy of guilt. Desperately in need of love and understanding from her father, Alex had been held at bay as if it were a sin for Connor Ross to allow his daughter to replace his dead son.

After the tragedy Rose Anne had tried her best to unite the family. An impossible task. Alexandra, the

young girl he had known so well, had been full of
the joy of life. She could draw lightning-swift sketches
of the people around her—many of him, to his surprise. She drew anything and everything that caught
her eye. He remembered her many studies of the
sylvan creek with its sculptural boulders, and banks
overhung by trees that were a magnet for the swarms
of gorgeous rainbow lorikeets. Alex had inherited her
gift from her great-grandfather Rory O'Farrell, who
had been from all accounts a fine watercolourist with
exhibits in the National Museum of Ireland.

Hot and bothered or not, he thought she looked
extremely beautiful and extremely desirable, as sexy
as a woman could look without even trying. It was
impossible to take Alex in at a glance. There was too
much to cover: the flush over her high cheekbones,
the flawless skin dewed with sweat. She had beautiful
feminine shoulders. Beautiful small, high breasts. He
could see she wasn't wearing a bra. The tight buds of
her nipples peaked against the damp singlet. He
looked away, his male body experiencing a near-
painful erotic charge. What man wouldn't feel it?
What man wouldn't want her? Alex had her father's
height. Her mother had been a petite, small-boned
woman. Alex was tall, narrow-waisted, with a strong,
very slender body. One long, thick, lustrous braid of
blue-black Irish hair hung down her back. Her vivid
blue eyes blazed out of a face that wore what he called
her "hoity-toity" expression. It suited her, he thought,
half amused. There was a depth and dimension to
Alex quite apart from her beauty.

Sasha Ross was a very pretty woman with a vampish
look to her. Short, fluffy, curly blond hair, light blue

eyes, a curvy, petite figure. Alas, no conversation but gossip. Certainly not issues of any weight. Someone must have told her men didn't like brainy women. Not true for him. Rather the contrary. Sasha couldn't hold a candle to Alex in any department. She could never have held a candle to the beautiful, tragic Rose Anne. What Connor saw in Connor's second wife remained a mystery to him.

"Don't let us hold you up then, Sandy. There's no real need for you to work so hard," Sasha said, wishing to show her concern.

"I can handle it."

Connect with

U s

Visit us online at
KensingtonBooks.com
to read more from your favorite authors, see books
by series, view reading group guides, and more.

for sneak peeks, chances to win books and prize packs,
and to share your thoughts with other readers.

facebook.com/kensingtonpublishing
twitter.com/kensingtonbooks

Tell us what you think!

To share your thoughts, submit a review,
or sign up for our eNewsletters, please visit:
KensingtonBooks.com/TellUs.

Romantic Suspense from
Lisa Jackson

Available Wherever Books Are Sold!
Visit our website at **www.kensingtonbooks.com**

Books by Bestselling Author
Fern Michaels